I0564194

ECHOES

Echoes

An Anthology of Short Fiction

Novelitics Writers Collective

EDITOR

Kim Taylor Blakemore

SYCAMORE
CREEK
press

First Edition 2023

Copy Editor: Kerry Cathers

ISBN (ebook): 979-8-9877480-6-0

ISBN (paperback): 979-8-9877480-7-7

ISBN (paperback KDP): 979-8-9877480-5-3

Copyright © 2023 by Sycamore Creek Press

All rights reserved.

No part of this book may be reproduced in any form or by any electronic or mechanical means, including information storage and retrieval systems, without written permission from the author, except for the use of brief quotations in a book review.

CONTENTS

FOREWORD

Novelitics Writers Collective began in response to the pandemic and the shut downs that forced each of us into isolation. Contrary to the prevailing belief that writers are solitary creatures, we do, in fact, thrive when we share our creative and publishing paths with other writers. I wrote in my local library. I taught in person through PDX Writers (a local writing organization based in Portland, Oregon), and through my own, very tiny, company, Novelitics.

Then came the pandemic and, like everyone else, I found my world turned upside down. I paced my office and house. And wondered if anyone else felt as out of sorts. I needed connection. I needed to know we were all okay.

So, I sent an email to writers I had worked with and taught. It said simply: "What are you doing and do you want to meet this Wednesday? Here's a Zoom link. I've never used it, but we'll see how it goes."

Wednesday rolled around. I sweated over the Zoom techs and troubles (remember them?). I worried no one would join the call.

I needn't have. One by one, faces filled the screen—my writing tribe, looking as disconcerted as I did, putting on brave faces, their faces too close to the camera or cut off at the forehead. No one had headphones or halo lights, or figured out the window behind them caused an inordinate amount of glare. None of that mattered. What mattered was we were there.

We caught up. Pretended this was just a few more weeks of annoyance. Shared where we were on our various novels and stories. Promised to meet again the next week. I named our Wednesday meeting Writers Well.

One Wednesday became another and another. We reached out to other novelists to join us. Our local Portland group soon had writers from Georgia, New Jersey, Ohio, Tennessee, Toronto, and California. We were, and are, a mix of aspiring authors and published authors, of traditional and indie, of historical fiction and sci fi and memoir.

Novelitics grew with the group—Saturday online workshops, morning writes, guest speakers—and this, the first annual Novelitics Writers Collective anthology.

This is a labor of love on all our parts. I wish to thank Kerry Cathers, who gave so much time and attention to copy editing and proofreading these remarkable stories, and Tonya Mitchell, whose eagle eye caught so much. And I wish to thank, from the bottom of my heart, each and every member of Novelitics. From that very first tenuous Zoom call to now, your support of each other's success, your expertise shared so generously, your laughter and words and spirit, floor me. I am more grateful than you can possibly know.

- Kim Taylor Blakemore, Editor

INTRODUCTION
By Robert Gwaltney

Far back as I can remember, I have longed to tell stories. With equal fervor, I have angled for a spot on the bench at a table meant for writers—a place of fellowship with like-minded folk.

We are a peculiar sort—storytellers. Within cool shadows, we dwell. Gazing out and into windows. Eavesdropping on life.

From solitary rooms or coffee-shop tables, we knit imaginary worlds. Tell tales. Straddle fences—traversing reality's terrain while quilting imaginary landscapes in our minds. This writerly existence is not for the weak of heart. This variety of dwelling lends, at times, a terrible sort of lonesome. A calling out into cavernous, unlit places— no one with whom to keep company but echoes.

These last few years, I have been fortunate to find my people, a community of writers calling back to me from their side of the murk. Deep calling to deep. Within the pages of this anthology, you will experience my friends at work, an enclave of gifted storytellers, a community of which I am proud to be a part.

The stories within this collection are as diverse as their creators. The only rule required of each contributor is that their work integrate a necklace: literal or symbolic. I am smitten with this device of a necklace, an echo of sorts, a series of links joining one author to another. One story to the next. This is the gift of stories, a thread tethering us to each other—anchoring us to our humanity and to this world.

Listen to the voices calling to you from these pages, stories of redemption and loss. The stuff of life. Pay mind to the echoes, and make your way out from the dark.

You, dear reader, are not alone.

- Robert Gwaltney, 2023 Georgia Author of the Year

WINGS

SHARON WOODARD

My wings appeared after they found the little girl's body under the foot bridge. The tiny angel was dead long enough to twist and stiffen up under the bridge. Whatever horror took her sweet innocence, shocked the village. There will be growls and whispers seeping through the pub for weeks as everyone posits opinions. But now, at the funeral, among the black umbrellas, no one stays to witness the miniature coffin sliding into the muck.

My wings aren't what you'd expect. They hang gray and sullied, not raven black, but not angelic either. That's why I hang back behind the hedgerow hidden among the foliage. I'm even further back than Constable Rorrick as he surveils the dismal clot of mourners.

I can't say why I'm here. I didn't know the girl. Little Jenny. Tragic with her being deaf, and from the orphan home. This far back, I pick out only those bits and pieces from the hushed conversations. I imagine they'll use a dozer or a backhoe to cover her up. Such a tiny grave but even so, Stanley, the groundsman, can't do all that digging and un-digging on his own. He can barely stay upright in a breeze.

The service goes short and everyone shuffles off leaving a few flowers drowning near the tiny muddied headstone. Stanley limps off to fetch his machinery to end this. Rorrick leaves with the rest of them.

Here I am with wings that ache and itch, bedraggled as they are in this brittle rain. Sprouting right out of my scapula, they reach a foot above my head and sweep the ground. Birds have hollow bones and feathers made of air. But mine are damn heavy; exhausting to lug around and hang wet and stiff. I couldn't say what they stretch out to. Or if they even do. The headaches alone bring me to my knees. If the feathers lighten and dry maybe all this will ease. Maybe that's the way of spontaneous wings. Arriving wet with life fluids, then drying to a supple lightness. Maybe even lighten enough to flex.

After everyone wanders off home, or whatever, I creep to kneel and peer into the grave.

The unstained pine coffin is nothing particular or singular. No one sprang for a showroom model. She lived at the county home, after all. In the ground, it's too small. Barely a life begun.

She didn't speak, our little Jenny. She is ours now, the whole town's. Our Jenny. Our shameful tragedy. She had no voice, our angel, maybe that's why she wasn't missed soon enough to be heard or protected. Now that she's gone, she has friends.

One wonders where they were before.

The wind rustles, the rain splashes, the soil splooshes the air. I strain for a clue. What happened little one? How did you come to be under the bridge? My bridge.

These damn wings itch like a mother. And pull, so I fight their backward drag. They pin me to that sad day. She dies and these wings appear. Maybe connected?

Mud splats the coffin because I am leaning too close, so I edge back. In some part of the cemetery, the backhoe fires up. Beside me, I hear something else. My wings shift pitching me forward. Damn things, so heavy and unmanageable. Kneeling, on the wet ground, my ears pressed near the open grave, it's unmistakable. Water, echoing and pattering over rocks, but both the creek and the Derryghal River it feeds into, are too far to hear.

Stanley grinds toward me, toward his sad chore. The sound of water passing under the bridge rises from the coffin. I don't hear it as much as feel it. The creek song rustles my wings whispering something I can't quite hear. Stanley's at the end of the row turning toward me. The water song whispers through my feathers, tugging me from the grave.

———

THE POLICE TAPE IS GONE FROM THE BRIDGE, THE BROKEN BODY too, of course. It's just a place now. Water and moss under an old foot bridge, but my body is electric. A current floods me from the wings. The violence here, the disturbance, the oak and ferns, the algae on the rocks, all of it shocked. I know something I don't know. I'm dizzy with too much coming in, too much to track.

"Oy! There! I dare you to go down to where she was."

Two boys, Angie's Charlie from the pub and O'Connell's middle one, Micky or Nicky or such, stand above, up on the road. I crouch behind bushes.

"You go if you're so bent." Charlie scorns shifting his rucksack's strap.

"Charlie, you're such a weasel. Scared of ghosts. Even a dumb ghost girl."

"Not scared." He shuffles his feet and I see him. The golden glow of him, his sweetness. It catches my breath how full of light he is. Then, it's gone and he's just a filthy town rat with muddy jeans and a ripped jacket. The other one shoves him, a smirk marring his face. A seed of darkness is in that one, like a shard of onyx, right next to his heart. I can't take my eyes from it. He looks down at me and freezes. A moment of utter silence. Even the water-song empties from the air.

When he looks away, all of it rushes back, the water patter, the green smell, the dirty leaf mold under my boots. The boys push at each other, but neither makes a move down the trail toward the water.

"Oy! Better! The drunk's shack. Maybe there's still some bottles to snag."

"Just go on, Micky. Just leave it."

That leads to more shoves. "Scared of ole drunk ghosts too? You weasel."

"Stop being an ass. Weasels aren't scared, they're clever. Besides, me mum says let things lie. Enough bad for now."

Charlie turns to go and Micky, moves like he's going to push him to the path but stares down at me instead, his dark heart sucking light. Everything goes quiet. Then he turns and they clump over the bridge toward town.

I realize two things. First, the bushes couldn't have hidden me, not with these ridiculous wings and Micky looking right at me. He sensed something maybe, but he didn't actually see. Come to think of it, no one at the funeral had either. Second, and more worrisome, the boys were talking about a drunk ghost and my house.

Talking about me.

Which made me realize a third thing. Time jumps around. I remember waking with wings, but not traveling to the funeral. Or leaving it. Or going to the creek. And here I am at my house. It's down a hidden path from the bridge. I didn't follow that path. I'm just here.

I have to turn sideways to get in and my wings send bottles clanking along the filthy floor. Dank air, full of peat smoke, rancid sweat, and a stink sends me gagging and stumbling to the door to breathe. The wings catch and I have to wrestle my way out into the evening. The rain tap tap taps the tin roof. This is no cabin. It's no home. It's a filthy makeshift shack in some no-man's land. It's pathetic and ugly and disgusting. It reeks and my mouth fills with bile and I'm vomiting and vomiting. Heaves and sweat and tears mix in the rain.

Drink. I need one like I have never needed one before. How could this be my life? I hold my breath and struggle into the cabin ransacking stacks of papers and books and boxes. I unearth a half bottle of wine and pour it down my throat. Red and sour, it's a searing fire and comes spewing up just as fast.

The despair of this place, the stink and suffocation of it, the grim darkness and the weight of these goddamn wings grind me to my knees. My head is compressing, an imploding void in this hovel, this monument to the catastrophe of my existence. My stomach roils as I'm smashed into the filth of the rotten floorboards and soil beneath. I open my eyes expecting spillage of life blood or something more precious. But I'm wrong. I'm lying on the ground in a shed with a tin roof, in the rain, pounds of feather and sinew plastered onto me. Instead of my life fluids, something shiny winks at me in the gloom where it's fallen from my hand.

Stretching, harder now with my burdensome back and rioting stomach, I pick up the tarnished silver chain with its St. Christopher medal. Something every man in the village wears.

Everyone, but me.

I sit up to get a better look. It nestles in my hand, warm and full of secrets. The saint is rubbed nearly flat, the chain dull and smooth and all of it loved and owned and out of place. It knows things. But I can't decipher anything. Not here.

IN THE CEMETERY, TREES SPIN AROUND ME. I'M DIZZY AND FAINT. My knees buckle but instead of pitching forward, I anticipate the wings and counter balance. My cramping stomach steadies. In my hand is the St. Christopher necklace. I'm still holding it. I've brought it here. Why?

The backhoe pats the mound of fresh earth. Stanley backs up and shuts it down. He steps from the cab and the rain splatters his gum boots. As he stands at the foot of the little mound, the rain pours off his hat, tracing down his stooped shoulders. A raven lands in the tree above.

I edge up just short of the grave.

His head stays bowed. Of course. He can't see me.

It's so quiet, I lean into the necklace's whispers. Closing my eyes and clasping it to my heart, I listen as hard as I can. Stanley makes a rustling noise and I look up. His hands wave about and it takes a minute to understand he is signing something to the dead girl, to Jenny. Sadness lines his weary face. We were kids together at the orphanage, me and Stanley. Why did we never become friends? I always felt sorry for him, doing this throwaway job at the bottom of the food chain. Thinking I was better off.

Filaments of light spin from his heart, through his hands and into the grave. A spiderweb of the same light weaves between him and all the graves.

He is the grave keeper.

It hits me sideways and in awe, I understand. He is a node in an immense net here. He is comforting her and I am intruding. The medal warms my hands and I close my eyes to keep from crying.

"She needs you to tell what happened."

Startled, I look at Stanley and he's looking at me. Right at me. His old blue eyes are sane and clear.

"You can see me?"

"Just the outline. My eyes aren't what they used to be."

"I thought no one could."

Stanley nods. "Probably not. Working in a cemetery going on thirty years, you learn to see things."

I want to ask him everything. "I'm dead? Is that what this is?"

He looks at me for a long minute, then shrugs and trudges to the backhoe.

"Wait!" I run after him, ungainly and ugly. "I don't understand. Why do I have wings? What do I have to do with this girl?"

He stops and turns, his shoulders slumped and tired. Not even fifty, but drained by some sickness, he is not long for this world. "Look. If you're stuck between here and whatever's next, there is something for you to do. She's not resting easy. Not by a long shot."

"But how? Why me?" I try to reach him but a wing catches and I tumble onto the mounded dirt. The engine roars to life and backs out heading to the service road. I lie, my whole body too heavy to move.

The grave is electric, like my wings, but more frantic and wrong. This is what Stanley means. This grave doesn't rest easy, not by a long shot.

Closing my eyes, I try to hear, to see, but I'm met with silence. No. Not silence, an emptiness where there should be sound. An electric emptiness setting my teeth on edge. Wrong, like chewing foil. And so much fear.

Heavy boots splash past me and a shiny flash drops where I lie. Fear. So much fear. More than my own. The boots nearly trample me. The shine falls. The boots run past.

The grave's electric charge pulses through me but this grave is not the muddy place I saw. I try to sit up.

A flash of memory? From Jenny or me? My head aches and I slump. I don't know how this works. The wings tug from behind and I close my eyes.

On the path above the creek, heavy boots, moving fast, splash past in the mud, something shiny falls and I grab it.

WHEN I AWAKEN, HALF MY FACE IS IN THE MUD OF THE GRAVE. IT'S full dark and the crescent moon hangs in the dark oak. Sitting up, I find the necklace in my hands. I run my thumb over the medal. It slides into a worn groove. Someone is missing this. How do I have it? Is it connected to Jenny's death? The shard of memory roars through.

Heavy boots splashing past in the mud above the creek. I grab the falling necklace.

Shaken, I jump up. In the tree, a raven caws, then swoops, landing beside me. Its wings flap as it hops forward.

"Show off." I roll my shoulders struggling to organize the wet chaos sprouting off my shoulders. It seems, I almost move them. The bird hops into a tree further on and caws. The necklace is warm in my hands. The bird flies further on. The necklace pulses. The bird glares at me, cawing and humping in its creepy frantic way. I glance at the grave and back to the bird.

"Follow you?"

THE BIRD PERCHES ON THE ROOF OF THE SPOKE AND LADDER. MY old pub roars tonight, busy after the funeral. It's been years since I drank in public but the raven glares down at me. The dizzy nausea is a bit less with this jump. I am adjusting. This is my life now.

I pocket the necklace and go inside.

Noise and lights shove me up against the back wall. No. Not lights. The pub is a room of dark paneling with battered wooden tables and chairs. Lamps spaced too far apart create pockets of shadow.

The lights are more a field, a pulsing thick plasma of color and depth winding through the room that I sense more than see. I feel everything and all at once. Despair and grief, sadness and fear, relief and suspicion, and anger thread through the fog of alcohol. All of it swirls and flows through the room and hits me, waves cresting and crashing. It's too much and I fall backward.

My wings catch me. They brace me, absorbing the waves and passing them through like great wind passing through empty air. My wings seem made for this. I lean back letting them bolster me. I take in the room. I'm adjusting and I'm using my wings to do it.

A roar of laughter catches me and there at the bar sit Patrick and Ilian raising pints. Ilian's liver is nearly gone. I see it. Not just his yellowed eyes but the spreading darkness of his right flank. His light flickers at Patrick then shrinks. Idiot. He should have stopped drinking years ago before Becky left, before he lost the farm. Plain as day he's brought himself to this.

"More for the rest of us!" Patrick bellows and leans to clink Ilian's glass.

Ilian's laugh is anemic. "You're a real Christian, Paddy!"

Patrick guffaws. "I'll say it again. That big oaf was a twat and we're better men without him!"

Ilian chuckles. But behind the bar, Angie turns away, moving down.

I fall heavy into my wings as a wave of jocund disgust washes through. I need a drink but shudder, remembering the wine's searing trip through me.

My eyes shift to a small table in a pool of lamplight. Two women hunch over glasses of sherry. They were part of the sparse crowd at Jenny's funeral. Haughty pinched faces huddled together, dirty maroon filaments weaving between them but not into the rest of the room.

"It was generous of the Ladies' Society to front the headstone."

"A little one, alone in the world like that, perhaps this was a kindness rather than facing a destitute life." They sip their sherry as if of one mind.

"But that bum, a waste of skin that one. I told Father Donavan not a bit of my coin was to go to that drunkard's expenses. Let him rot I say." They drink to that. I brace for the wave of sour piety to reach me, but it flattens and pools murky and maroon around their feet soaking back into their funeral coats, leaching up their bodies winding out of their mouths twining them tighter together and further from the rest of the room. Their gossip is cold, heartless, yet my own heart softens with pity for them, confusing me.

"Talk is, Kelso did it. His boot prints around the body led right to his shack. That's how they found him." It's the grocer, McKinney, and his wife at a table near me sharing a shepherd's pie.

"Kelso?" Claire pauses, her fork in the air. "He lived down there, of course his prints would be all over. Don't be spreading nonsense old man. Kelso was lost, not evil."

McKinney fills his fork. "You've always been too soft. Sometimes they are one and the same."

Claire sets down her own fork and stares at her husband. She glows a warm peach color, vibrant and lovely, the crinkles of her face and generous folds of her body warm with it. McKinney softens in the look and an ocean flows between them, mixing and swirling. She rolls her eyes. I see how much she loves him even when trying not to. Kindness is her zero state and she doesn't swim against it. She reaches her hand across the table inviting him in. "Two lost souls passed from us. Prayer for their rest to be easy, that should be our focus tonight."

I close my eyes. The wave of good will is sunshine cleansing straight through to my feather tips and I feel it flow clear to Jenny in the cemetery. It settles and warms and grounds us. I open my eyes to find Claire staring at me.

McKinney cranes to see. "What? What are you looking at?"

Claire's eyes cloud and she shakes her head, furrows her brow. "I don't know. Nothing. A light flickered."

McKinney growls, "The wiring in this dump. Some day." He shakes his head.

I pull back, scooching my wings behind my arms. I felt her sight or sense or whatever. Like the boy on the trail. But then I'm onto what McKinney said about my footprints.

I'm in the creek tugging the little body from the water. I'm screaming for help. I don't know what to do. Dead drunk, I can barely stand all my thoughts a jumble of shadows.

Falling back, the wings steady me. The pub stinks of mildew and stale beer. I scan the room and everyone drinking, the sight makes me heave. Drunk. Me pissing drunk when it mattered most. The disgust roils up, a dark cyclone of rage and shame. I have to get out. I have to do something. As I pitch toward the door my eyes zero in on something across the room.

Matron Ellis, in a chair by the stone fireplace, holds court. At least sixty, she's robust and mean. The St. Christopher medal on her chest sparkles in the firelight. One hand rubs it absently. I loathe that medal, the way it dangles down in a righteous taunt as her meaty hand slaps me again and again. Thirty years but I feel it like yesterday, my cheeks singed and red, my bottom raw and bruised. Her cruelty is sickly green, drab, and turbid, mottling her skin, fouling the air around her. It spreads through the room, the noxious mist winding through. Her eyes hunt behind it, she can't help herself. I shrink back unsure if she can see me.

"Matron, I'm so sorry for your loss. What is this world coming to?" O'Connell's wife bends to Matron offering her hands.

Disrupted, Matron returns a tight smile full of false grief and spiders. "I fear for my charges. My desperate little ones."

My chest heaves. Desperate. Yes.

"I'm just glad the monster who did it is dead as well. That's a blessing." A flicker of glee washes through her, a wave of pleasure speaking of me, but a stumble in the sureness. A shadow passes over her heart and through mine, the chill of lies, intended to convince herself and the surrounding women.

O'Connell's wife brightens. "I'll send a donation to indulge your little ones with sweets and toys. Help them to move on."

Matron pats the woman's hand. "A kindness, Mrs. O'Connell. Together we'll soften the blow of the world's horrors."

As Mrs. O'Connell moves on, Matron continues her scan. I shrink, breaking my gaze. She passes over and pauses on the corner where Eddis Rorrick hunches over a barely-touched Guinness. She watches him, and, satisfied, scans on.

I linger, because even though he appears alone, hunched and defeated, he isn't. His attention casts throughout the room. He did the same at the edge of the funeral today. Not back as far as I was, but not at the grave either. Though with us nearly a decade, he still plays the outsider. He wouldn't be up at the bar with the regulars nor at a table with a woman. No one notices him noticing them. He shines out, plumbing this room, tracking everything.

I like this man, the steadiness of him. We've been on opposite sides of too many scuffles to count, but fairness and justice color him. I wonder if he thinks I hurt Jenny and uncomfortably, I do, too. His gaze reaching out into the room is uncertain. He doesn't know, not for sure, and that's a comfort.

Matron makes a big show of lifting herself from her seat, pulling a cane from against the brickwork. Big and gangly, and, except for a few farm lads and me, she towers over everyone. "This has been a solace on a difficult day, but I must get my old bones to bed." The women seated near her flutter and scatter as she lumbers to the door. She wobbles, dependent upon the cane. Father Donovan appears out of nowhere to offer his hand.

"Allow me to escort you, Matron Ellis. I too would put this day to rest."

The thing passing between them is so tangled and sullied, it steals my breath. The sick red light of him punches my sore stomach. Her smile, a wry and twisted thing, shines over his head to the center of the room where Mayor O'Connell is ensconced. His benign jowls and gray caterpillar brows meet her flutter of sickly green snarls with a wall of gray, a battlement, on high guard. In turn, she sneers and hunches a bit to get through the door held open to her. Across the room, Rorrick watches over his beer.

The door closes and the whole room freshens as if there's more air to breathe.

I AM IN THE SHADOWS OF A PATHETIC PEA GREEN WARD OF THE orphanage. Two even rows of four beds mirror each other in the darkness. A shard of blue-white light slices into the room as Matron opens a door and steps in. Sturdy and sure with no cane now, she prowls along the sleeping girls, pausing at the empty bed. Her hand caresses the chipped metal frame, tender, thoughtful. Without a backward glance she leaves, shutting the door as silently as she's arrived.

I tiptoe past the sleeping girls to the empty bed. Jenny's, no doubt. The familiar olive blankets, too rough, too thin, reek of the austere bleak coldness that isn't just absence of heat. Still, gentle breaths create wispy clouds of sweet light.

"Are you an angel?" A sprite next to me sits up, rubbing her eyes. Her short, messy hair is greasy like all the girls here. Poorly cut, poorly cared for.

"You can see me?"

Her brown eyes widen. "Did you take Jenny?"

I look at her and wonder.

Before I can answer, she scoots from her blanket and shines her sunflower face upward. "Have you come for me?"

I kneel at her bed and surprisingly, the wings cooperate, folding soft and silent behind me. Her light collapses far too short of her face. I don't know how it should look but I know this isn't right. I want to scoop her up and escape from here. Far from this cold, empty place of beatings and darkness.

Instead, I fold my hands in my lap and whisper. "No, little one. This isn't your time. That's not how your life will go."

"How will it go?"

I see her running in the heath. I see a young woman holding someone's hand, an old woman rocking on a porch under a blue sky. The sadness around her eyes is wrong, but her light is strong. I aim for reassuring. "It will get better. You will make something so much better than this."

"Will there be a puppy?"

Light grows around her eyes. I think about the wave of Claire's kindness filling me in the pub. I picture a floppy puppy running. I smile. "Yeah. Of course, there will be a puppy."

She hugs herself and the light spills onto me. It flows through my wings making them tingle. My eyes fall to the empty bed.

"Was Jenny your friend?"

"She only just got here. Then she got sick and now she's gone."

I touch her head. Her hair is soft, barely even fuzz. "You'll remember what I said?"

Eyes all black pupils, she looks up. "I'll make something better."

"So much better." I help her climb under the blanket and tuck in the edges. I stay beside her bed until her breath drops and evens out. I summon all the kind thoughts I can for her. And for the girls in the other beds. And across town to the girl in the cold grave. The room hums with warm light winding glorious in my wings. When I stand, they don't yank as hard or pull on my head and make it ache.

It's still dark in the police station. Rorrick hunches alone with a mug of coffee and an open file. A sergeant walks in flipping on the overhead lights.

"You early or a holdover from last night?"

"Couldn't sleep, may as well work."

"Well, Doc would fight you on that but what you got there?" The sergeant pours a cup of coffee, smells it, grimaces, and plops down at Rorrick's desk.

"That little girl. Doesn't add up."

"Seems open and shut. Orphan runs away, gets lost, the big freak finds her, drowns her in the creek, stumbles off to his shack to die of alcohol poisoning. Case closed."

My heart gives way. Alcohol poisoning seems about right. But drowning a little girl. My wings can't hold me and I crumple to the floor.

Rorrick grimaces. "Makes no sense. Kelso was a mess, but no killer. Why would he? And there is this." He pushes the folder across the desk. "Medical report. She died of a brain aneurysm, not drowning."

The sergeant picks up the paper. "A what of the what?"

"A defect in a blood vessel to her brain. Might have burst anytime. Likely died instantly."

Boots running, heavy like they are carrying something, the necklace drops and I grab it.

It's in my hand. But they can't see me, neither one of them. And what would it explain? What does it explain?

"But his boot marks. At the creek leading to his shack?"

Out the dingy window, daylight blooms through the grime. "Maybe he found her. Tried to pull her out?"

Yeah.

Maybe I tried to help. I crush the necklace in my hand, demanding that it tell me.

I'm pulling the little body from the water. It's so light, so still, so cold. Thick boots run past me, the necklace drops and I grab it.

No. That came before.

I grab the necklace as the boots run past. Under the bridge, I pull the little body out of the water.

The sergeant sets his mug down and stands, shifting his gun belt. "Maybe he hurt her then went on home to drown his shame."

Rorrick doesn't say anything, just looks out on the brightening day. He is my lifeboat. I wouldn't hurt that girl. I'm a fuck up, but I wouldn't do that. The necklace cuts my hand. Rorrick turns and the sun shines off his chest. His heart beats just under, vermilion and true.

Except the shadow.

I sit up straighter, my wings tingling. Beside his heart a darkness hides, not stone like Micky's, not hardened and sucking in light, but soft and private. Rorrick's shadow is a soft pain he holds close, rocked by the flutter of his lungs, each breath a caress. This is grief. A defining grief. I am an expert on grief and I recognize it from across the room. I'm intimate with this pain. Its sharp corners and tenacious roots strangling his heart. I don't know when I stand or extend my hand, but there I am reaching toward that darkness. It streams to me across the room gathering into a furry ball of shadow in my hand. It shimmers and whimpers and vanishes.

I fall back on my wings and Rorrick gasps, clutching his chest. The sergeant spins around. "Eddy?"

Rorrick gags, clutching his chest. He falls against his chair shaking his head. "I..." He catches himself, gulps in air. Coughs. "God damn heartburn, we gotta get better coffee." Holding his chest, looking dazed, he stands. "I need to see that old bat. Something is amiss."

My wings are the only things holding me up. Tears stream from my eyes, blurring the room.

ACROSS THE ROOM, FATHER DONOVAN BALANCES A TEACUP ON HIS knee. I am at the window next to Matron who is stroking her St. Christopher medal. Her meticulous compulsion makes me shudder. Thirty years and even death doesn't shield me from this woman's cruelty. She pulls aside the brocade curtain as a car crunches the gravel. I see the horrible necklace, harbinger of punishment and nightmares. I turn away and watch Rorrick shut his car door.

I turn back because Matron is not wearing the necklace of nightmares. This one, the one lying over her olive dress, is a shiny new Celtic cross with St. Christopher carrying Jesus in a gaudy silver oval at its center. Not worn and worried. Not the necklace that dangled in front of me for years as I'm slapped and scorned and starved. Not the necklace that broke me. That necklace I would know. My stomach lurches as I gawk at my hand.

Rorrick knocks at the door and Matron growls. "What does *he* want?"

"Likely come to say the case is closed." The priest sets his teacup on a table and rises.

At the door, Rorrick is saying he has a few more questions. At the window, I'm staring at the necklace in my hands. It is the stuff of nightmares. Worn and worried. Ancient. I cast it away, but it clings, stuck fast and cutting into my hand.

The necklace is menacing in front of me, swinging back and forth.

No.

It's stationary and I am going back and forth, hands grip my shoulders, too strong, too violent. Matron screams, her face red in an absence of sound. Her hand slaps hard and my hand tangles pulling the necklace to my chest before it all goes black.

No. I would never touch this terrifying thing.

This is not my memory.

Rorrick settles in a chair as the priest leaves the room. Off to tend his flock, he chuckles, and Matron pours tea. I struggle back by the curtain. Sitting upright, Rorrick shines bright in the room. Matron is slippery, moving around him, careful with the tea things. He watches, his heart brilliant in his eyes.

"She didn't drown."

Matron clutches her medal, rubbing, worrying it. "Poor dear. What did that horrid monster do? Oh, sweet Mother Mary."

"You said she was in the infirmary, away from the others the night she disappeared."

Matron nods, all smoke and spiders.

"What was wrong with her?"

Matron slips into her chair and takes her tea. "Stomach ache. Sometimes new ones need time adjusting to the food."

This is rich, calling it food. I clutch the necklace. Her necklace. It's as solid in my hand as he is sitting in that chair. I want him to see it. I want him to ask her about her necklace. Instead, he asks, "Belly ache. Common in littles is it?"

Matron sighs, eases back, takes a sip. "Yes. We separate them so as not to upset the others. I checked on her through the night."

"Your room is just across the hall?"

Matron smiles, all maternal concern. "Yes. I left my door open to hear the dear should she need me." She shakes her head. "And all the time, that little minx, faking and fixing her bed to look like she was in it fooling me until morning." Wispy smoke spills onto the floor around her.

Rorrick pauses. Then, "And her hand?"

Matron's eyes tighten, black and raven sharp. "Hand?"

Rorrick, as calm as you please, holds out his hand. "The medical report said a deep cut through her right palm."

That can't be. I replay the memory. No, it's the left hand tangled in the silver chain yanking it free, then cutting and burning and pulling into my chest. Her chest. Jenny's chest.

"Yes, yes, of course. She hurt it earlier. The rope swing. I dressed it myself. She took off the wrap. Like I say, a little minx." She shakes her head fondly smiling into her tea.

"Her birth certificate doesn't list a father."

Matron looks up, too quick, holds his gaze a shade too long.

Rorrick leans in. "That's a bit odd, isn't it?"

She collects herself. "No. No. Not for these girls. Born to a sinful woman who died in childbirth. Tragic, but not unusual."

"Ah." Rorrick sits back. The air bristles with lies. She isn't aware, but he is. They both sip tea.

Matron sets her cup down, stands, and smooths her dress. "I'm sorry, but I need to tend the children."

He stands and smiles. "That's a handsome St. Christopher. A new take on it."

Her hand cups the medal. "A gift. From Father Donovan. Saint Christopher is dear to me. One feels such comfort from the saint's service, doesn't one?"

Rorrick pats his chest. "Never leave home without mine."

Heavy boots run past. The necklace drops and I grab it. Later, I pull her from the creek. She is still. Dead drunk, I'm utterly useless.

Get help. Yes. I need help. I go back to the cabin. Why? Why do I do that?

Jenny is being beaten and she grabs Matron's necklace.

And what? Drops it? No. She holds it and holds it and then there on the path, near me, she drops it and I pick it up. No, she'd have been dead by then, unable to hold it. But it stays with her somehow. When I try to help her, I fuck it up like I do everything. I wake up with wings.

I need more from Jenny.

———

At the grave, I lay down listening. Begging her. Tell me. But she doesn't speak, our Jenny. I know Matron did this. The necklace has told me. I gather my wings and pour myself over the grave. Why, Jenny?

She can't tell me.

Not because she can't speak. Because she is scared. No. Bigger.

Terror. A shard of ice shoots up from the grave spearing me. I clutch at my breast and roll off the mound.

Matron strikes her, furious, and Jenny is terrified.

Why? I steel myself and roll back onto the grave, spread my wings over it. What did you see Jenny? Show me. I breathe into the wings and listen with every fiber. Show me, Jenny.

A picture roars up.

An open door across the dark corridor into a dimly-lit room. Matron hunches on her bed removing her enormous shoes. Then, pulls off leggings. She tugs off the olive dress. The pale white cotton slip casts a ghostly glow and she removes that. She takes off her chest tossing it to the bed and stretches. She reaches for her face and a scream erupts all over. Matron is on her feet grabbing at her gown and rushing across the hall.

Jenny screams with no sound, only terror.

It goes on and on. I roll off the grave holding my ears, afraid they will burst. My heart thrashes so hard it threatens to fly out. My wings enfold me, evening my breath, softening everything. What have I seen? What does it mean? No longer trapped with her in the grave, her vision shimmers in the air above me. I watch it over and over.

A raven swoops through and flies toward town.

I need to tell Rorrick what I know but he can't see me.

Stanley can.

PEOPLE PACK THE SMALL ROOM WHERE STANLEY LIES IN BED. ALL OF them are luminous and translucent except for a spidery woman, one of the sherry women from the pub, who circles through them pocketing things. A Swiss Army knife, a money clip. The others only have eyes for Stanley. Filaments of golden light interweave between them, engulfing the bed. The sherry woman finishes her scavenging and settles into the stiff chair at the bedside. Father Donovan steps into the room and the people part for him. The light swirls but touches neither him nor the sherry woman.

"Thank you for sitting with him, Miss Grelen. I'm sure it eased his last moments."

Miss Grelen rises, pious and proud. Sickly maroon tendrils ensnare her. "I welcome God's work."

Father Donavon pats her shoulder. "You are a treasure." As she leaves, he steps toward Stanley holding his Bible and speaking a prayer in a low voice.

Stanley stands beside me. He is radiant.

This is a nightmare. "Stanley you can't leave. I need you to talk to Rorrick."

Father Donavon drones over gray Stanley as luminous Stanley stands surrounded by his crowd woven together in broad rays of light. The filaments from the graveyard grown stronger. He points to a small girl and says, "She looks better." The girl ogles me in awe then shimmers away. My heart crumples.

Stanley pats my shoulder. "The fully dead know what we can do, even if we don't. But don't stay too long."

The room empties except for Father Donavon, Stanley cooling in the bed, and me. No one had wings, just luminous light they faded into. I fall back but my wings tug and ache and keep me upright.

I want to rip them off.

RORRICK HANGS UP THE PHONE AS THE SERGEANT COMES IN WITH AN envelope.

"Another all-nighter?" He tosses it on the desk. "Special delivery from the Bureau of Records. This about the little girl?"

Rorrick rips the seal. He is brilliant with light. "I had a hit last night. Did some research. Nothing on the girl but look at this." He pushes the paper across the desk.

"Marvin Ellis." The sergeant shrugs. "I don't understand."

Rorrick leans back. He is the sun this morning. "Marvin..." He taps the paper. "Is Matron Ellis. Born a man."

She took off her slip and then her chest.

What Jenny saw. Matron removing a prosthetic not a terrifying monster shedding its human form. But then, infuriated, Matron grabbed the girl and struck her. Oh God. A girl with a fragile brain. Oh God.

The sergeant stares back. "She is a he?" He turns back to the paper. "I heard of that. My sister shares a flat with one. Saved the whole building from a fire last May. A hero."

"Matron's no hero. She's our murderer."

The sergeant shakes his head. "A secret sure, but murder seems a leap."

"A life built on secrets leads to a sticky web. If this got out, old Donovan's legion of pious ladies will run her out of town."

"But how does the girl factor in?"

I lean toward Rorrick, praying, willing him to get this.

"The girl was alone across the hall, the door was open. She saw something. Something that gave it away. Scared and angry at being discovered, Matron grabs her. With that aneurysm, it wouldn't take much."

"But how'd she get in the creek?"

Rorrick is resplendent and I love him. I love him with every feather in my wings. "I'm thinking," he says. "She panics, runs her to the path tossing her in the creek. A runaway accidentally drowning. Not bad for thinking on the fly."

"Except for..."

Rorrick smiles. "She said she's never been to the creek, but the Wellies she wore to the funeral and the pub, were slick with the red clay. That iron ore only bubbles up at the creek. Nowhere else."

Heavy boots run past me and down to the creek.

"So, she had been there and recently."

"Right."

"And lied about it."

The sergeant drops into the chair. "Motive and method. Hmm."

"There's more."

"Bring me home, Sherlock."

"Matron is at mass every Sunday and Wednesday, has nightcaps at the pub on the regular. She is enormous. You can't miss her. What is she always fiddling with over that olive dress?"

The sergeant settles, thinking. "Her St. Christopher medal. Kind of weird for a woman. Most of them wear simple crosses."

"For ten years I see this giant sour woman around town brandishing a traditional St. Christopher medal. Like mine and yours. All of a sudden, she's got a new one. Different. A gift, from the priest."

The sergeant looks bewildered. The necklace is slicing into my hand, but I can't take my eyes from Rorrick. He slides a photo from the file across the desk. "What do you see?"

The sergeant examines the photo. "The girl's hand. Sliced across the palm and a..." He pulls it closer. "A bruise."

Rorrick pulls his medal over his head and holds it out. "Shaped like this?"

The Sergeant looks at Rorrick's necklace then, at the photo. Their eyes meet. "Could have been Kelso's."

Rorrick shakes his head. "No. Kelso would have none of him. Told me himself. Plenty of nights drying out in the tank." Her gestures to the holding cell.

Offended, the sergeant touches his chest, locating his own medal. "St. Christopher is patron of travelers and children. He carried Jesus across a river."

"Before that, he worshiped a king, then the devil himself. Kelso said he couldn't abide a saint like that. Willing to serve whoever seemed most powerful."

"So, you think it's Matron's missing necklace in the girl's hands?"

"It's not the whole case, but we need that necklace." Rorrick grabs his coat. "Get the metal detectors and meet me at the creek."

Boots run past, the necklace drops, and I grab it.

I have it. The only real evidence and I've fucked that up too. I try to slump back but my wings don't let me.

THE MEN ARE WORKING THE METAL DETECTORS ALL OVER THE RIVER bank. The necklace slices into my hand, blood dripping and vanishing before it hits the ground. The pain is nothing compared to what I know. I have the necklace and I can't give it to them. They need what they won't find. So close, and, because of me, it will come no closer. I sulk on a damp log beside the water listening to the metal detectors hum. The men sweep in the water up and downstream and the bank where Jenny came to lay. Slow and painstaking, they creep up the footpath.

My back collapses heavy under the burden of defeat and, for once, not because of the wings. Lightened and sun-warmed, they shift a little in the breeze. Almost pleasant. The men work their way along their futile mission. The creek winds across rocks. The necklace, the key to all of this, rakes my hand and I know this will be my burden forever.

A soft hand slips into mine, a damaged one, bruised and cut and black with death. The girl connected to it is small and golden, her face soft with no lingering trace of terror. Where she touches me, gold light whispers and twirls and binds us as the bruising and insults wash clean. Her smile breaks my heart because I will fail her again. She looks at me with such love I weep. I pull her to me and my wings enfold us and inexplicably, I start to know.

Even before her hand is fully healed, even before the stigmata of my hand lightens and releases the necklace, even before I hear the telltale mechanical pings of the metal detectors and the triumphant hoots of the men, I know.

I NEVER WENT BACK TO MY SHACK AFTERWARD. MY BODY WAS already there. Already dead. Lost and wondering, I came upon them, the distraught saint with Matron and a very dead girl.

The necklace dropped and I grabbed it.

No. The saint stumbled, because even saints stumble. He stumbled and fell but I caught him. I was there and I caught him and with him I caught Jenny. St. Christopher carried Jesus across the river but he couldn't carry Jenny. Not like that. He went looking for a god to serve and worship and he picked wrong. Now we three stand here. Jenny and me and a saint who only means to serve.

When the whoops come, I don't look. The necklace is with Rorrick and his brilliant vermilion heart. I've carried St. Christopher to him and together they will finish this. My part is done.

I scoop up this golden child, this creature of wonder and stardust into my arms and rise, wings fully unfurled. I know. I, Christopher Kelso, know exactly what my wings are for.

The Vanishing

Carrie Hayes

"I promise." My brother, Sean, was emphatic. "I'm *not* having a party."

I couldn't hear our Dad's response. We were crossing First Avenue and I trailed the pair of them, straining to eavesdrop without seeming to do so. We entered the news shop where I barely caught Dad's, "un hunh." Sean's petition was dismissed, the case closed.

I chose a pack of gum and put it on the counter.

Dad gestured to his preferred can of pipe tobacco. "Hey, Rishi. Happy New Year."

"And to you," said the newsagent. On the wall behind the counter were treasures, trinkets, jewelry, lighters, key chains, and those pens that, when tilted, revealed a scantily dressed woman or a fish. Junk mostly, depending on one's point of view.

Back at the apartment, we prepared to load the car. My mother was always either leaving or arriving, which involved the detailed business of packing. It was one of the enduring rituals in our parents' frayed relationship. The four of us lived in disparate corners of the globe, yet somehow, we were still a family, at least during the holidays.

Sean said, "I'm not going uptown." My mother turned toward Sean. Like her, he was formidable in the way he packed stuff she wanted from the apartment. Perhaps that's why he had her sympathy. "It'll just be a couple of old friends. Ben is coming. You like Ben." After graduating college, Sean had rented a room in a cold water flat, way, way uptown in what some people called Upstate Manhattan.

Our mother actually did live upstate, while our dad was mostly here in his apartment off Sutton Place. It was a one bedroom, but in some ways, it was perfect. I was at boarding school, and with us kids not around, our parents' lives were quite separate. But when I showed up, they cobbled together a strange semblance of normalcy. We'd go to the theater and do city things, staying at my dad's where Sean and I camped on the sofas, our parents retreating behind the silence of their bedroom door.

Sean made one final plea. "I swear I'm not having a party." His eyes are blue and heavily lashed. "Really." When he looks straight at you, his gaze is warm. It commands trust, faith even.

After what felt like forever, Dad said, "All right." Then he added a bond to which Sean agreed. Rather than go upstate with our parents, I would remain for the evening's events. Sean was twenty-two years old, and I was fifteen. Nobody asked me to weigh in. They could see I was thrilled. It was written all over my face. They knew Sean was serious in his role as older brother and he and I both knew, that if the need arose, they'd use my witness testimony, with their mistaken belief that I was a terrible liar.

It was very warm that year. We didn't wear coats when we loaded the car. The doorman watched from under the awning as the station wagon pulled into the street and we waved our parents goodbye. We watched the car turn left on to Sutton Place where it would head north up York and over to the FDR.

Sean turned on his heel and handed the doorman the agreed upon sum. With a wink and a nod, New Year's Eve, 1979 was now under way.

Ben was the first to arrive. He carried a small goatskin bag and embraced my brother with a happy open smile. He lumbered over to me and took me in his arms. "Sister," he exclaimed. Ben always addressed everyone as if they were a member of his family. His teeth were a wreck, and his nose was too big, yet with his golden skin and honey-colored hair, Ben was terrifically handsome.

He and Sean had graduated the previous spring. But while Sean had scrambled to carve out a life in New York, Ben had wandered the world.

They both opened their bags. Sean's was filled with balloons and rolls of raffia to hang from the ceiling. Ben had souvenirs, like statues and marbles, odd-looking trinkets. He lit some incense in a gleaming crystal ashtray my mom had placed on a table. Sean opened the bag of balloons and the three of us began blowing them up.

"Where did you come from?" I asked Ben. I tied a knot in my first balloon.

He let some air out from his. Just a little, so it sounded silly. "I was with my folks on Long Island."

"Oh." I made a slight nod of ennui, anxious to show my empathy and my sophistication, too. We handed our balloons over to Sean.

"But before that I was in Kabul. And before that I was in Tehran. And before that I was in Damascus."

"Really?" Visions of these places swirled before me. Ben was so exotic.

"Hmm..." We filled more balloons and wordlessly knotted them.

I brought him the step ladder and twisting some raffia, gave it to him. He taped it to the ceiling, first one length and then another. I said, "I thought the Russians—"

"I left before they got there." The ceiling was festooned in purple and yellow lengths of ribbon. "I was staying with a mullah, and he got me out."

"Really?" Plastic cups and paper napkins were set upon the dining table.

"Yeah! I was pretty lucky. I hid under a blanket in his camping van."

The doorman called announcing a delivery of ice. "Send him up," I said, while Sean remained focused, the mountain of balloons growing beside him.

"What was that like?" I asked Ben. We put the ice in the bathtub.

"You know, the people were incredible," Ben paused, then added, "The air was really different from here. I felt perfectly at home."

"Wow. I can't imagine doing any of that." Chatting with him was effortless.

He described his adventures with as much wonder as I had hearing them. "Now tell me about you. What's going on with you these days?" Ben waited, as if what I'd say mattered, as if I were someone who actually had something to say.

I resisted the urge to not answer. With his soft eyes and broken smile, I didn't feel awkward or self-conscious in the way I normally did. Looking back, I have no idea what my response was, but his answer would have been kind and witty. I know I must have laughed, happy to be in his company.

The room was soon lavishly festive. The three of us went to our respective corners, re-emerging in our party clothes. Mine was a silk ensemble, tailored to resemble men's pajamas. Tricked out with a string of pearls and impossibly high heels, I teetered, then got my footing and strutted a few steps.

Ben gave a soft whistle, "You look like you're in a play by Noel Coward."

I gestured to his dinner jacket. "So do you."

He put his hand on his chest. His bow tie rested around his collar which was open. "I don't know how to tie this, though. Do you?"

That we should resemble two of a kind had me beaming from ear to ear. We'd become glamorous, possibly louche, and undeniably elegant.

I shrugged, "Sean? Can you tie a bow tie?"

Sean poked his head out from the kitchen, he was wearing a corduroy blazer. But his style was such that Sean was elegant regardless of his clothes. He was my brother, and that's how I saw him. He smiled at the pair of us, resplendent in our finery.

"Sorry kids." He went over to the record player. "I still need Mom for that."

The music was something warbly and understated.

A melancholy woman sang, "*Oh give me something to remember you by...*"

Then Ben's hand was around my waist, and he sang to the record, stepping forward with a graceful turn. "*When you are far away from me.*"

Despite my heels, I followed his lead. We danced, almost like floating, until the doorman buzzed and the guests began to arrive.

Sean took coats while Ben stood at the door, "Happy New Year! Amy, I haven't seen you since graduation!" Or, "Hello. Come on in, brother. Happy New Year, my name's Ben." He cut quite the figure, with his dinner jacket and bow tie and collar still open. Bottles upon bottles were handed to him, which he passed to me. I noticed a thin silver chain with a rose-colored stone resting at the base of his throat.

Anxious to seem efficient, I scurried to the bathroom, placing the booze in the tub filled with ice. Returning to my place between Sean and Ben, I imagined myself a junior hostess of sorts, grateful to be included.

People continued to fill the apartment, and I moved back and forth, nestling the bottles in and against each other, much like the guests at our party.

A group surrounded Ben, and I slid into the space on his right. He described wandering through Mongolia, falling in love in Nepal, living at an ashram in India. Each anecdote was more extraordinary than the last, yet none of the telling seemed pompous or crazy. Rather, Ben found it as miraculous as we did.

One of the women looked me up and down, "You're Sean's sister." She stood on Ben's other side. "How cute."

"What's that?" Another woman pointed at his necklace.

"It's a rose quartz. It's from India."

He slightly bent his knees. She leaned forward, squinting at the stone.

"It's for peace and joy." He smiled at me. "And emotional healing."

Did Ben know that I'd been hurt? Did he sense I had poor

judgment? I still winced, ashamed and embarrassed when thinking of a boy who I'd let do things to me I rather wish he hadn't.

"Ben, do you need to be healed?" The woman was flirtatious, a coquette.

Ben threw back his head and laughed at this, replying, "You don't know how to tie a bow tie, do you?"

Sean tapped me on the shoulder, pointing to another rush of people at the door.

A guy named Jimmy introduced himself and handed me a bottle. He was funny and goofy. Another guy named Jimmy was intense and wore a beret. That Jimmy introduced me to his girlfriend who'd been editor of the college paper. They were friendly and kind, having begun their adult adventure while I was still in my childhood one. The ruckus and the crowd continued to grow. I squeezed next to someone who wore a tuxedo. Someone else stood on my toe.

"Ouch."

"I'm sorry." His smile was caught in that space between boy and man. Standing in my heels, we were nearly the same height. I felt very sophisticated, very sophisticated, indeed.

The crush in the living room became worse. Suddenly, Ben shouted, "Let's go to the roof!"

Everyone agreed and we piled into the elevators up to the floor marked PH. When the doors opened, there were only three apartments in the hallway instead of the usual five, and two separate doors to the roof. One went to the front of the building and the other opened onto the back where the airshaft was, which was the roof we stumbled onto. The night was mild, but you could still see your breath. We were rowdy and it was fun. The discussion turned to Time and illusions, how Time was actually fake and that all of it was a lie.

Ben looked up at the moon, then back at the rest of us. "We should throw away Time." His eyes sparkled. "It's being robbed from us, anyway. Let's make it disappear!" There were cheers and whistles at this, everyone shouting their agreement.

People removed their watches. For one brief moment, Ben put his hand on his throat, gave a little start, as if something had surprised him. He leant toward me. "Give me your hand."

Obediently, I did.

"I want you to have this." He pressed his necklace into my palm. "Keep it. You might need it." He added, "It will remind you, just in case." He frowned, "I think the fastening's broken."

I slipped it deep into the pocket of my pajamas, securing it with a button. Turning back to the others, he then removed his watch. It was nearly midnight.

Someone began the countdown. "Ten! Nine! Eight!" Everyone joined in. Timex and the like were held up in the air. I didn't wear a watch then. "Three! Two! One! Happy New Year!"

There were horns and shouting, fireworks in the sky. Everyone flung their watches over the side of the building. They dropped into the air shaft, like so many pebbles, somewhere far below us.

"What are you doing?" The door to the hallway was open. An old woman stood in its threshold watching us. She wore a black house coat with a zipper that ran up to her throat. Ben came forward and introduced the group.

She waved us across the hall to her apartment. "Come in, come in." By now we were only a dozen or so. Our hostess sat down, and Ben curled up at her feet, everyone else was cross legged on the floor. Along the far wall was a fire in the fireplace, flanked by French doors leading out to her apartment's portion of the roof.

"Will you tell us your story, Mother?" Ben asked in that same way he spoke to me, as if what I said really mattered.

"How about I tie that bowtie for you?" He happily moved closer to her as she began the folds and tucks of tying a bowtie. "And first, why don't you tell me where you've been and where you want to go?"

He gazed at her, his smile strangely bashful. "I just got back from traveling the world."

The tie was now in place and she touched his cheek with her hand. "I did that once. Long, long ago. How does it feel to be home?"

"It feels like I need to leave again." His voice was soft, I could barely hear him. "My journey has just begun and I don't want it to end."

Someone had opened the door to the terrace. Garden furniture was covered for the winter but the boxwood hedge was green and alive.

I stepped outside. The high-rise next door had yet to be built, and, from where I stood, I could see the Pepsi Cola sign reflected on the river.

"*Fire!*" There was a shout, but it seemed far away. "*Fire!*"

Somewhere below, out on the street, were sirens and alarms. I went back inside. The party was peaceful. No one was ready to leave. Then Sean crossed the room. He took my elbow and led me into the hallway.

"What did I do?" I was afraid there would be a lecture. Rather than answer, he pressed the button of the elevator. Then he changed his mind.

"Come on." He took my hand and we crossed to the stairwell. Down, down, down the flight of stairs. Seventeen floors in four inch heels, hanging on to that handrail for dear life. We saw no one else, as if the building were empty. At last, we burst onto the sidewalk. Flames leapt out of a window two stories above us. The distant sirens grew louder. Save for the doorman standing by the awning, we were the only people on the street. Sean looked at the East River, then west at the firetrucks barreling toward us. I shivered in my heels and silk pajamas.

"Stay here," he said. "I'll be right back." He approached the doorman. A pair of firetrucks pulled up outside the building.

In the distance, one of the Jimmy's came from across the street. He saw me standing by myself. He waved, his face shining with joy, oblivious to the commotion, and the hydrant being opened. "You won't believe where I was!"

"Where was that?" The night sky had begun to fade. Firemen ran behind him, pulling their hose from the truck.

"Studio 54! It was *amazing*."

"Oh."

Jimmy looked over his shoulder, at the red flashing lights.

"There was a fire," I said, coolly detached, an expert, fifteen-year-old witness.

He frowned.

I beamed at the thought of the cozy penthouse apartment, the elegant young people visiting the old woman. "And everyone's on the roof."

Moments passed. "All clear!" came the shout. The firemen returned their axes and hoses back to their trucks.

"Well, let's go in then," Jimmy said.

"I have to wait for Sean."

Jimmy shrugged at this and went inside. Moments later, Sean waved me over and we took the elevator. My shoes felt unbearable. I got out at our floor. "I'm gonna get my sneakers."

He nodded. "See you upstairs."

I was cold and needed something warmer than a pair of silk PJs. The door of the apartment stood open. A handful of people were in the living room. My clothes were in the bedroom, as were a naked couple in the bed. They looked at me, irked at the interruption. Silently, I gathered my things, closed the door and took the elevator back to the penthouse.

Everything was much as I'd left it, only Ben was standing near the French doors. "You've returned!"

"Yes." My innocence dangled by a thread, breathless, happy, ready to be lost.

"Let's watch the sunrise." He held his hand out to me and we stepped outside. We were the only ones there. Long Island City and Roosevelt Island had yet to become the bustling neighborhoods they are today. All one saw was the wreck of Blackwell's Island and the Pepsi sign shining across the river.

The sky turned to dawn then to gold. He put his hand around my waist, humming the tune from my brother's record.

When he spoke, I could see his breath. "Are you warmer now?"

In my sweater and jeans, I definitely was. "Yes, I am." The air was crisp, but I was warm.

"Happy New Year." His kiss was tender, chaste.

It was 1980, the first day of a new decade. It was time for the party to end.

At the door, Ben embraced the elderly woman.

"I will see you again," she said.

"Yes, Mother," he smiled down at her. "You will."

It was brilliantly sunny outside. All of us squeezed round a table at the diner across the street. The chatter and the breakfast, the cigarettes and coffee took pride of place, but I barely noticed, still glowing from that moment on the roof.

Ben removed his bowtie and stuffed it in his pocket. "Sugar?"

I nodded, blushing.

Someone asked Ben what he'd do next. My brother leaned back to listen to the answer.

"I've been offered a job with the State." Ben sighed and put out his cigarette. "I start on Monday."

The conversation resumed, moving in a thousand directions. Ben stretched and sighed, "I don't think I'm going to do it."

Someone paid the check. Outside, bright daylight warmed our shoulders and the morning filled with possibility. At the corner, we went east to go back to the apartment, but Ben kept walking north.

"Hey Ben!" Sean called. "When are you coming back?"

Ben stopped. He turned to face us. Smiling, he shrugged, "Later?"

He turned back around, his long stride heading uptown as he grew smaller and smaller in the distance.

None of us ever saw Ben again.

The couple in my parents' room were gone. We scoured the apartment, vacuuming, polishing, spraying, and scrubbing. Ben's goatskin bag discreetly waited in the corner behind the lamp. The ashtrays sparkled; the pillows were plumped.

My parents were suitably impressed.

My mother poured my dad a scotch, and he toasted my brother.

"Well, I had misgivings," he said, "But you did the right thing." Taking his first sip, his eyes moved up in the way they do as you lower your glass. A bit of purple raffia, smaller than a dime, was still hung from the ceiling.

Rather than react he looked at my brother, and my brother met his gaze. They both remained silent.

The next week, Ben's father called. Ben had not returned to Long Island. Had he made mention of his plans? Sean opened Ben's bag. His passport and savings account book were inside. The balance was several thousand dollars.

Weeks passed. I returned to boarding school and wondered what stories Ben might tell the next time we met. When I came home, it was springtime. Sean mentioned him several times in passing. His parents had collected Ben's bag, but no one had seen nor heard from him. A detective interviewed Sean, but nothing came of that. Eventually, Ben's mother asked Sean to meet a psychic on TV. Friends advised him not to, so he demurred.

People described Ben as someone who could vanish. It turned out he had done it before. He had the means to do it again. There was much talk about his fascination with the East. If Sean or I saw a group of Hare Krishnas, we always stopped and looked, to see if Ben was among them. But he never was.

Eventually, there was a police report, but in truth, there was nothing, only that brief, "Who knows?"

Time passed, and with it, another New Year's Eve. As the years went by, Sean said little of his missing friend. I embarked on my own adventures, often filled with terrible choices, because that was the path I set for myself. Sean grew to be successful, but was still the perfect brother, wiping my tears when things went wrong, waiting in the shadows should I seek reinforcements. As the decade drew to a close, Ben's name would come up, always followed by the unspoken question: What could possibly have happened?

Eventually, it was New Year's Eve, 1989. Our Dad had died earlier that year and Sean took over the apartment, using it as an office of sorts. He wondered, if the stage were set properly, would Ben return?

Sean went up to the penthouse, but the lady who had been so kind to us had died by then as well. There was no disputing it. Life went on and so did we.

What was one decade became two. By the third decade, most of us who'd been at the party were married and divorced at least once. I counted myself amongst them. Several had died of AIDS. Many just moved away and were now out of touch. Someone, perhaps it was Sean, sent around an email, asking if there wasn't some way to find out what had happened to Ben. There was a friend in forensics, another in the coroner's office. Enquiries were made. But there was nothing. One of the Jimmy's had known Ben in high school and had recently gone to Ben's house. He knew Ben's parents still lived there, waiting, hoping that Ben would come back. Otherwise, they worried, he wouldn't know how to find them. Jimmy knocked on the door, and the woman who answered was one of Ben's sisters. She was in her late fifties. When Jimmy offered to help with some yard work, she declined, saying that if her parents saw him, it would remind them too much of Ben.

Jimmy's email described this to the group; how Ben's parents waited, every day, just to hear something, anything, that might bring back their son.

Someone in the email chain knew a psychic in Texas who was coming east for the New Year. Sean jumped at this and invited the psychic to come to the apartment.

I answered the buzzer.

"Ellie le Farge is here," said the doorman.

Ellie's coat had a wide velvet collar and she seemed a caricature of whatever one imagines a psychic to be.

"Do you have an item of Ben's clothing, or some possession he may have left behind?"

Sean went to a dresser in the hallway. He removed something from the top drawer and handed it to her. It was the silver chain with the rose-colored stone. My heart began pounding.

"Oh give me something to remember you by."

The three of us held hands in a circle and Ellie whispered, "Let us pray." We bent our heads.

Time. The years. Ben's golden smile with that rose-colored stone resting at his throat. His hand upon my waist. In a life made up of many mistakes, that brief moment with Ben had not been one of them.

Ellie spoke, "It was not far. He only went a block or two from here. There was much energy, much commotion, lots of noise and a crashing!" She looked up at us, her eyes were sorrowful. "Now there is nothing. There is nothing for you to do."

She put the necklace on the coffee table. I realized it wasn't the same one. Its fastening was intact.

After she left, Sean poured himself a glass of the scotch our father used to drink. When he gestured, I nodded and he poured me one, too. I lit a cigarette and tossed the match into the ash tray. It was a favorite of our mother's, heavy and beautiful, no doubt a relic from that party.

Sean said, "When you lose your parents you're orphaned and when you lose a spouse, you're widowed." There was a catch in his voice, his beautiful eyes were haunted. "But there's no word for friends who've lost friends or for parents who lose children, is there?" He finished his scotch. "Imagine them waiting, every single day."

"Sean, how did you get that necklace?"

He stood up. "Come on. I want to show you something."

It was New Year's Eve, thirty years to the day since that party. It was cold and overcast. Crumpled wrappers and litter blew across the street. Most of the places on First Avenue had changed hands. But a few of them were the same. The same dry cleaner, the same diner, the same newsagent. We entered the shop. Rishi's son, also named Rishi, sat behind the counter.

"Let me have one of those." Sean gestured to the charms hanging on the wall behind him. Rishi turned and took one down. Inside the clear plastic was a fine silver chain with a rose-colored stone, identical to the one Sean had given to the psychic.

"Two ninety-nine."

Back on the sidewalk, Sean handed me the necklace. "Ben always had tons of these. He gave them to people he liked."

We crossed the street. I felt inside my pocket. I had never mended the fastening of the one Ben had given me. Most days it sat in a box on my dressing table, buried somewhere amongst a jumble of jewelry. But sometimes, I took it out and held it to remind me. Sometimes, it summoned that beautiful winter night. But most times, it just reminded me how precious every fleeting second is. Because suddenly, without warning, all of it could vanish.

THE LEAVENWORTH NECKLACES

GAIL LEHRMAN

U tley, the jittery cage-kicker stationed outside the cell block, barks "Keep back," before he slides the bars open to admit a latecomer. His panic is a source of universal amusement. Because we're denied the privilege of the exercise yard, the imbecile assumes he's guarding the prison's worst ogres. He's too dense to grasp that we're in chains because we spoke against the vile savagery of war, and we're confined to rec time in our cellblock corridor because the warden fears our unpatriotic blasphemies might corrupt the prison's regular population of thugs and murderers.

"It's a compliment, really," Nardo Albinoni asserts as he gnaws the stem of his empty pipe. "The Oppressors fear that our pen is mightier than their sword."

He would know. Albinoni's editorial urging workers to ignore their government's command to fight a rich man's war earned him a five-year sentence under President Wilson's mighty Espionage Act.

The gate scrapes the concrete floor. Eli Edwards traipses in, covered in muck and reeking of shit. A strapping hayseed newcomer, he got stuck cleaning the latrines in the quarry long after we came in for rec.

"*Madonna.*" Nardo glances up as Edwards passes. "I thought you were our resident burly peasant, Leo, but that goliath puts you to shame."

Back in his cell, Edwards bends low over his sink to wash up. It's true. There aren't many here who can touch my bulk, but he makes me look small.

I move my black checker forward on the diagonal. Bam, bam, bam, bam. Albinoni's red king circles the board. Losing checkers to Albinoni is one of the great consistencies of my imprisonment, along with the rats, lice, bedbugs, and maggots—both insect and human. I set the board for another game, noticing that Edwards has pulled his Bible onto his lap. We all get to keep some preferred reading matter, but, since his arrival two weeks ago, that black book has been Edwards' single companion.

"Do you believe in God, Nardo?"

"My father was an anarchist, and his father before him. What do you think?"

"Nor me. You know—*religion is the opiate of the masses...*"

"*Ai, si,*" he razzes. "Yet another of your dictatorial Marxist decrees."

Arguing revolutionary philosophy with Albinoni is another great consistency of our acquaintanceship given the ideological chasm between his anarchism and my Marxism.

Across the corridor, the new man's lips move in what I assume to be prayer.

"Poor bastard." I push out my checker. "Surrounded by communists, anarchists, atheists, and Jews."

Albinoni double jumps me. "What do you suggest, Leo? Convert him to the Gospel of Marx instead of the Gospel of Jesus?"

I glance at the black bars, the grey walls, the single inch of daylight from the filthy slit they call a window. "Communist or Christian, to survive this place you need the gospel of something."

He slaps the empty bowl of his pipe against the table as if to clean it, then sneers at this pointless habit. "Or else the Gospel of Nothing."

———

NIGHT. CRIES. CURSES. THE MOANS OF SELF-ABUSE AND THE scritch of vermin scuttling across the concrete. Deep into my sleep, the smokey blackness congeals to become my wife, her hair piled high on her head, her arms outstretched. She glides toward me, a hovering accusation. *You said you'd be here.* I bat the empty air, gasping into wakefulness.

That's when I hear it.

"Jephthah, Joshua, Matthew, and John. Mary, Martha, and Grace."

I rub my eyes, frightened I'm still prisoner of the dream. The dirge comes again.

"Jephthah, Joshua, Matthew, and John. Mary, Martha, and Grace."

It's the next cell over—the farmer. Arms out to find the wall, I grope my way forward to the bars.

"Jephthah, Joshua ..."

"Edwards," I whisper. The chanting stops dead. "Edwards, what are you singing?"

Silence but for his ragged breathing.

"Are those saints from your New Testament? I don't know your Christian prophets. I'm a Jew by birth and an atheist by choice."

Still no answer. It's just as well. In this smoldering darkness, the man could be anyone, a friend, a comrade, even a minion of the God that I eschew. I curl up to the wall and wrap my arms around my knees.

"I was dreaming about my wife," I say. "She was eight months with child when I was taken at an anti-draft rally. It's been almost two years. They only let us write once a month." The rest chokes in my throat. I can't utter it aloud, not to my friends, not to my comrades, not even to the indifferent prison night.

A quivering whisper swims back through the dark. "I was reciting the names of my young'uns."

My head jerks up. Jephthah, Joshua, Matthew, and John. Mary, Martha, and Grace. God Almighty.

"How did you come to be here, man?"

"Like Lord Jesus, betrayed by a Judas." His nasal twang sounds alien to my city ears. "After the Spirit entered me at a revival, I took to preaching the Gospels. This one Sunday the lesson was John 3:15. 'You know that no murderer has eternal life abiding in him.' I asked the gathering if they thought Lord Jesus might not deem it fit to kill, even in war." His voice shudders. "A neighbor reported me to the draft board. I got a year for obstructing military service."

A foul, sour rage overtakes me. *I said...I wrote...I believe...*

"We're all victims of the same wickedness, comrade."

I offer my hand through the bars, not sure if he'll see it, but his calloused fingers find their way around mine. "Thank you, neighbor."

Soothed by his faceless company, I drift off to sleep on the hard stone floor.

"RISE AND SHINE, YOU CHICKEN-LIVERED SHITS."

My eyelids shoot open at the shrill clang of a bayonet clattering along our cages. Bull Bradshaw leads a squad through the cellblock, his eyes burning with venom.

"Stand forward for the count."

Groggy as I am, I snap to. Pulled from the trenches of France with a ruined leg, Bradshaw's brutality outstrips every other cage-kicker's here. Bradshaw limps the line, tapping his cudgel against his leather boot. He slides past me, but halts at Edwards' cell.

"On your feet, you milksop daisy."

I allow myself a sideways glance. Eli is still on his knees, palms pressed together.

"I am praying to Jesus Christ, in whom we are all saved."

"Praying, are you?" Bradshaw waves a hand. Two lackies open the cage and drag Eli forward. Smack. The cudgel slams his gut, doubling him over. "This is Leavenworth Prison. You want salvation, you pray to me." Bradshaw motions to the guards. "Punishment."

———

CLANG. THWACK. THE PERCUSSIONS ECHO OFF THE QUARRY CLIFFS. Overhead and down, I smash one boulder into three and those three into three more. In two years, the Espionage Act has tripled Leavenworth's population. The fortress bulges with the added human freight so, like the Hebrews in Egypt, we grind the bricks to expand the walls of our enslavement.

I wipe an arm across my sweaty brow, study the hillside in the direction of the Punishment Building. "It's been five days."

Albinoni is hauling the wheelbarrow that collects the stony fruits of my labor. "Why so concerned, Hirsch? We've all survived Punishment."

Five feet by nine. A slop bucket. A plank bed. The inner door of bars, the outer door of solid wood. When that's slammed shut, the white-hot cage becomes a shuttered black tomb and the vermin who hide from the light come clicking and crawling and slithering out of the bricks. Miriam's phantom appeared my first night in that black hole and I haven't had a full night's sleep since.

Still, there's a difference.

"We arrived here prepared for Capitalism's barbarities. Eli Edwards is an innocent."

"Not anymore," Nardo snorts. "By now he'll have discovered the Great Truth that we already knew—the only real God is power. The rich have usurped it." He makes a fist. "We must snatch it back."

"Nardo—" My response is interrupted by the clink of manacled feet. Utley slides down the gravel slope, dragging Edwards, his wrists and ankles chained. As they stumble to us, Utley unlocks the shackles.

"Sergeant says he's broken in. Put him to rock picking."

Nardo and I wait until the ox has stomped off, then we grab Edwards by the arms and lower him to the ground. I dash to the water station for a ladle. Edwards guzzles, liquid spilling down his chin.

"Easy." I let him take another swig.

Nardo is busy examining the raw flesh of Edwards' wrists. He looks up at me. "The Leavenworth jewelry."

I kick at the white dust in fury.

They invented the torture just for us. Thrust against the cage with your arms above your head, you hang from the bars by handcuffs they dub their "Leavenworth bracelets." After twelve, thirteen hours hogtied and wetting yourself, your knees become molten pokers, your arms iron pikes.

Eli's face is as grey as the quarry walls. He opens his mouth as if to speak, then shuts it. I put a hand on his shoulder. It's then I notice the welt around his neck, raw as his wrists. He blinks. His gaze centers on the farthest crag of the quarry.

"Eli?"

"They...I...He..." Eli can only manage a strangled rasp. "I was trussed like a pig for slaughter. That Sergeant Bradshaw pulled out this newspaper about how the Krauts slaughtered our boys in some Frenchy place. 'While you assholes strut around, safe as the Kings of Arabia.' He throws this rope over a hook in the ceiling. Nooses it round my neck. Pulls me to my toes. 'Long as you're here, you'll stand at attention to honor our dead heroes. Enjoy your Leavenworth Necklace, you cowardly shit.'"

A biting pain constricts my chest. "The whole time?"

"Released every night, trussed up every morning. Finally, I swore if they strung me up again, I'd make an end, though Devil might take me for a sinner." His shaking hand gloms onto my collar. "I closed my eyes and offered up my final prayer. 'Twas then it happened. God's clarion voice enveloped me in splendor. *I will throw open the floodgates of heaven and pour out so much blessing that you will not have room enough for it.* A Holy Light flooded my pit and I understood: God was scouring my soul to make it ready. I had only to hold fast in my faith until He revealed his Holy Purpose." Eli unbuttons his trouser waist. He has a long section of rope, noosed at the end, shoved into his pants. "It snapped just after I was cinched this morning. That Utley fella didn't pay me much mind at my release. I grabbed it soon as my hands were free."

A rain of pebbles drizzles down from the guard patrolling the path above.

Nardo jumps behind us so the guard won't see anything. I move to Eli's front, twisting to cover up the rope.

"Dump that thing. If they find it, you're a dead man."

Eli's big paw pushes me off. "You can't understand. God's chosen me to enter His Circle. I'm anointed to rid the world of that Devil."

"Bradshaw? You mean Bradshaw?" Nardo and I exchange a look.

"His Voice has commanded me, *Smite them and take their heads. Like clay vessels will they be smashed.*"

"Eli, you can't do a damn thing with one piece of rope."

"The Lord turned water into wine. He fed bread to the multitudes. Who knows what miracle can be wrought with a piece of rope?"

———

"Look at his face." I can't pull my eyes from Edwards across the mess hall, scrubbed and rested, still wrapped in his ecstatic mirage.

Nardo studies his soup and flicks out a worm. "The man's *pazzo.*" He taps a finger to his forehead. "Crazed."

"He'll get himself killed."

Shoving the bowl away, Nardo pulls out his empty pipe. "That might not be such a catastrophe."

I snap around. He ignores my angry scowl and leans closer so as not to be overheard.

"Thousands languish here, suffering the army's barbarity. Conscientious objectors, union builders, pacifists, men of conscience one and all. Our friends out in the world have been shouting about the injustice for two years. Now that the war nears its end, there's an opportunity to catch the public's ear. Imagine the outcry if the army murdered a good American farmer. A Christian preacher no less. A martyr like that could open our path to freedom."

"You mean to use him like a sacrificial lamb?"

"I'm not using him as anything. It would be an outcome of the man's own actions. One that would work to our advantage."

"I'm a Marxist. I don't betray one comrade to save another."

"You and your Communist dictums. What gives you the right to step between a man and his beliefs?"

Under the murmur of voices and clatter of plates and forks, I hear Eli's midnight song. "His seven children."

"Plenty of men have children. My mother had ten." Nardo rises. "Forget it, Hirsh. Whatever your tender proletarian feelings, if Edwards wants to use that rope, there's nothing you can do." He seizes his tray and strides away.

I look back to the big farmer across the room. "Maybe. Maybe not."

SHOES LACED, FULLY DRESSED, I LIE TENSED IN MY BUNK, EARS perked for the morning squad. Down the corridor, the outer cage screeches on the floor. Boot heels strike the concrete. "Up for the Count." Luck is with me. It's not Bradshaw's voice.

When they're five cells away, I hop to the crapper and shove my fingers down my throat so I'm bent and retching when they reach me. It's a tactic we perfected when we discovered that the army assigned us a physician straight out of school and the cub retains something resembling a conscience: on occasion, he will treat the sick.

I sit in the infirmary, bare to the waist, while the doctor knocks on my chest and listens through his earpiece. "Whatever you ate will pass out your gullet or your gut. I'll give you a day's work pass."

"I was so sick, I thought I'd go crackers." Buttoning up my shirt, I look around as if making casual small talk. "I bet you get a lot of loony guys in this hole."

He wrinkles his nose at my choice of words. "The congenital weakness of the criminal mind is often outside of his control. If a man's condition is that dire, we send him to the asylum." He's busy writing out my pass. "Hardly any gift. A prison term has a limit. The insane could be asylum-ed for life. Here. Show this to the guard."

He hands me my paper and shuttles me out. It was far-fetched, but worth the tiny effort of asking. I glance down at my yellow work pass. This is the real goal. I can go alone to the empty cellblock, where the cages stay unlocked while the inmates are in the field.

Eli's cell is just like mine, a shelf for personals, sink, crapper, bunk. I frisk all the usual spots, upending the mattress, running my hand under the blankets down to the foot of the bed, turning out the pillow case, feeling the wall behind the sink and crapper. Damn. I tap my foot on the floor and give the cell a final once-over. There, on the shelf, tucked between Eli's shirts, a hint of something pale. I stride over. My hand closes on a thin white envelope. Not exactly the prize I came for but...I glance over my shoulder. Still alone. I perch on Eli's bunk and unfold a single page scribbled in smudged pencil.

> *Dear husband,*
>
> *I have written the army to ask after you, begging they might give you to us for harvest if you swear to return once it is done. I wrote you were a good husband and steady father until you felt the Good Lord's call. I set out how you sermonized about the war in ignorance, being that you were not a trained preacher. The crops are due and we have lost the cow to bloat. Grace is still at my breast, but the rest suffer for the lack of milk and we scarce have money for flour and salt.*
>
> *Please, as your young'uns are so missing you, and me too, can you ask their indulgence as an act of Christian charity?*
>
> *Your loving wife,*
>
> *Hettie*

The sheet drops from my fingers and gooseflesh pebbles my arms as the worn, haggard figure of Hettie Edwards comes to life in the grey cage, surrounded by waifs, an infant at her breast. My wife, Miriam, floats beside her, but Miriam's open arms are empty. 'You said you'd be here.'

When I walked away from her, spouting my Marxist doctrine, was I as lunatic as Eli Edwards?

Hettie Edwards' letter lies at my feet. I reach to retrieve it. A knot of determination hardens in my chest. One grieving mother is enough.

THEY ROUST US OUT TO WORK AT DAWN, THE WHOLE CELLBLOCK, shivering with no jackets against the autumn air. Under the charcoal sky, no one but me thinks to question the lump under the shirt Eli Edwards has buttoned up to his neck.

Utley is squinting at his clipboard, laboring to read our assignments. "Sergeant's up at the north rim. He needs two bruisers for boulder smashing." He blinks into the sun rising diamond bright at our backs, doing his best imitation of thinking. Finally, he points to brawny Edwards. "You."

"As it is meant." Eli steps forward, chin high. "God's will be done."

Befuddled, Utley's brows furrow, but my stomach drops. In a desperate move, I shift my weight and fake cough to catch Utley's attention. It works. The donkey jerks his thumb for me to step forward.

"You too, Hirsch. And see you're quick about it. Sergeant don't take kindly to malingerers."

It's a hike to the far side of the quarry. Eli double-times it, wordless with intent. I trot at his side, cursing that his brawn makes him too powerful to simply wrestle down. I bat my brains. Come on, Hirsch. You've spent your life as an organizer. Your words are your best weapon.

We round a bend and Eli stops dead, his color rising. Up on the cliff-face, Bull Bradshaw, alone, silhouetted against the morning sky.

Eli's shoves a beefy fist into my shoulder. "Neighbor, best stay here."

I dance to hold my footing on the slope. "You'll hang like wet laundry in the wind."

His face could have been etched quarry stone. "I am the resurrection and the life: he that believeth in me, though he were dead, yet shall he live."

"Jephthah, Joshua, Matthew, and John. Mary, Martha, and Grace. You sang their names, remember?"

"I am elected. His will be done, on Earth as it is in Heaven."

I skip a circle, scanning the sky, the rocks, the air for an idea. I'm about to throw a punch, futile or not, when it comes to me.

"How do you know it was God's voice you heard in the Punishment cell? I mean, I'm not a believer, but they say the Devil comes in disguise, right? Isn't that in your Bible...the serpent in the Garden, tempting Eve. How do you know it wasn't the Devil that you heard?"

"There's godly and ungodly. A man needs only cleave to his heart. It'll take him to the right."

"I don't know, Eli. You are locked here because you spoke against killing. Now, you're planning to do murder. Does that sound like something your loving Jesus would want?"

My heart leaps as a wave of uncertainty ripples over Eli's face.

"Listen to me. The night I was arrested, my wife begged me not to go. You should have heard me proclaiming. 'No. We Marxists are the proletarian vanguard. It is my duty to be there.' Want to know what my proud declaration meant? It meant I never set eyes on my son. Samuel. Little Sammy. In the depth of sleep, I feel his ghostly infant fingers against my cheek. My wife buried him without me. Night after night I cry in vain, begging her forgiveness. Tell me, if that's not the Devil's work, what is?"

A breeze swirls dry dust at our feet. The distant clang of hammer against stone rises from the quarry floor. A crow crosses the horizon, cawing into the wind.

Eli's hesitant hand moves to his shirt. I hold my breath, as the long grey rope slithers from round his waist and hangs in his fist, it's noose-end swaying in the breeze.

Slowly. Slowly, like with a skittish child, I breathe, "I'll take care of it."

"No, you chicken shit assholes. That gadget belongs to me."

We swing round as Bull Bradshaw slides to a halt, spewing pebbles in the heavy scree, a pistol in his hand.

The air shoots from my lungs. I step backwards, half tripping over a jutting stone as Eli drops to a crouch.

Bradshaw flicks the gun and holds out his free hand. "Give her here. I know just where that baby needs to go."

Eli offers up the rope, but instead of surrendering it, he leaps, thudding into Bradshaw's gut, bringing him down with the force of a boulder. Bradshaw's face goes wild with shock as his finger jerks the trigger, sending a bullet whizzing uselessly off a boulder.

A troop of cage-kickers passing below us stops dead. "Hoy, what's the trouble up there?" Their feet scuffle the rocky soil as they barrel up the hill, guns clattering against their gear on the steep and treacherous slope. I watch frozen, as Eli, rising first, wraps the noose around Bull Bradshaw's neck and heaves.

Bradshaw's face goes crimson and his eyes bulge white and round. He gurgles, scratching his fingers at the rope. His bowels release. Eli leans backwards with the full weight of his body, holding Bradshaw in a death grip, when, ping, ping, ping three rifle shots slam into Eli's chest. Arms flying open, he's hurled backwards until his body lies spread-eagled on the hard, rocky slope.

Coughing and spitting, Bradshaw yanks the rope from his neck and rolls over, gasping for air. The platoon of guards reaches us, as Bradshaw heaves himself up and lurches over to Eli's body. He swings his one good leg and kicks in Eli Edwards' face.

Bellowing an animal howl, I hurtle myself at Bradshaw.

The rest is bedlam.

MY CHEEK IS PLASTERED AGAINST THE COARSE IRON OF THE BARS. The bracelets have scraped my wrists to the bone and my Leavenworth Necklace grinds the soft flesh of my neck. I have no idea how long they'll keep me in Punishment. It doesn't matter. When Bull Bradshaw defiled Eli Edwards' corpse, my gut burst into white-hot flame. If I survive, I will make my wife understand. No price is too costly, no sacrifice too deep. My phantoms are gone.

When night comes and I'm shuttered into this dark cage, I will sleep undisturbed.

A Voice

Elyse Garrett

Southern California
May 1961

We had a stupid fire drill at school after lunch. Too bad my family never got to practice before the fire.

I hurried home from school, but not to my real home, just a foster home. I slapped the soles of my new saddle shoes against the concrete sidewalk and jumped over the cracks. My favorite necklace hung around my neck and swung back and forth across my chest like the metronome that used to be on our piano.

The necklace was a tarnished chain with a silver St. Christopher medal. My oldest brother, Scott, had bought it for me and said it would keep me safe. "Every surfer wears a St. Christopher medal," he'd said, and slipped the chain over my head. "Now that you're a surfer, you'll never get wiped out from a wave." He'd had my name engraved on the back. *Ellie.*

We weren't Catholic. We were good surfers. I wore my necklace every day, even if I wasn't surfing. I wore it to a slumber party at my best friend's house. That was the night my house burned down. Killed my family. And our dog. I regretted going to the party and wearing the necklace. Saved me, but not my family.

My green Girl Scout uniform smelled new and felt stiff. I couldn't be late for my first Girl Scout meeting, but I had to get my sweater. If I felt scared or thought about my home in Huntington Beach, my family, or my dog, that horrible wave of fear would grab my stomach and make me throw up. I needed the sweater to help me feel safe and calm. Mom's sweater. The only thing that belonged to Mom that didn't burn. She had left it in the car parked along the curb. I loved the soft angora and Mom's lavender scent, so I kept it next to my pillow at night to calm myself after a bad dream.

That horrible wave also happened when I was in a new place or around new people. And, since everything and everyone was new, that wave hit me often, and got worse.

The foster family's gardener, Terrence, pushed his mower across their lawn. He mowed every week and wore his blue Dodgers baseball cap backwards. He stopped, letting the mower idle. His eyes followed me. Creepy. I squeezed my necklace and rubbed the medal between my fingers. *I'm safe.*

I sprinted toward the front door and grabbed the handle with both hands. Locked. I grabbed the key from under the yellow flowerpot on the porch, fumbled with the lock, and, after several tries, the door unlocked. I pushed it open and slammed it shut behind me.

Chills crept up my back.

As always, the foster family's house was quiet. Cold. No dog to greet me. No one was home. A cold hamburger or a sandwich always waited for me in the refrigerator. Since the social worker had brought me here, I ate dinner alone, in front of the TV, almost every day. No one hugged me, or sat at the table for dinner, talked about the day's events, or laughed together.

The foster mother said I could join the Girl Scout troop and go to the meeting at a neighbor's house. The neighbor would make tacos for the troop. But my mom made the best tacos in the world. *She used to.* Every Friday night, my brothers and I invited friends to Taco Friday.

We stuffed ourselves with Mom's tacos, made root beer floats, and played games.

That horrible wave rolled in my stomach.

The sound of Terrence's lawn mower stopped. I peeked out a window. His truck with THREE T's LANDSCAPING painted on the truck's doors was gone. I slipped my arms into Mom's sweater. A few sizes too big, but I wore it anyway.

Outside, I slipped the key under the flowerpot in case one of her sons came home early, like the foster mother had instructed me. A brisk chill in the air and a few dark clouds hovered in the distance. As I rushed past the rose bushes, a thorn caught the sweater's sleeve. I eased it from the soft yarn.

Something stronger grabbed my arm. Terrence stood in front of me. Blocked my way. His fingers dug deeper into my arm. His other stinky hand covered my mouth before I could scream. I kicked his knees and shins. Aimed for the area between his legs, used all my strength to pull away from his grip, and yelled a muffled scream. He squeezed my arm so tight I thought he would snap the bone.

He carried me down the sidewalk, threw me on the front seat of his truck, and slammed the door. The stench of fertilizer and cigarette smoke stung my nose and throat. I reached for the door handle. Nothing there, just a hole where it used to be. I kicked the door. It didn't budge. I pounded my fist against the window. Panic prickled down the back of my head and my spine. I screamed, "Help!" Again, again, and again.

He jumped into the truck next to me and pointed his dirty hand with black under his fingernails to my chin. He snarled. "Not a sound. Hear me?" I held Mom's sweater sleeve to my mouth. A neighbor must have seen him carry me to his truck.

He gripped the steering wheel, his eyes darting between the road and the rear-view mirror. He grabbed a brown paper bag from the floor and set it on the seat against his leg. The truck bounced down the street, onto the highway and smelled like the dark fertilizer he had spread in the yard.

"Where are you taking me?"

"Shut up." His eyes bore into me. A wave of pain struck my stomach. I was about to throw up, so I rolled down the side window until it stopped halfway.

"You ain't gettin' out, so don't try."

I tilted my head back to breathe in the fresh air and squinted against the late afternoon sun. I counted the highway markers to keep from looking at his face. That horrible wave of pain grabbed my entire body. *Will he kill me?*

Mom had warned me many times. "Never walk alone. Some crazy man might grab you and take you away."

Just like those girls who disappeared near Huntington Beach. Someone took them while they walked home from school. Maybe they'd sat in this truck, too.

A sign read San Bernardino County. After what seemed an hour, he turned off the highway onto a two-lane road with a gas station and a café on the corner. When Dad drove our family to Lake Arrowhead, he'd always stop at this gas station to fill the car's tank, before we'd all walk across the parking lot to Dottie's Café, where we'd eat the best homemade buckwheat pancakes in the world. Dottie always wore a pink apron with sparkly fringe that matched her pink cheeks as she made her way around the café, carrying a steamy coffee pot. She'd stop at each table to chat with her customers. She'd seemed to enjoy waving at the cars and trucks that pulled in and out of the parking lot through the café's full-length windows.

I spotted people inside the café near the window. "I'm hungry. Can we stop here?"

"Shut up," he growled. "You make another sound and I'll choke you."

I covered my throat with both hands, breathed in the lavender and recalled Mom telling me to "Call for help." I waved my arm out the window and screamed as if I was being killed. "Help! Dottie! Help!" My throat burned.

He grabbed my sweater and yanked me across the seat. My head bumped against the paper bag. Something full of liquid inside. His fist slugged my shoulder. "God dammit. I'll slice your throat if you try that again."

I sucked in a breath and folded my arms over my stomach. My throat felt heavy, like I had swallowed oil. Did anyone see me? Dottie?

He stepped on the gas and drove up the hill on a winding road with tall trees shading old houses in need of fresh paint. Rain drops streamed down the windshield. The wiper blades swept back and forth in a rhythm that sounded like shush, shush, shush. I gripped the edge of the seat as he raced around the hairpin turns. I kept my eyes on the road until it straightened out again. The rows of trees thickened into a dark forest with small run-down cabins back from the road. I rubbed the St. Christopher medal on my necklace. *Please keep me safe.*

He stomped on the brake pedal and skidded to a stop on the wet pavement. My knees slammed into the dashboard. He held his hand over the brown paper bag. A white McDonald's bag and a red flashlight rolled from under the seat onto the dirty floor mats. "Dammit." He pulled a piece of paper from his shirt pocket, like a gum wrapper, squinted at it, then eyed a rusted mailbox on a leaning post with faded numbers. "That's it," he said.

I searched into the forest, between trees, shrubs, and cabins, for someone to help me. No one. He shoved the piece of paper back into his pocket and turned the truck onto a bumpy gravel driveway. The shape of a cabin was barely visible at the end of the driveway. He twisted the steering wheel and spun the truck around to face the road, then backed it close to the cabin.

"Why are we here?" My voice sounded like sandpaper. Almost a whisper.

"I'll kill you if you talk again." He jumped out, ran around the front of the truck and yanked the truck door open, grabbing my arm and pulling me against his chest with one arm while the other went under my legs. "Quiet." He carried me into the tiny one-room cabin. "Don't say a word." He smelled like a dirty horse stall.

He's going to kill me.

He bolted the cabin door and turned a key in the lock. "Don't even think about gettin' outta here. It locks from inside, too." Bug spray fumes settled in the back of my throat. Dust floated in the air when he patted the overstuffed small sofa. "Sit here and shut up. Got it?"

I couldn't speak. I nodded and gulped down breaths to stay quiet and held the necklace to my lips. Mouse traps lined up under the bed. Moldy wood floors smelled like moss in the creek where the neighborhood kids and I caught crawdads.

He set the McDonald's bag and big brown paper bag on a wooden table barely big enough for two people to eat at, and two chairs, then he sat on a narrow folding bed that sloped in the middle. A dusty lantern hung from the ceiling, along with strands of spider webs, like a haunted house. He hung his blue baseball hat on a hook next to the locked door and stood in front of me, leaning his face close to mine. "Chuck will be here in the morning." His yellowed teeth and stinky breath made me gag.

"Who's Chuck?" I shivered.

"Shut up. I told you, don't talk."

Bile rose in my throat.

He straddled the narrow bed and leaned his head against the wall. He crushed an empty beer can and threw it under the bed along with the others, then grabbed a full can from the paper bag, peeled the tab, bent his head back, and guzzled. His Adam's Apple bobbed up and down.

IT SEEMED HOURS HAD PASSED WHILE HE READ A NEWSPAPER AND shoved two McDonald's hamburgers into his mouth. Shadows danced on the wall. It must be close to sunset. My teeth chattered and my hands trembled. I held my arm against my face. The soft angora yarn and the smell of lavender made me feel like Mom was with me. *Help me, Mommy.*

I tucked my icy hands between the sofa cushions and felt

something. I waited until he guzzled again and pulled up a pink barrette and pushed it into a pocket on my Girl Scout skirt. Did it belong to one of the missing girls? I wiped the tears rolling down my cheeks. No one would find me here. I had to get out.

Tonight.

The dark sky was visible through a space between the red and white curtains, but not the trees. Would the Girl Scout leader call my foster mom? Tell her I wasn't there? How would they find me locked in this scary place with this crazy man?

Mom had warned me about crazy men like Terrence. She had always worried that someone would take me, like the two ten-year-old girls. Same age as me. Linda had disappeared first. The police found her lunch pail on the curb by the school. Then Susie. She'd left her new bike on the side of the road.

Mom had told me, "No matter how scared you are, kick him. Between his legs. Grab something and hit his face, and scream. Loud. Get help. Run away as soon as possible. Don't wait." It had seemed silly then. I'd never thought someone would take me. But Terrence did.

He sprawled out on the narrow bed with his head against the wall. After a few minutes, he slept with his mouth open and his eyes closed, his arms hung over the sides of the thin mattress. An opened beer can was wedged between his legs. Outside, a coyote howled. His leg jerked and his eyes opened. I pretended to be asleep and listened to his breathing until he snored again. I peeked through my eyelashes at the locked door. The keys must be in his pocket. I glanced around the cabin. The window. A rusted latch, but not locked.

I pulled the curtains back and twisted the latch, then checked him.

Still asleep.

I dragged the wooden chair under the window, an inch at a time. Stopped and listened to him snoring. I pulled myself up with both hands onto the dusty window ledge and straddled it. I lifted my other leg over and jumped down into the mud. My leg burned where I scraped it. I reached back in and pulled the curtains together, and the closed window inch by inch. I squeezed my necklace and stood still. No sounds except his snoring.

Run. I checked for lights. None. Just dark shadows.

I sprinted across the road to a tree with a wide trunk. I peeked at the cabin. No light. No sounds. My shoe sunk into the mud. I reached down and pulled it out, then pushed my foot back into the muddy shoe. I took some deep breaths. Which way? My gut told me to run back toward the highway.

I sprinted toward the next driveway, hid behind a pile of tires, and peeked back at the cabin. A light switched on. I sucked in a breath. The door flung open and bounced against the cabin wall. "Dammit."

My heart pounded into my throat. He got his flashlight from the truck and aimed it at both sides of the cabin, then down the driveway, the mailbox, the trees, and the road. The light bounced up and down as he walked to the end of the driveway. Then the light went off.

I held my breath. It wouldn't be hard to find me wearing a Girl Scout uniform and a big sweater.

The truck's engine kicked over. The roar filled the forest and might get someone's attention. Headlights pointed down the driveway, and then turned onto the road. Toward me.

A flashlight beam shone from the truck's window and creeped closer to me. I put my hand over my mouth to hold back a scream when the beam made small circles on the trees just inches from me. He scanned the pile of tires and an empty woodshed, the beam stalled a few feet away, and landed on a metal trash can behind me. The beam went out. Listen. I shivered and held my breath. He cursed. I tucked my knees under my skirt and waited. His flashlight shot back on again. Brighter. It zig-zagged up the wide tree trunks. I wrapped my necklace around my fingers and kept my eyes on his truck.

The headlights and the flashlight's beam slithered further down the road, shining between the trees, Taillights faded into the darkness and almost out of sight. Did he give up? I stretched the soft sweater sleeve over my throat and stared at the road and listened. He might be hiding.

Red brake lights illuminated the forest and startled me. He's coming back for me. Bright headlights aimed at my hiding place. I lay flat on the pine needles and waited until the truck crept past me and stopped next to the mailbox. He backed the truck into the driveway and turned the engine off. No lights. The cabin door slammed behind him.

I waited until I felt safe enough to sprint between the trees and out of sight. Mud squished under each step. The distance from Dottie's Café to the cabin had not seemed as far when he was speeding around the curves in daylight. How much time before sunrise?

My legs cramped. I pulled the sweater's sleeves over my freezing hands and forced myself to put one foot in front of the other.

Chills up my back. I stopped and listened. Was he running behind me?

A wooden ladder leaned against the back of a burned-out cabin. I climbed the rickety rungs to the roof and checked the road behind me. No headlights. No sounds except frogs. In the other direction, over the trees, I spotted a steady stream of headlights and taillights. The highway.

I pushed myself to keep going, checking over my shoulder every few minutes, and listening for an engine behind me. Low-lying shrubs brought me to my knees twice. There wasn't time to check the damage on my burning and stinging knees. Blood trickled down to my ankle. I kept my eyes on the highway at the bottom of the hill and ran along the edge of the road. My lungs and throat burned, but I refused to stop.

The sky became a golden haze when the sun peeked over the mountains. In the distance, I spotted the tall highway sign, trimmed with pink lights. *Dottie's Café*.

My muddy shoes slapped the asphalt, my knees throbbed, but nothing could stop me. Lights went on inside the café and cars pulled into the parking lot. The length of a football field away. I kept my eyes on the café. My necklace bounced against my chest.

The sound of an engine broke my concentration. I glanced over my shoulder. Terrence's truck.

The café was within reach. I scrambled across the parking lot, skidding on the gravel and dodging around parked cars. His truck pulled into the parking lot. I pushed the glass café door open and ran to Dottie behind the counter.

Dottie's eyes widened. "What is it, honey? Are you okay?"

I opened my mouth but couldn't speak. *No voice.* I reached toward Dottie's pink apron and took the order pad from her pocket and grabbed the pen above Dottie's ear.

With trembling hands, I scribbled: *Call police.*

A FEW DAYS LATER, I SAT IN THE SOCIAL WORKER'S CAR AND twisted the necklace around my fingers. Mom's sweater warmed my lap. What would Mom have thought about what happened to me?

The social worker turned the key in the ignition. "Ready Ellie? I didn't think I'd be transporting you to another foster home this soon. But that's not your fault. And besides, I think you'll be happier with people who know you."

I didn't answer. I couldn't. *So frustrating.*

"Do you remember my name?" she asked.

I nodded. How could I forget? Veronica. Like the Archie comic books. Even looked like Veronica. Long shiny black hair.

"Is that a St. Christopher on the chain?"

I nodded and held it out for her to see.

"My son wears one, too. He's a surfer. Are you a surfer?"

I nodded and attempted to smile. *Wished I could ask her where he surfs. Laguna? Huntington?*

"Ellie, I don't know if the doctors told you, but you have what's called Psychogenic Aphonia caused by emotional trauma. You should be able to speak as soon as your world calms and you have people who love you, and you feel safe. You've just had too much trauma in such a short time. But eventually, you'll trust those around you and feel safe again and your voice will return. Did the doctors explain that to you?"

I won't ever trust anyone again. So, I guess that means I'll never talk.

"The detectives showed me the drawings you provided. You're quite the little artist. So many details. Especially your drawing of Terrence, and his truck, and the cabin, inside and out. I'm sure they told you that they were able to find his landscaping company and arrested him along with a man named Chuck that you mentioned, and three others. They'll need you to testify in court. And when you do, I'll be right beside you. You're not getting rid of me so soon." She laughed. "And you were so smart to keep that little barrette and give it to the detectives. Now, they have more evidence. One of the girls' mothers identified it as her missing daughter's."

I wanted to ask more about the two girls. Linda and Susie. *Were there others?*

Veronica drove through a suburban neighborhood to the white house that I had drawn for an art class. The teacher said it was a 1920's California bungalow. Giant olive trees shaded both sides of the narrow street. Veronica pulled into the familiar long driveway, a strip of grass down the center, and parked behind Uncle Frank's prized possession. A bright red 1955 Chevy, parked in the driveway for everyone to admire. *Especially me.*

I had joined my brothers in building model cars with glue that made me dizzy. I made a red '55 Chevy, just like Uncle Frank's. I kept it on my bookcase with my favorite books. *That's all gone now.*

I reached out and ran my fingers along the side of the car as we walked by.

The front door of the house swung open, Aunt Anna, arms outstretched, grabbed my shoulders, and pulled me close to her. "My little Ellie. I've missed you so much."

Like Mom's hugs. Almost.

Uncle Frank, with his big Irish smile, stood behind her. "Please, come in and sit down."

Inside, everything was exactly where I knew it would be. I didn't feel that wave of pain. Danish modern furniture, family photos displayed on walls, piano, and end tables. Something sweet baking in the oven. Aunt Anna loved to bake and used to teach me her secrets.

"Jenette," Uncle Frank called out. "Your cousin is here."

Footsteps ran down the hall until my teenage cousin appeared with her perfect smile. Straight white teeth. "Ellie!" She wrapped her arms around my shoulders. "So, you're not talking, huh?"

"No. Not now. But she will," Veronica said. "She's a really smart kid and mature for her age. I'm sure you know that. You're her family, on her mother's side? You've known her since she was a baby. Right?"

"Since the day she was born," Aunt Anna said. "She's my favorite niece."

"Just curious, why didn't you take her after..."

"We wanted to, but we live in Los Angeles County and by the time they figured out we were related to her, they had already placed her in Orange County. An emergency placement. Someone overlooked or delayed our paperwork." She glanced at Uncle Frank. "So they said."

"Well," Veronica said, "the doctors are confident that she will talk again, but first she needs to feel secure, wanted, and loved, and I'm sure you will be best for her. Stay within her sight as much as possible so she can establish trust. For now, I strongly suggest just low-key activities. No large crowds. Never leave her alone. And I think it's best to keep her out of school, at least until after summer. We'll see how she's doing in the fall."

Oh good. No school. I'd look stupid if I couldn't even talk.

"We'll do whatever we can for her," Uncle Frank said. "We're glad she's here with us."

Wish I had come here first. Terrence wouldn't have taken me.

Veronica shifted her weight and smiled. "Okay. I know you'll all be fine. Just call me if you have questions. I'll call before I visit." She walked down the driveway, with her eyes on the red '55 Chevy, then turned and waved to me. *She must like it, too.*

"Jenette, you'll need to take Ellie everywhere you go, except school. Understand?"

"But Dad. Everywhere?"

"Yes, absolutely."

———

JENETTE SAID I COULD SHARE HER PURPLE ROOM SO I WOULD FEEL safe. She had always been like my big sister. Five years older. A purple bedspread covered the double bed and silky, purple pillows leaned against the headboard. The lamps, picture frames, and curtains all the same shade of purple. Ricky Nelson and Frankie Avalon posters covered the wall on each side of her dresser. A stack of movie magazines filled the bookcase. A chair in the corner with soft purple cushions rocked with a soothing motion. Like Mom's rocking chair. I sat there when Jenette was in the kitchen or living room and didn't feel embarrassed when tears ran down my face.

Jenette kneeled on the purple vanity bench in her bedroom and faced the mirror. She used an odd little thing to curl her eyelashes.

Maureen, her best friend for as long as I could remember, sat on the edge of the bed. "So, whatcha gonna do with her?" She snapped her Juicy Fruit gum.

"What can I do? Mom and Dad are busy with that weekly poker game on Saturday nights. And I'm supposed to take her wherever I go."

"But tomorrow's Saturday night and Hollywood is waiting for our arrival." Maureen extended her hand out to an invisible Prince Charming for a kiss.

Jenette poked Maureen's shoulder. "She's going with us."

"Are you serious?" Maureen spoke to Jenette's reflection. "We can't get a ten-year-old into those clubs. We can barely pass, even with the fake IDs. How're we gonna get her in?"

"I thought of everything," Jenette said. "Johnny made her one, too." She reached into a drawer. "He took her photo yesterday and look...better than ours."

"She's ten!" Maureen threw her arms out, just missing my head. "How's she gonna look eighteen?"

Jenette pointed to her makeup box on the dresser. "I put gobs of makeup on her for the photo. Believe me, she's a blonde bombshell; the guys will swarm around us this weekend." She smiled at me as if she had created the answer to her prayers. "Wait until tomorrow night; you'll see what I mean."

I hated that goop on my face and eyes, but I wanted Jenette to like taking me with her.

Maureen opened the bedroom door to leave. "I hope you're right." She leaned back into the bedroom and whispered. "Oh, and please leave a light on. Last week, I tripped over the garden hose in the driveway."

How could Uncle Frank and Aunt Anna not know Jenette snuck out and drove the car? But then I guess the poker game in the family room at the back of the house, with a view of the pool, distracted them. Jenette's purple bedroom faced the side of the house, next to the long driveway, out of view of the adults.

SATURDAY NIGHT ARRIVED AND JENETTE KEPT CHECKING THE CLOCK on her dresser. 9:05. Aqua Net hairspray swirled in the air like the magic dust from Cinderella's fairy godmother. A faint tap on the window. Jenette crawled across her bed and lifted the window with both hands.

Maureen must have stood on the faucet and pulled herself up to the ledge. Her bouffant hairdo made its appearance long before her face. With that much makeup, she looked like a movie star. "Are you both ready?" she asked.

Jenette sprayed another round of hairspray over her head. "Thank God you're here." She grabbed a roll of electrical tape off the dresser. "I need help gettin' this one dressed." She motioned to me.

Who else would she be referring to? After all, I was the only "this one" in the room.

Maureen crawled over the window ledge onto the purple bed. "I can't believe you're taking her." Maureen pointed to my chest. "What can we do with her boobs? Quick, get a box of tissue; we'll stuff her bra, like my mom does."

"She doesn't even wear a bra yet." Jenette said. "She's still a little girl." She held up a black lacey bra. "I bought her a padded bra today that will knock your socks off. She'll certainly get the male attention if you know what I mean." She winked at Maureen and, like always, they laughed at one of their secrets. Jenette made cleavage for me with electrical tape that pulled my skin.

My reflection in the full-length mirror shocked me. I ripped off the *Frederick's of Hollywood* tag dangling under my armpit. *A perfect costume for next Halloween.* I'd look like a witch in a shiny black tight skirt, a black lace halter top, black high heels with rhinestones, and my blonde hair all teased and sprayed. *No one would guess that I was buried under all that stuff.*

Jenette pointed to my necklace. "You can't wear that. It doesn't go with the outfit."

I wrapped the tarnished chain with my beloved St. Christopher around my wrist and tied it. *Will a bracelet do?* I balanced on the bed and put one leg out the window and straddled the windowsill, right behind Jenette and Maureen. I struggled to climb over the ledge when my heels caught on the bedspread, and the black lace bra stuck out in front of me so I couldn't see my legs. The electrical tape pulled on my skin. I dropped Mom's sweater out the window and then slid from the ledge down to the driveway below, careful to avoid the faucet. Jenette caught me.

I stood next to the red '55 Chevy that glistened under the moonlight. Jenette's purple dress was too tight, it looked like she had painted it on her skin. And, of course, her high heels matched her dress. Her long hair cascaded like ebony waves down her back. Like a Hawaiian hula dancer.

Sharon, another long-time friend of Jenette's, waited on the other side of the car and tapped her fire-engine red fingernails on the hood. Her wavy red hair rested on her shoulders. Silver hoop earrings dangled from her ears.

Jenette tossed a can of hair spray to her. "Where were you?"

"I had to get some money from my dad's wallet," Sharon said. "He chose tonight to hang his pants on the back of the door. Usually, they're on the floor. Just like him to change his routine tonight."

"Shh! Let's hurry before anyone hears us." Jenette spit out her wad of Juicy Fruit gum. She rolled it next to the front tire with her foot and pressed the gum onto the concrete. "Marks the spot where Dad parked." She put the car in neutral and let the brake off. We pushed the Chevy down the long driveway, onto the street.

We all jumped in and closed the doors gently. "Oh, my God! Who is this?" Sharon's penciled eyebrows shot up to her hairline. She hesitated, then slid into the back seat, next to me.

"She's my cousin, Ellie," Jenette said. "Remember?"

"Oh yeah, but I thought she was much younger."

Jenette started the engine. "She's only ten, but tonight she's eighteen. And with those shoes and her long legs, she's a knockout."

"We've got some tough competition tonight, girls," Maureen said from the front seat. "We don't stand a chance next to that gorgeous blonde." She snapped her gum.

Is that good or bad? I spread Mom's sweater across my legs. An awkward combination of perfumes competed with the heavy fragrance of hair spray inside the car. I rolled the window down and stuck my face into the fresh air.

"My hair!" Maureen screamed with a high-pitched voice. She held her hands over her bouffant hairdo as if it would fly off her head.

"Shit, roll that damn window up!" Jenette yelled.

Sharon poked her fingers into her hair as if she were trying to revive it and inspected her face in the rear-view mirror. "My eyelashes got stuck together." She scowled in my direction.

She should get rid of those stupid-looking lashes. They look like spider legs.

The red '55 Chevy sped along the Freeway toward Hollywood. Jenette turned the radio to KRLA and twisted the other knob all the way to the right. Chubby Checkers sang "The Twist." Jenette and her friends sang along, dancing in their seats. I'd seen no one doing that while driving a car. I pulled my necklace out and rubbed the medal between my fingers. *Please Keep me safe.*

We passed the Hollywood City Limit sign. Sharon rolled her window down, pulled her bra and blouse up to her chin, and leaned out the window. Jenette slowed the Chevy next to a diesel truck. The driver leaned out his window with big eyes and a huge smile. He pulled the air horn. The girls responded with screams of laughter.

What was the big deal? She got to open her window, and nobody complained about that.

People in cars and on the sidewalk stopped to stare at the red '55 Chevy. After all, it was the "Car of the Year." Jenette weaved around traffic with ease. A man in a beat-up Ford with a construction hat gave us the big green pickle, as Jenette called it, when she cut in front of him. Sharon returned the greeting by pushing her boobs out the window again.

THE WHEELS ON THE RED '55 CHEVY CRUNCHED THE GRAVEL IN THE crowded parking lot until we found a space. I stepped out and leaned against the car door to get my balance with the high heels on my feet. Jenette pulled a cigarette out from her purse, lit it, and handed the smoking thing to me. "Here, stick this in your mouth. You'll look older."

But I don't smoke. My mom and dad don't...didn't smoke.

"Just stick it between your lips, but don't breathe in, okay?"

Sharon lit her cigarette with a silver lighter that had *Budweiser* on both sides. It hung out the side of her mouth, her eyes squinted. "Watch me, Pipsqueak. Take it out between these two fingers and flick it with your thumb so the ashes fall off."

Maureen threw her head back and blew smoke into the air. "Yeah, it makes you look really cool."

They all looked ridiculous, and it made their breath stink.

Jenette took the sweater from me. "Leave it in the car."

I pulled it back against my chest.

Jenette smiled and hugged my shoulder. "Okay. I get it. Don't worry, you're safe with us."

Maureen shook her head and Sharon scowled. I tried to act older than ten because I didn't want them to think I was a baby. But everything scared me. I squeezed the sweater against my chest and twisted the necklace that I had wrapped around my wrist. *Safe.*

Somehow, we synchronized the clicks of our high heels on the pavement as we walked toward the entrance of The Whiskey. We held our cigarettes between our fingers with our wrists bent up, and the four of us approached the front door. *I'm just like them.* But my black skirt was so tight I walked like a geisha girl with a sweater over my arm.

The guy at the door was huge, like one of those men who wrestled on television every Monday night. His arms bulged under his black jacket. *The seams are about to split.* He motioned us toward the door as we pranced toward him.

Jenette whispered in my ear. "Don't worry. You don't need to talk. Just smile."

This time, I don't want to talk. I nodded and all the poofiness on my head jiggled.

Maureen held her ID between two fingers of her left hand, matching the cigarette in her right hand. Her hip bounced at the same time she smacked her bubble gum. The Wrestler nodded.

Sharon was next. She showed her ID in her cupped hand. Her knees and toes turned inward, and her shoulders slumped. The Wrestler nodded again.

Jenette stepped in front of me and pointed with her thumb over her shoulder toward me. "This is my cousin." The Wrestler glanced at her ID and nodded, then glanced at mine. He didn't nod. Instead, he looked me up and down. Twice. *He must like my costume*.

"Hello, sweetheart." He pulled the door open for us, winked, and blew a kiss to me.

Jenette poked Maureen's back as they paraded into the lobby. I followed close behind Jenette. Loud music bounced off my eardrums, and cigarette smoke hovered over everyone's head. *Why didn't someone turn the lights on?*

A waiter led us to the second tier and a booth. A blond server brought our drinks on a tray. Kinda like Bob's Big Boy, except she wasn't wearing skates. Her shocking pink lipstick was so bright you could find her in the dark.

Maureen stuck her gum under the table. "For later."

Jenette set a drink in front of me. "Here's your root beer float. Stay here. We'll be right down there on the dance floor. You're safe."

I had a perfect view of the dance floor and the bar. Guys with tight pants and girls with tight dresses strolled around the tables and along the edge of the crowded dance floor. One guy wore a dark suit, but no shirt. Gold chains hung around his neck. *Must have been in a hurry*. He wrapped his arms around two blonde women standing by the bar. Both wore dresses that were way too small. *Didn't they try them on first?*

Spotlights in different colors circled over heads that bobbed up and down on the dance floor. Like *American Bandstand*, but much bigger, louder, and darker with clouds of smoke. I used to dance with that show every afternoon and every week at the Sinclair Dance Studio. I could dance better than most down there. Watching everyone move and the loud music made my feet tap to the rhythm and a hint of laughter hid just under the surface.

Jenette and her friends pushed their way into the middle of the floor and shook their bodies in places I didn't know could shake.

Boys with slicked-back hair in the next booth blew smoke from their mouths, like koi fish swimming along the surface. White rings floated up into the air and hovered like little UFOs.

I took a cigarette out of Sharon's pack of Marlboro's on our table. I burned my finger with the lighter, so I stuck the tip of my finger on the ice cubes in Maureen's glass and tried again. I sucked in smoke from the cigarette and tried to push it out, like the slicked-back guys, but it didn't soar or even look like a ring. Instead, it blew out like exhaust from a truck when I coughed. *Like Terrence's truck.* That horrible wave twisted in my stomach. The slicked-backs blew more rings out over their table. *Why can't I make rings?*

"Want some help with that, sweetheart?" A slicked-back with Elvis eyes slipped into our booth and put his arm around my shoulders. Just like when my brothers taught me to spit watermelon seeds and whistle. That horrible wave disappeared.

I nodded. *Sure, that'd be cool.* That's a word Jenette and her friends always said. *Wish I could talk.* A few more slicked-back boys squeezed into our booth. Two others jumped onto the table and faced me to show me how to get the rings out with my tongue and lips. Elvis-eyes blew a giant smoke ring over my head. "Here's a halo for an angel."

When a perfect ring finally lifted out of my mouth, floated up and hovered over the table, we celebrated with a toast. Their giant beer glasses slammed against my root beer float and spilled beer foam onto the vanilla ice cream.

The band took a break. The dance floor cleared. Jenette and her friends ran up the second tier of steps. "Damn. Look at her," Sharon said. I assumed she meant me.

My cool friends smiled and whistled when Jenette, Sharon, and Maureen bounced up the steps. "Well, how-dee-doo," one of them said.

"The Pipsqueak can really draw them in, can't she?" Jenette smiled at me. "Next week, you'll come to the dance floor with me."

Good.

The slicked-backs brought chairs to the booth for the girls to join the fun and ordered more drinks. I made several really cool rings, one after the other, that floated over the table and melted into the server's face when she brought another tray of drinks. *Oops.*

One boy grabbed the root beer float off the tray and set it in front of me.

"So, sweetie, where do you work?" he asked.

Jenette answered for me. "She doesn't work, she goes to school."

"Going to college, huh?" He leaned against my shoulder, and I got a strong whiff of his Aqua Velva aftershave, a combination of vanilla and Windex.

I nodded.

"Hey, this one here is a smart broad," he said. "She goes to college."

———

Several hours later, all that was left on the table was a plate of cold pizza crusts and three empty packs of cigarettes. Everyone stood and headed for the exits.

Jenette, Maureen, and Sharon staggered out to the gravel parking lot. I blew bubbles with the pink bubble gum I found in Maureen's purse and trailed behind them.

Jenette dug into her purse. "Now you gotta pay your dues. Here's the keys."

"Hey, Pipsqueak ain't driving the car, is she?" Maureen asked.

"Yeah, she can drive." Jenette said. "She loves to race go-carts around a huge racetrack, and I was the one who taught her to drive the Chevy in the school parking lot. She's a brainy kid." Jenette hugged me with one arm and stumbled.

"Geez, I haven't even passed Driver's Ed." Maureen threw her high heels on the backseat.

"I drank way too much tequila tonight," Sharon said. "I might puke out the window."

"Shit, I forgot to bring the pillow for her to sit on," Jenette said. "Give me your purses; we'll stack them on the seat. She's gotta be able to see over the dashboard." She motioned to Sharon and Maureen with her waving hand. "Help me push the front seat up to the steering wheel."

I unwound the necklace from my wrist. It got in the way of the steering wheel. Jenette took it from me and hung it from the rear-view mirror. She kissed my cheek. "You're safe."

Perched on top of the purses like a princess on a throne, I drove out of the parking lot with Jenette in the front seat next to me. "Stay on the freeway," she said. "Until the exit sign says Norwalk Boulevard. Slow the car down like I showed you and wake me up. I'll show you the way back to the house."

Maureen and Sharon had sprawled out across the back seat. Mom would've said *in unladylike* positions. Their bouffant hairdos had deflated, and makeup smeared under their eyes. Jenette kicked off her shoes and stretched her feet under the dashboard. Her arms dangled like limp noodles. Her head dropped against the window. I covered her arms with Mom's sweater.

The freeway lights sparkled like a runway at LAX. The pink sky rested on the top of the San Bernardino Mountains. Jenette, Sharon, and Maureen were my three fairy godmothers and I, Cinderella, drove the pumpkin coach, a red '55 Chevy, back to the purple bedroom in Norwalk.

Every Saturday night. All summer.

BY THE END OF THE SUMMER OF '61, I HAD WON SIX TROPHIES IN the Palladium dance contests, and four trophies at The Whiskey. It was during one of those crack-of-dawn drives in the red '55 Chevy that I surprised myself by singing out loud with BB King, *Stand by Me*.

Jenette sat up. "Ellie. You're singing! You have your voice again!"

Caboose

Sue Ann Higgens

Well, look who it is. My firstborn. C'mon inside, kiddo. Haven't seen you in, what, a month?

I saw Dad's truck was gone.

Come in. My Rice-a-Roni is about to burn.

I'm always hoping I'll come by here, Ma, and there won't be a real live train car in your backyard. But there it is in all its glory.

Oh, here we go. First thing in the door, that's what you've got to say? You and I both know no one's going to outlive the caboose.

But, Ma, it's an embarrassment.

Well, your father's at the store at the moment. Feel free to stick around and tell him your thoughts.

No, I'm good.

Anyway, good to see you, Bryan. Need money, or just a social call to remind your dear old mother there's an actual caboose in my backyard?

Ma, c'mon. I'm never just here to ask for money. I found something for you the other day and wanted to drop it by. How long since my sister has graced your doorway? Huh?

Well, Mellie's not back home much. She's making a living in the city, which you may have heard, keeps a person busy.

Oh, real nice. Wasn't my fault the mill closed.

No. But that was four years ago.

I'm looking, okay? And, at least, I don't have a caboose on a fifty-foot concrete slab out back of my house. I thought you said he'd grow tired of it and send it down the tracks.

Well, I was mistaken. Your father loves his caboose; thinks it's a symbol of something. Of his uniqueness. And the good ole days. The glory of his 'historic curation.'

What a bunch of bull.

He has little enough in life he enjoys. If a caboose toots his horn, what do I care?

Jesus. It's like advertising that crazy people live here.

Is it so bad if people think we're different?

Different? Your purple front door is different. Your hundred pots of petunias. A ten-ton peeling caboose in the yard—that's not different, Ma. It's a symptom. He's all about giving people ultimatums. 'My way or the highway, son!' So, I'm just saying, talk to him in a language he understands. Give him an ultimatum. You know, like it's you or the caboose.

Why would I do that? Why would I invite him to say he wants that metal monstrosity here more than he wants me?

He wouldn't last a week without you.

Do you even know what a caboose is? It's like punctuation—like a tail that waves goodbye. So, let him have his big finish.

Ma...

No. You won't hear me making ultimatums about it. I live here. I intend to stay here.

Well, he kicked me out for no good reason.

I think we both know you can move back in anytime you want to deal with your crap out there.

Right. Jump through his hoops but ignore his rusting junker of a choo-choo. And he used, what, half your retirement to deposit that thing in your yard? With a crane?

Yes, Bryan, I was here. And it's not like I had any retirement from J. C. Penny's. They just closed the store and that was it.

What an eyesore that building's become, down on First Street.

Yeah, for fifty years it drew people to our little downtown. Now what is there? Your dad and I go all the way out to the mall like everyone else. Your sister thinks we should move to the city where she is.

Yeah, right. Dad hates the city. Says it's because of the traffic. But his big reason is probably the zoning that says: NO TRAINS IN YOUR YARD.

Leave it alone, Bry.

I figure he's still hoping his favorite child, the train-loving Mellie, will come scampering back. Why else have a caboose shouting to all the world: HERE LIVES A WEIRDO AND HIS LONG-SUFFERING WIFE?

He's happy when he's out there dinging around. Caboosing, I call it.

Does he ever do anything for you, Ma? Besides mow the lawn?

Look, Bry, marriage is about looking away as often as it is about seeing someone. Time was, I couldn't take my eyes off that old geezer. Couldn't wait for him to get home when he was first driving long haul. Dreaded him leaving every time. But I learned to do it. Got to where I preferred it.

I don't blame you.

Oh, hush. And now, what with him having the cancer, what have I got to win on something like this? Plus, I've got my quirks. My *hundred pots of petunias* for instance. I've never had more than sixty, by the way. He's never liked the smell of them. And my collection of Roseville vases. He hates those things. Remind him of a Depression-era funeral parlor, he says.

Jesus. I know what he says. They are ugly. But at least they fit in your two china cabinets. It's not like you filled entire rooms with them, let alone the back lot.

Well, I might just put petunia boxes on the caboose. That would look nice. White ones against its orange and black. If he ever finishes painting it, I'll do it, too. Here, stir the rice for me, will you? I need to set the table.

He'd have a cow.

You staying for dinner?

Oh, sure, and listen to Dad chew my leg off over nothing? No, just dropping something off for you.

It's the usual: hot dogs, this rice, and Jell-O salad if you change your mind.

It's best if Mr. Caboose and I keep our distance. I just wish he'd think of you for once.

Well, besides my petunias, and my Roseville vases, I've got all my lockets.

Yeah, there's what, a dozen of them hanging in the hall?

Started with the necklace from my Gramma Bowers. She tucked a tiny photo of her and Grandad inside it.

I know, Ma.

Well, time was, and I mean even ancient times, a locket was a prized possession from a loved one. People understood symbols of affection in those days. Over the years, I'd sometimes find a nice old locket in an antique shop.

You mean a junk shop?

You can be rude, you know that? I just love the way the little hasp clicks into place when you close one. I used to just hang them from push pins. You remember that?

Yeah, when we were little, we used to open and close them. Then Mellie wanted to hide a message to you in one.

Don't remind me. I was almost sick when she snapped the front right off the little hinge.

She nearly peed her pants.

Well, I was mad. Some of them are worth something, you know. A few of mine have initials or a tribute engraved on them. Gold plate or sterling silver. But they're fragile. After that one broke, I thought, why not frame them? Anyway, turn the burner down to simmer and put the lid on the rice now.

That's why you framed them?

Yep. Oh, come here, son. I saw in a collector's magazine this was the right way to display them. The dark velvet behind them looks pretty, doesn't it? I need to dust these, but people spent a lot of money on them—gold chains, fancy edges. This one has *1874* engraved on it.

Right. And your whole set of them in these ugly Victorian frames, takes up, what, some eight feet on the wall in this hallway? It's not exactly the same as...

The last time lockets were popular, you know, was when the young people left for World War One. They sold like hotcakes. I told your dad once I thought up stories about who had owned the lockets. Like that one with the long chain. What's it say? I left my glasses in the kitchen.

It says: *From E.L. to J.M., with Warmest Regards.*

See? It just makes you wonder, doesn't it?

Not really, Ma.

Well, I do. I mean, did E. L. survive? Is he moldering in some cemetery in Belgium? Or did he come back to J. M., work his parents' farm and have five kids, but one had rheumatic fever and couldn't run at all? Did the war make E.L. cruel? Or incredibly kind? Maybe he came back with a bum leg but got work as an assistant to a veterinarian. He might have brought the worst dogs home to his family who loved them, you know? But what if the Weimaraner bit the little girl on the arm and, and maybe she got rabies? There was a lot more rabies back then.

Jesus, Ma. Take it easy.

Well, anyway, I'd like to hang them in the dining room. But he'd never stand for that.

What? You mean you can't put your lockets up where you want in your own house? But meanwhile, you stare down the peeling side of a Union Pacific all day?

Oh, never mind all that. Get me a bowl for this rice. Your dad will be home soon. It's nice to see you. Nice of you to just drop by to chat for a change.

Oh, because the favorite, Mellie, comes out to the hinterlands so often?

Stop it with that jealous crap, Bryan. He never had favorites. She loved trains, too. That's all. And he's got the caboose fixed up enough he can sit in it with his little heater and organize his train books. He's rigged up some lights. And has a little fridge with his Cokes and Coors in it.

Yeah. I see the genius has run not one, but two, bright orange extension cords across your yard to his damned caboose. Jesus. How the hell does he even mow around it? Your lockets are a little sad. But they're not, you know, bigger than your house.

Sad? Keeping a part of history alive isn't sad. Longing and love are as old as time, son. Things that help us remember. Even if you don't appreciate old things, I hope your sister will want my locket collection someday.

You might have noticed your daughter's not the most sentimental person alive.

Well, in our generation, you appreciated what your parents passed down to you. You kept things because they had stories, even if they weren't quite to your taste. My great grandparents used that mirror we have over the bathroom sink. I hope one of you two kids will want it someday.

Mellie is pretty indifferent to stuff, Ma. It's weird, though. She was *so* into trains, even more than Dad. She collected all those boxes of HO scale track and scenery with her allowance.

I made Mellie that little engineer's hat. That was the last thing I made your sister that she liked.

She grew up, Ma. Don't take it personally that she doesn't like the crafts and stuff you do. She can't stand trains anymore either.

She had so many model cabooses. Drew pictures of the ones that had a little cupola on top.

Must be boxes of her stuff around here. How come the old man doesn't hound her to get her stuff out of here?

She sold them. When she went to hairdresser school.

Please, Ma, she's a *stylist*. Not a hairdresser. Get with the times.

Well, whatever you want to call it. Not sure why she can't style things here in town. I guess the city suits her better.

Yeah, she must really miss this yard with a life-size caboose in it.

Cut the smart mouth, Bryan. You can be tiresome.

I swear that's why Dad got it. He thought she'd love it and come home more.

Dammit, Bry. You're nearly thirty years old. Enough.

But you know I'm right. She's only seen it once in, what, the six years it's been here?

Seven years next month. But who's counting?

Damn. Seven years.

The cancer changed some things, son. I don't think you've registered that.

Well, he's had the cancer two times before. He'll probably live another fifteen years just to spite all of us. That's what grinds me. It's not the caboose. It's the spite. He knows it needles you. It's frickin' petty, Ma.

Well, it helps us stay out of each other's way. He tinkers on it like it's his job. Drinks beers out there most evenings. Reads his Westerns. But if you think you know better how he should spend his precious time, fly right at it.

Anyway, Ma, I found something for you. That's why I came by. You're not gonna believe what's in this bag. Careful. It's probably kinda fragile. I don't even know if it's real. Don't...don't drop it.

Heavens, Bryan. It's Roseville for sure.

Do you have this one?

Good Lord, no. A Bleeding Heart pattern Roseville bowl? And in blue! I've only ever seen them in pictures. Hard to find. I think these were only made around nineteen forty. Where in the world...

It's a crazy story, Ma. I'm working on a car with Jonesy—he's got the most perfect '66 Chevy SS. Big pipes; bright orange with a white racing stripe. We're tuning the carburetor and he wants to drive it by his girlfriend's house, see?

Oh, so still no job, but you're fixing other people's cars for free? Bryan, you've got to get your life together.

Ma, listen, okay? So, we go over there, to this little house; it's just south of Fourth Street. His girlfriend lets us in. And I can see right away she lives with some old lady—her aunt, she says. The aunt's sleeping in the easy chair. Jonesy is talking to the girlfriend in the kitchen. So, I'm just standing there, looking around. Lots of old photos, big old-fashioned sofa, and a piano. The place feels real crowded. And then, wham! There, on top of a bookshelf are two bowls or vases or whatever. And I think maybe one of them is a Roseville.

I didn't know you had an interest in my pottery.

I don't, okay? But I've been staring at this stuff all my life. Anyway, the old gal opens her eyes and looks at me. 'Hi,' I say. And she says, 'Is Kara here?' I tell her Jonesy and the girlfriend are in the kitchen. I keep looking over at the bowl. She finally says, 'You seem interested in my Roseville bowl. That's the blue one.'

I say, 'Yeah, my mom collects Rosevilles. But I've never seen the blue type, so I wasn't sure it was actually a Roseville.'

'Oh, my, yes,' the lady says, 'several of their patterns came in blue, though you are probably more familiar with the green and pink ones.'

'Yeah. My mom has two hutches full of them.'

'Wonderful. Wonderful.' She's real quiet. Her eyes are kinda wet so I'm afraid she's crying or something. 'Well,' she says, 'the blue is the most valuable in this Bleeding Heart pattern.'

I say, 'It's real pretty. You must have quite a nose for it if you found a blue one.' I'm just making small talk, you know. 'No,' she says. She got that bowl as a wedding present, before her husband left to fight in Japan. 'He was never the same after that,' she goes. 'That bowl helped me remember him as he used to be.' Her eyes are closed again. I don't know what to say, if she's asleep or whatever. Then she opens her eyes and says, 'If your mother might like it, why don't you take it to her?'

Ma, what could I say? I go, 'Oh, I'm pretty sure you should keep it in the family. I bet your niece or someone would love it.'

'Oh, no. They don't appreciate these things of mine,' she says. She sounded real sad. 'They'd have sold it off by now if they knew it was valuable. To them it's just some old bowl of Aunt Myrna's.'

Goodness, Bryan. Was this old Myrna Rodgers? I knew her from church when I was a kid. Didn't know she was still around.

I didn't get her last name. Anyway, she tells me to open the front closet door and get out a paper bag. I have to move stuff, an ottoman and her slippers and magazines, to get the closet open. She tells me to put the bowl in the paper bag. Says if her niece or anyone asks me about it, to say I volunteered to drop something off at Goodwill for her. 'They'll probably never notice it's gone,' she said. 'And if you'll give it to your mother, that will give me some peace of mind that it's in good hands, and someone will still appreciate it.'

You know, they used to say Myrna Rodgers' husband was a mean cuss. Died young if I remember right. Maybe that was a grace.

She seemed sad, you know?

My land, Bry. I have one piece of the Bleeding Heart; it's pink. Look, it's on the back of the lower shelf in that cabinet on the right. This is really something. Thank you, son.

It's okay. I guess I was paying a little attention around here.

I always thought I'd assembled a good collection. But this is—my word. And see this number on the bottom here? Don't drop it. I can use that number to look up the pattern and shape and find its value. And he can't growl at me for adding to the collection, because it's a gift.

Yeah, he'll say, 'What jackass brought another piece of that godawful pottery into my house?'

Don't mimic his voice so he sounds like a stupid hick. He's annoying, but he's your father.

Well, the guy's got a caboose in his yard, so...

Anyway, this is incredibly nice of you.

Glad you like it, Ma. Seems like you deserve it with all you put up with around here. But I should probably take off. No need to run into the old man and get his fresh ideas on how I should run my life.

He cares about you, son. That's all. That's why he badgers you.

Anyway, before I go, I could use fifty bucks for gas this week.

Ah, the real reason for your visit comes out.

C'mon, Ma. I came because I had a nice gift for you. I mean, you said this bowl is probably valuable.

Oh, hold on. This bowl is for sale? For fifty dollars?

C'mon. It's not like that. You said yourself it's a good one.

Here I thought my son had brought me a gift. Should've known.

C'mon. It's just that I'm between things, you know that.

Well, since wheeling and dealing is your thing, I've got an idea.

Don't start, Ma. Please.

You know what else we need to get rid of around here? My garage full of motorbike stuff you haven't touched since you were fifteen, okay? I should put up a sign: DIRT BIKE DAYS OF YESTERYEAR. I can barely fight the lawnmower in and out because your crap's still piled up in my garage.

Wait, *Dad's* not even mowing the grass? *You're* doing all the mowing? And going around that hulking train car? And the godforsaken extension cords? Unbelievable.

He's gotten a lot weaker, in case you haven't noticed. I can mow just fine, but what I can't do is get around all your motorcycle carcasses out there. Fenders and oil pans and god knows what all. It's like you think it's someone else's job to deal with it.

Look, Ma. I've got a lot of memories in that stuff out there whether or not you appreciate it. You guys wouldn't let me do motocross anymore after I broke my collarbone, remember? And you know some of those parts are rare. I'm not just gonna give them away.

Well, as I've said a hundred times, I don't care how you get rid of it.

Look, Ma, I'm staying with Wes. I just don't have the space...

Well, you can talk about your father being petty or spiteful when you've gotten your crap out of our garage. In fact, how's next Tuesday sound? Since you're *between things right now.* You sell it or remove it, or I'll put a box of it on the curb every day for the next month until it's gone.

You'd never do that.

Try me.

Ma. You're being unreasonable.

Well, sometimes you have to give someone an ultimatum or they never have the motivation to do something.

Very funny.

I'm not kidding. Everyone thinks I'm a joke, not just because I have a goddam caboose in my yard. No, sirree. Also, because I've parked my car on the street in the snow and heat for ten years because of all *your* crap in my garage. As you said, I need to lay down the law. My way or the highway.

Where would I put it all?

Not my problem. Consider yourself duly and truly warned, Bryan Christopher. One box a day, on the curb until it's all gone. Or you move it all by Tuesday.

There's no way I can move it by Tuesday. That's ridiculous.

Well, as you've reminded me, ridiculous is my middle name. I'll get the boxes lined up. And once I've put a few out, I'll probably have people lined up for all that valuable crap. Line down the block.

Ma...

Scrap metal guys will have a heyday. Enduro enthusiasts will fight over it. Newspaper might come by and interview me. Yes, you've been a big help here, son. Can't thank you enough for thinking my problems through. Don't know what I'd do without you. Finally, I'll be famous for something other than the caboose in my yard.

La Femme Assassin

Tonya Mitchell

The dagger was new and felt strange in my hands. I breathed in a sharp gasp as the blade tested the tension of the skin at his cheek. He was pinned to the bed, my body straddling him. Had he been awake, he would have overcome me had he wished. But he would not move now. I positioned the dagger at his throat, poised to slice.

She spoke then, her voice so close I felt the tendrils of my hair dance at my temple.

"One simple thrust, my dear, and it is done." She placed her hand over mine to guide me. "You will feel little resistance. Only a slight tug of the skin before the puncture. Then, no resistance at all. You'll see. Just like all the others, you will feel immediate peace for having rid the world of him."

I didn't need to look at Madame to know that her eyes twinkled in the candlelight, that her smile—and what a beautiful smile it was— transformed her from lovely to magnificent. She possessed only one flaw, if indeed it was a flaw: the gold tooth that winked when she smiled. As rumor went, she had lost the original when a man extracted it with pinchers for beating him at cards. Long, long ago. Before she dealt in the Gentlemen's Trade.

But this man, though a lecher like all the rest, was different. The others I put to eternal rest by poison. Their lives had not been snuffed out as quickly as a candle. They had gasped and writhed and whimpered in agony.

My hands trembled as my eyes took in the reposed figure of the man. His face was flushed, his lips slightly parted. His sideburns were gray and this, along with his midsection that was running to fat, classed him a practiced *roué*. Only his pants and boots remained. He had removed his waistcoat and shirt with haste, eager to have me. As he'd untied his cravat at the window with his back to me, he'd boasted of the delights that awaited. Fool. I had dropped laudanum—infused with cinnamon and clove to mask the bitter taste—into his wine glass. He turned, winked at me lasciviously, and downed the glass in one go. Already unsteady from the bottles he had imbibed earlier at his club, he'd fallen back onto the bed like a gutted boar. In that instant, I realized I had forgotten his name.

"Collingsworth. Samuel Collingsworth," Madame said, as if she had read my thoughts. "But it does not matter. You are doing his wife a courtesy. She paid handsomely for your services, my dear. They all do. You must never forget why you do this." She gestured to Collingsworth's still form. "His body is but a vessel of lust and betrayal. Once you finish him, his wife, the city, the very world will be the better for it."

It was true, yet I did not stir. The sudden clatter of a carriage passing below the window brought me up sharp. The strike of hooves against cobblestones I had heard all my life. Strange. No matter which area of London one found oneself—from the mansions of St. James to the rookeries of St. Giles—the horses sounded the same. It was only the passengers who differed.

It was simple. One slash. Clean and done. I thought of my sister, Sophie, the need to protect her from such scoundrels, and anger swelled within me. I steadied the knife, but just as I was poised to cut, I dropped it to the bed. Poison was one thing. Butchery another.

"I can't." A strange mixture of relief and regret swept over me.

"You can and you will," Madame answered. She turned from me and walked away from the bed, her crimson dress making a whoosh as she walked. She looked out the window, placed her hands on the sill for a moment, then turned to me. Her hair, blonde and arranged on her head in a delicate array of curls, caught the candlelight. In the half-light she looked younger, her face as perfect as it must have been twenty years before when she herself had rid the city of the debauched. "You've done it before, and you will do it again, Marguerite."

My breath caught and I recalled tapping white powder from my poison ring into a faceted ruby goblet that flickered in the firelight. A man lying on his back in an alley, convulsing as foam issued from his mouth. Another's agonized moans as I lay naked in bed beside him, recoiling from his outstretched arms as his eyes pleaded for help.

So many. Dead by my hand. Though it was their own deeds, not mine, that had sealed their fate.

I HAD COME TO MADAME LACROIX AND HER ESTABLISHMENT ONE year ago. Like so many others, I arrived filthy, exhausted, and hungry. It was midday. Her girls were still abed. Like roaches, the brothel's patrons had vanished at first light. Madame reclined regally upon a tufted sofa in a room of dark wood and tapestries, sipping something from a fluted glass on a table next to her.

"And you are?" she inquired with a quirked brow.

I gave her my name, begging God's forgiveness as I said it. I had sunk so low. I was selling my soul—and more besides. Surely, He would understand my predicament.

"And what brings you here, Marguerite?"

"I have nowhere to go, Madame."

"So say them all." Her eyes swept my tattered coat, my unkempt hair. "You have been living on the streets."

I bowed my head, deferential. Pride would not save me now.

"Look at me," she commanded. I raised my head. She rose from the sofa, the sensuous sway of her hips carrying the scent of her jasmine perfume to me. She hooked a finger under my chin and turned my face from side to side. "I have seen you somewhere before I think."

"I doubt that, Madame."

"No." Her brow furrowed. "I am not wrong. Tell me where."

"I was a performer at Bartholomew Fair in Smithfield. Before the theatre burned down."

"Black's? You are an actress."

"Of a sort." Her brows rose in question, so I continued. "I was a pantomime, and I did some comedy. Mostly, I did some—"

"Conjuring?"

So she *had* seen me. The realization of it, the bawdiness of the acts, the lewd crowd, brought heat to my cheeks. "Begging your pardon, Madame. I didn't think you would frequent—" Black's wasn't the kind of establishment she would patronize, as it wasn't where her clientele would go. There was Convent Garden and Drury Lane for that.

"I am well aware of the shows in Smithfield."

I made no reply. I kept my eyes to the floor while she made a slow circle around me. "As I recall, you made birds disappear. Scarves and such. But money, money was your best trick. The one the audience loved the most."

"Yes."

I would call a man up on stage and ask him to place his wallet inside a small box that he himself locked. After I'd cast a spell with a feather, he'd unlock the box to find his money gone.

"How long did you work at Black's?"

"Three and half years."

"And did anyone ever discover your trick?"

"No, Madame."

Her arms crossed as she stopped in front of me. "Your accent doesn't belong to the lower classes."

"I was born in France, Madame. Paris. My mother was French."

Her eyes widened. "You speak French?"

"Yes, Madame."

"*Alors dis-moi, pourquoi tu veux être une putain.*" Then tell me why you wish to be a whore.

"*Je n'ai nulle part où aller et je meurs de faim.*" I have no place to go, and I am starving.

"Your mother?"

"Dead."

"And your father?"

"He was the proprietor of Black's, Madame. He perished in the fire."

Madame narrowed her eyes. "You must have sought employment at the other theaters around the fair. Why did they not take you in?"

"My father nearly drove them out of business. Cheaper tickets, better brandy. They laughed when I appeared on their doorstep."

"Mmm." Madame walked away, her arms hugging her frame, eyes to the floor. She took a sip from the flute, then said, almost to herself, "You are not beautiful, nor are you plain, which could suit. And, of course, the sleight of hand..." As if she had come to a decision, she turned to me. "I have an opportunity for you. A job for one night only. Not this, something else. Something dangerous. I will pay you well. If you succeed, there is the opportunity for more on a regular basis. I will pay for your lodgings, your gowns, anything you require. But I demand complete secrecy." Something stirred behind her eyes. "And I will always be watching." She named a sum I had never hoped to earn in a year, let alone a single night. "Does that sound amenable to you?"

Before I understood what it was she wanted of me, I nodded. Sealing my fate.

———

I AWOKE ON A BENCH BESIDE THE THAMES, MORNING MIST RISING from its surface like smoke. I had fallen asleep in my clothes. A feeling of déjà vu filled me. I had been here before, hadn't I? Memories of my encounter with Collingsworth tugged at me, but I shrugged them off.

My head ached and I was hungry. I walked in the direction of my rooms, but when I passed a newsstand, my eyes fell on a bold headline:

LONDON ROCKED BY ANOTHER GENTLEMAN MURDER
THIRTEENTH MAN SLAIN
*HAS THE ELUSIVE LADY KILLER ABANDONED POISON
AND TURNED TO THE BLADE?*

I placed a coin in the seller's hand. As I took the paper and stuffed the change into my coat pocket, I felt something. I withdrew a handkerchief speckled with blood. Two dark initials stood out against the white background: 'SC.' Samuel Collingsworth.

I began to shake and, quickening my steps, soon arrived at my lodgings. I slammed the door behind me and shrugged off my coat. The hand that had touched the handkerchief was bloody, and with a sudden urge to wash, I fled to the bedroom. There, in the mirror over the washstand, I saw that my gown was streaked crimson. Tracks of blood, as if splattered there from a violent gashing, covered my bodice and skirts. Even my neck, laid bare by my gown's low neckline, bore the marks of Collingsworth's gore. *Dieu merci.* I had murdered him. My Sophie would be safe.

But...I hadn't killed him. I had refused Madame's demand. Hadn't I?

My horror was just beginning. Before me lay hours of restless anxiety. I watched the pavement below my window darken and the gas lamps come up to reveal empty walkways and cafés, food stalls boarded up, street corners abandoned. Another gentleman murder had shuttered all of London. Not even a stray dog stirred.

Then, a shadow. The silhouette of a woman seated on a bench. Not moving. A trick of my imagination, surely. Until she smiled and a flash of gold winked in the darkness.

I extinguished my lamp. Like a heavy fog, the night crept into my room. Madame had vanished. What a fiend, the imagination!

A tap at my door.

"My dear, Marguerite," Madame Lacroix said behind it. "Let us take the air, shall we?"

My heart seized. "I am unwell," I said.

"Then you must admit me," she snapped. "I must have a look at you."

I turned the bolt, the chain still latched. Through the gap, the light from the hall sconces blazed a sickly green, just enough to illuminate her lips pushed up into a smile, her gums the color of dark blood. One blue orb stared unblinkingly at me.

When I unlatched the door and opened it, I felt a prick on my arm. Her slender form dissolved into darkness, and I knew no more.

I awoke alone in a carriage. Around me, the stink of rotting meat roiled, and my stomach turned. The slaughterhouses of Seven Dials? It was dark and the streets empty. I had no recollection of the last hours—or had it been days? Jumbled images. A woman's bare clavicle, pale as a shell. Madame Lacroix putting pen to paper. The glisten of diamonds. None of it made sense except the recollection of my dagger; its white bone handle, its blade glinting in my hand.

The carriage came to a halt. I threw open the door and alighted, pulling my coat around me. I had the uncontrollable urge to hide. As I crossed the street, I looked back at the driver. The silhouette was unmistakably a woman's, but not just any woman. The winking tooth was the tell. Madame Lacroix sat atop the box, her gloved hands holding the reins, her smile a void of darkness save that single gold tooth. She was staring right at me.

I flew down the street, veering into an alley. It, too, was deserted, but there was enough light from a gas lamp to see that the fence at the end wasn't too high to climb, not if I used the crates stacked against it. I stumbled onto the wooden pile, making a racket that pierced the night. I lifted my skirts and hefted one leg over the top, then the other. I pitched myself over, landing hard on my feet.

And I ran.

Seven Dials was blocks from Covent Garden. People would be there. Others with whom to mingle. I continued through the streets, and soon I saw the façade of the theatre. A crowd milled about. Gas lamps illuminated a press of people advancing inside. I was soon a part of it, looking back only once. Madame had joined the throng and she was gaining on me.

I reached into my coat pocket and withdrew a ticket to the show. How had it come to be there? Had I purchased it earlier? It didn't matter; I must get away. It seemed that Madame Lacroix had me in her clutches, but I would not be caught.

Inside, the lobby teemed with bodies. The doors to the seats were still barred. Madame would spy me here among the crowd most certainly. I advanced through a side door and sped down a dark, narrow corridor that led to another door marked BACK STAGE. Here I would lose her, I was certain.

Beyond the door, the way opened to a high-ceilinged space. Costumes hung from open wardrobes. Actors clothed in gray wigs and pantalets hurried about. A woman practiced her soprano in airy trills. Having made my home at Black's, this melee was familiar. I hurried ahead. A door leading to the back alley would present itself. As I wound my way through scenery and moving carts, I caught a glimpse of a young woman and my steps paused.

It was my sister. Sophie.

She stood in profile in a gown of voluptuous white, and when I uttered her name, she turned. Oh, that pale oval face. I would know it anywhere. She wore heavy face paint: skin alabaster, brows artfully curved, lips the bud of a rose. Her upswept hair was heavily powdered, her teeth small and perfect. The large diamonds at her throat—made of paste, for they were large enough for the highest seats in the theater to view—winked in the flickering gas jets.

A laugh behind me stilled my heart. *Madame Lacroix.*

I turned but saw no one. I advanced toward Sophie, thinking to protect her from my villainous huntress, but as I did so, her smile vanished. Her eyes grew dark, and her bodice bloomed a rich red. Her diamond necklace vanished, a red gash in its place. Sophie backed away, one pale hand upon her breast. In the next instant, the shadows swallowed her whole. I flew to the place she had been only a second before, my heart knocking in my chest. I stretched out my hands but there was only air. I began to shake. My vision dimmed, black shadows crowding in at the edges.

"*La femme assassin*," Madame called softly. "Margueriiiiite..."

I staggered through the wings and found a door that opened to the night. The air was brisk and stirred me to run. And I did. I cannot say what things caught my eye, what streets I passed. I only knew I could sprint no more when I came to Westminster Bridge. I bent, hands on my knees, and drew air into my lungs.

The wind was up, whipping my skirts, but no one was about. Below, the Thames was a black coil. When the moon emerged from a smudge of clouds, the water winked like the diamonds of my Sophie's necklace. I tried to think, to remember, but it was all a blur. Like a dream after waking.

Where was Sophie?

I placed my hands upon the balustrade and looked east toward Lambeth. It would take some time for me to reach my rooms from here. I would need a carriage. As if conjured from my mind, I heard wheels on the bridge. A cold fear slithered over my bones as it halted. I studied the shadow of the driver. Was it Madame?

Would she give me no peace?

But it was only a man in a black coat and muffler bent to the cold. I gave him my destination and slipped inside the carriage. There in the darkness, my heart slowed, and I came to myself. I would return to my lodgings, pack a few items, and find Sophie. I would kill no longer. I was through with Madame and her game of cat and mouse.

"Ah, but you are not, my dear Marguerite. Not yet."

Moonlight sliced through the darkness of the carriage to the opposite bench. A sensuous mouth with a single gold tooth playfully glinted at me. My heart iced. I leaned forward and placed my hand upon the door handle, ready to flee.

"I have one last task for you, my dear," Madame Lacroix said. "One more only." Her hand rested on mine, cold as January.

"You will relieve me of my duties then?" I could no longer stomach the Gentlemen's Trade. I would rather be poor than endure Madame, but if one last slaying would free me from her clutches, I would do it.

She smiled. "*Vous avez ma parole*." You have my word.

As the carriage rolled, she told me of my intended victim. A man of high birth, esteemed in public, whose private life told a different story. "He is cruel and calculating, with the heart of a jackal," Madame explained, the words seemingly bitter on her tongue. "He dispatched his wife in a fit of rage." I shivered in the closeness of the carriage, but she went on. "The mother of the unfortunate wife wants him dead and has paid a tidy sum to see it done. Her daughter was an heiress, you see, and the blackguard had the gall to squander his wife's fortune in the span of a year." Madame made a tsking sound. "Can you imagine the nerve of such a man?"

I said I could not, for indeed the situation was inexcusable. Such tales were the only solace of my craft. Murder was ghastly, but were the deeds of these unconscionable men not equally so?

The carriage stopped. As I prepared to alight, Madame placed a hand on my arm. "A moment, *la femme assassin*." From the folds of her cloak, she produced my dagger. "You forgot something. Don't you remember?"

Jarring scenes obscured my vision. Collingsworth lying prone on the bed beneath me, the flash of a knife, a red stain flowing outward soaking the bed sheets. But I had not—

Madame slipped the dagger into my hand. "You will need your dagger in the presence of *this* last gentleman."

There was something in the way she said it—*this last gentleman*— that gave me pause. Before I could consider it, she laughed and told me to follow the cobblestones to the top of the street. I would know my destination when I arrived at it.

I clambered out, hurling questions into the air as the carriage moved. "How shall I know I've reached the right place?" Keeping in step, I rapped upon the equipage as if to wake the dead. "Madame, how am I to know my victim?" But the carriage gained speed and disappeared into the night.

The darkness slithered around me as I climbed, the cold leaching into my very bones. The fine houses along the street were shuttered and silent. I kept on, anxious to be rid of the horrid task that awaited me.

Ahead, something white bobbed. I quickened my pace and soon discerned two young women walking arm in arm. Their gowns glowed white in the beam of the moon. As I drew abreast, they paused and turned to me. How surprised I was to see that one of them was my Sophie. Why was she here? Memories wrestled. My heart thundered and my head felt as if it might explode. I must focus. *Focus.*

Sophie was much the same as I'd seen her in the theater, though her gown bore no stain upon it now. How could this be? And how frightened she looked. At once I knew the reason: the string of diamonds winked from her throat. No wonder she trembled. Vulnerable on the street, anyone might accost her to steal the precious gems. Paste they might be, but what thief would know in such poor light?

I must protect her. She was not safe here.

"Come," I said, ushering the women against the wall of a house where a roof jutted to blot the moonlight. "I have an errand to do just ahead, but I shall fetch you as soon as I am finished. The three of us shall walk together, and I will take you home."

I had not given much attention to the second woman until I finished this instruction. I could not quite fathom her features in the shadows, but I was struck by the notion that she was not unlike myself in height, dress, and hair. The pair could be Sophie and I returning from the theater.

A strange fancy, but I hadn't the time to ponder it more. Certain the two would remain where they hid, I raced up the street. At the top, a single house had a shutter open on the second floor revealing a light within. Was this my destination?

I stole to the door. I cannot explain it—the clear understanding that came over me that this was the correct house, and my prey was above. The door came open with ease, and I stepped over the threshold.

With Sophie so near, I must dispatch the gentleman before he harmed her.

There was enough moonlight shining through the door to light the way to the stairs. With a wild heart, I climbed.

At the top, the light from one room spilled into the hall. The house was a tomb. Not a creature stirred.

And then a male voice punctured the night. "Come in, my dear Marguerite."

As if pulled by some invisible force, I stole across the floor. I withdrew my dagger and entered the room.

A man sat comfortably in an upholstered chair. A glass of blood-red wine rested on a table at his elbow. A corner of his mouth lifted. "I've been waiting for you."

His words pierced me through. Madame had led me to believe this man would be like the others, that he would be duped by my cunning and surprise. This gentleman—this *last* gentleman—was altogether different. He was expecting me. And he knew who I was.

"Come," he said. He gestured to the bed. "It is there that I killed her. Would you like to know the details?" I did not move. He took a sip of wine and returned the glass to the table, licking dry lips and crossing one leg over the other. "It was so easy."

"You are—" I began.

"Satterfield?" He raised fine brows. "Yes, of course." He chuckled. "Didn't Madame Lacroix give you my name?"

Yes. Satterfield *was* his name. Madame had told me in the carriage. But never had my victims known of my relationship with her, nor my diabolical plans. My head pounded anew. I resisted the urge to abandon myself to the black shadows at the edge of my vision. I had walked into a trap. Madame might have given me the bone-handled dagger, but she had sealed my fate. I thought, *Run. With a head start, you can evade him in the shadows.*

But my Sophie was near and unprotected.

"You needn't be concerned," Satterfield said with another chuckle. His eyes flicked to my hand. "You have the dagger. Use it." When I didn't stir, he went on. "I'm a fantastic faro player, you know. And I do appreciate the ponies. What's a wife's fortune for if her husband can't spend it, eh? My Lizbeth was a beautiful woman of fine stock, but once the money vanished." He leaned forward in his chair and pinned me with his dark eyes, "Well, so did my passion for her."

He stood and I retreated a step. He was taller than I expected. He was in his shirt sleeves, his waistcoat having been discarded. "Don't be such a filly," he said with a sardonic smile. "*Femme assassin* indeed." He loosened his cravat. "You do realize, it's you who's doing the killing, yes?" He winked at me.

I wanted to fly at him. The bluster of the man. But what if I failed to gut him and he fled? My Sophie was near and unprotected. The fiend would want her diamonds!

He cast his cravat to the floor and approached the bed. This was his wife's room, for it was adorned in a feminine style, its pinks and flounces outrageously vulnerable in the presence of such a cruel brute.

"She lay here perfect in sleep," he said, with a sweep of his arm. "So very peaceful. And I left her that way, in the end."

My heart quickened with anger. I wanted him to die.

To my surprise, he lay down on the bed. With his arms folded under his head and his ankles crossed, he continued. "She awoke when she felt my hands at her throat. The panic in her eyes." A snicker. "Such an innocent. It was beautiful, you know. The light in her eyes that slowly died as I squeezed."

I had seen that look in my own victims' eyes. I was suddenly filled with self-loathing.

He patted the bed. "Come. I won't protest, I promise. I shall even unfasten a button or two to reveal my neck. Isn't that the way? A single slash to the throat?"

I did not move. Madame had coaxed me here to die. She couldn't trust I wouldn't one day reveal our relationship, that she had once been the *la femme assassin* of London. Finishing me would keep her secrets buried. I wondered how she'd coerced Satterfield to do her dirty work.

"*Marguerite*," Satterfield snapped. His light mockery had vanished. "I know Sophie hides on the street but a house away. If you do not do as I say, I will snatch that precious diamond necklace from her and use your dagger to slit her creamy throat."

With a shriek, I flew to the bed, landing on top of Satterfield before my mind had time to register what I'd done. I plunged the dagger down and made one swift and vicious slice across Satterfield's throat.

Then, just like the last time, and the time before that, and the time before the time before that, the bedroom door opened behind me. The smell of jasmine perfume wafted to me. In walked Madame Lacroix followed by two young gentlemen. Each carried a clipboard.

"Next on our list," Madame declared, flipping a page, "is Margaret Collings. Once a prominent actress, she joined us a year ago following the death of her sister, Sophie."

The men nodded, jotting notes. Oddly, they wore no waistcoats or cravats. Affixed to their shirts were small white cards marked cryptically with the words: VISITING RESIDENT.

No one noticed the dagger in my hands, nor what I had done. Slowly, stealthily, I concealed my dagger among the sheets. Spinning around, I gripped the metal bars of the footboard and peered through.

"Madame," I said, my heart beating a steady staccato, "what is the meaning of this?"

"Margaret," she replied, taking a step closer. "I'm very busy. Some other time." She smiled fleetingly, the gold tooth glinting before her lips fell. Her hair was no longer piled atop her head in the fashion but worked into a rather shoddy twist. She wore an odd white coat I had never seen before.

"How did her sister die?" one gentleman asked.

How absurd. I tried to catch Madame's eye, but she was focused on the man.

"Sophie went to the theater one evening to watch Margaret perform. By the time the show let out and Margaret had changed out of her costume, the streets were deserted. She'd worn a fake diamond necklace in the play—a rather gaudy one, I might add—and Sophie wished to wear it home."

I placed my fingers to my temples and pressed. The pain in my head was excruciating.

Madame continued, "Before they reached their car, a band of thugs approached and one of them—Satterfield was his name—snatched it from Sophie's throat. He thought it was real."

I couldn't breathe. Satterfield had never laid a hand on my Sophie. I had killed him to prevent it.

"Margaret tried to intervene, but the other men held her back. Satterfield, the sod, slashed Sophie's throat. She died on the pavement in Margaret's arms."

Nonsense. Madame was talking nonsense. My Sophie was alive. It was Satterfield who was dead, and by my hand. Like so many other *bâtards*. I began to rock. It was the only thing that soothed me when Madame spoke lies.

"The handkerchief she holds," she said, "was in Sophie's pocket that night. She won't let it out of her hands."

I looked down. A scruff of white linen was balled in my fists. Upon it were garish red stains. *Oui,* Madame was mad. This was Samuel Collingsworth's handkerchief, his blood. I pressed it out straight. The 'SC' embroidered in the corner leered at me.

"Madame," I said gingerly, for I did not want to anger her, "I wish to return to my lodgings. Would you be so kind as to call for a carriage?"

The gentlemen blinked at me. Were they next on Madame's list? Was she trying to tell me something?

"Yes, of course, Margaret," Madame said. A glint of gold. "I shall have one brought around." She turned to the gentlemen and said, low, "She fancies herself a paid assassin employed by a woman who runs a brothel in 1870's London. '*La Femme Assassin*' she calls herself. I imagine it's the guilt. For not being able to protect her young sister."

When the door closed, I waited for my Sophie. The sound of horse hooves striking cobblestones soon filled the room. I was again with Collingsworth, sitting astride him, Madame at my ear. The dagger was new and felt strange in my hands. I breathed in a sharp gasp as the blade, balanced in my hands, tested the tension of the skin at his cheek.

"One simple thrust, my dear, and it is done," Madame said.

LA COLLIER

MICAH THORP

I t was during a period of modernization that the idea of a freeway
ringing the city was first conceived. The decision was unusually
popular, even among the discordant members of the City
Council, who, after assiduously arguing over which council members
had proposed the concept, voted unanimously to approve it. Once
decided in accordance with the wishes of the council, the plan was
delegated to the Metropolitan Engineering Department to be carried
out.

Understanding the political importance of the assignment, Chief
Engineer Claude Savante turned to the department's rising star, Jacque
Collier, to design the thoroughfare. Described as a boulevard the likes
of which the city hadn't seen since the days of Napoleon, the official
naming of the manager was treated with the pomp and circumstance
of a ribbon cutting. Savante described Collier as a recent graduate of
École Polytechnique who had chosen to work for the city rather than
taking a more lucrative job in a private firm; a description designed to
invoke popular support during the inevitable civic disruption that
building a highway around the city would engender.

In other venues, Jacque Collier might have been viewed as a zealot.
His appearance, at the very least, bore the unmistakable

characteristics of a young man so utterly invested in the subject of his passions he'd set aside all else in their pursuit. Modestly unkempt, his tousled brown hair and stubble-covered face aligned with the flannel shirts comfortably hidden beneath wrinkled sport coats, which he seemed to wear primarily as a repository for the drafting pens and flash drives, embedding them in ink-stained pockets. His mildly disheveled appearance suggested he had little time for the niceties of politics. In contrast to his wardrobe, the penetrating stare of his deep-set dark eyes suggested that whatever his gaze landed upon was not merely of importance, but a point of concentration and the singular entity onto which the entirety of his focus was fixed.

A self-reported visionary, Collier often remarked that he had chosen employment with the city to build *les grands desseins*, a phrase intended to describe pieces of infrastructure, but interpreted by those who knew him as an admission of his blind ambition. In granting him managerial control of the highway, Savante understood he had named either a potential successor or necessary foil.

Once the proposed highway was announced and Jacque Collier named the lead engineer, a flurry of activity commenced. Work groups and managers were assigned, meetings were convened, maps were drawn, and contracts negotiated. In the center of it all was the young Collier, rushing from committee to committee, scrolls and files under his arm as a trail of assistants flowed behind him jotting down notes and trying to appear as focused as their principal.

Paris Match was the first to refer to the planned highway as "the necklace," perhaps in homage to its lead engineer, perhaps as metaphor. Regardless of its reason, the name captured the public's imagination. While initially ignored by city planners who regarded it with the derision held by those who believe that naming civic infrastructure distracts from the building of it, the term eventually took hold and was used in nearly all descriptions.

To ensure that any mention of the highway also included deferential reference to the engineer in charge of its creation, Collier took great care to personally announce decisions about where the highway would be built, which neighborhoods would be dissected, where on- and off-ramps would be placed, whose construction companies would be hired, where rock and gravel would be requisitioned, and so on. What followed was an inevitable line of favor-seekers outside the Metropolitan Engineering Department: neighborhood activists, city counselors, unionists, city executives, and builders, all seeking a brief moment with Collier. In time, the bland engineering offices filled with baskets of fresh pastries and bottles of wine. With the gifts came invitations: opening night at the ballet, dinner with civic dignitaries, and salons with artists and academics.

It was at such a soirée that Collier was introduced to Mademoiselle Marie Benoit, a striking thirty-six-year-old with hazel eyes and soft brown hair. A wealthy socialite and the daughter of a prominent politician, she was at once graceful and familiar, capable of holding a conversation about arcane academia or the latest acquisition of Paris Saint-Germain. After a brief introduction, Collier found himself entranced, hanging on her every word, transfixed by Marie's sparkling wit and devilish smile. Over the ensuing weeks he prioritized events where he knew she would be in attendance, ensuring that whenever she appeared on a guest list he was invited as well.

Marie undoubtedly noticed Collier's interest but was coy in response to his advances. Uncertainty fueled his interest in the effervescent young woman. As is often the case with infatuation, Collier began to ruminate at all hours about how he might win her affection. Where he had once seemed relentless in designing the great Parisian highway, he became distracted, at times staring into space in his office, ignoring the drawings and schematics scattered across his desk. In meetings he seemed uninterested and aloof. Colleagues noted the shift in demeanor and focus but were wary to discuss it with their headstrong boss.

Finally, in a fit of desperation, Collier decided to confront the issue. He left a message asking Marie to meet him that evening at the opera, intent on finding out whether she was simply feigning interest, or if she genuinely wished to pursue an amorous relationship.

Collier arrived early at the opera house and quickly found his seat. It wasn't until the theater darkened and the curtain was rising that Marie appeared and sank into the seat next to him. He wasn't immediately certain whether her arrival at the last minute was a sign of disinterest or merely an effort to encourage his advance. Even as they watched *Les Troyens* and her hand descended onto his he remained confused. During the climactic moment she leaned against him, gripping his arm. For a moment, he felt he might have forged a connection, but as quickly as she seemed to embrace his affection, she pulled away. Before the final aria, Marie retreated to the powder room and Collier found himself alone in the foyer.

By the time she emerged, the crowd had thinned considerably. Collier's anxiety grew as she took his arm. "Jacque, you seem upset. Let us leave this place. I know somewhere we can go and talk."

Collier nodded and followed Marie down the gilded opera house stairs. A short cab ride later he found himself at an intimate brasserie in La Chapelle, sitting at a table listening to Marie tell stories about trips to London and New York. After a half hour, he waved to the waiter and motioned for two glasses of Bordeaux. Before the waiter returned, he removed his tie and loosened his collar anticipating the questions he might ask Marie.

"What is that around your neck?" Marie asked, pointing to a silver chain.

"Saint Christopher." Jacque replied, pulling the small silver disc from inside his shirt.

"I did not think you were religious," Marie said with a sly grin.

"I am not," Jacque replied. "Except for this." He pinched the silver chain. "I have not taken it from my neck since it was given to me as a boy." He cleared his throat, ready to refocus the conversation.

Marie raised an eyebrow. "It must be worth a great deal to you."

Collier nodded. "It is a source of purpose, given to me by a priest from Lourdes." He leaned forward and said in a low voice, "It was blessed by the pope."

"Well then, you definitely must let me see it." Marie leaned forward and kissed his cheek. "Just for a moment."

Collier hesitated, suddenly certain of Marie's interest. Feeling the need to reveal more of himself, he held the Saint Christopher in his open hand. "My father died when I was small, and my mother worked as a seamstress. I got into a great deal of trouble. My teachers told me only an act of God would keep me out of jail. I assumed I would be poor and penniless. One day, my school visited Lourdes to see the basilica and grotto. As we toured the plaza, I became separated from my class and lost in the crowd. I wandered for what seemed like hours until I was found by a priest in the grotto. He took me to the basilica and stayed with me while someone went to find my teacher. As we waited, he gave me the Saint Christopher and told me that with it I would not fail, that the Holy Father had blessed it and that it held the guiding light of God. I knew in that moment that it was the act of God my teachers had told me I needed. From that day forward I pledged myself to keeping faith with that purpose. I have carried it with me ever since."

"What a lovely story. But how did your Saint Christopher provide you purpose and direction?"

Collier rolled the silver chain between his fingers. "It is simple and clear. Saint Christopher is the patron of the traveler on the road. It was a sign of what I was meant to do. It is why I was asked to build the highway, to help pilgrims and travelers. God intended it."

Marie smiled and playfully grasped his hand. "If you love me you'll let me have it."

Collier took a sip of wine and looked into Marie's dark brown eyes.

"Just for a moment." Slowly, he removed the chain from his neck and placed it in her hand.

Marie carefully cradled the small silver disc. "I can feel its energy." She paused and turned her mouth into a crooked smile. "Never mind. It's the wine."

Collier's face darkened. "Give it back. Please."

Marie placed the Saint Christopher in Collier's hand. After a moment, she touched his arm. "I did not mean to upset you. Let us enjoy the evening." She looked around the room. "This place bores me. We should leave and find something exhilarating." With a flick of her hair, she made for the door.

THE NEXT DAY, COLLIER WOKE IN HIS BED NAUSEATED AND disheveled. He stood, legs shaking as he made his way to the bathroom to splash water on his face. Looking at himself in the mirror his face suddenly whitened, and a rush of fear overwhelmed him as he stared at his bare neck, devoid of the silver chain and Saint Christopher.

For the next hour he meticulously searched his apartment, digging through his clothes, tearing apart the bed and scouring the floor for his lost charm. Not finding it, nor any clue about where it might be, he sat on the edge of his bed and tried to recall where he might have left it. He remembered very little after leaving the opera: a cab ride, laughing with a drink in his hand, the tinkle of Marie's laugh. He attempted to call Marie, but she did not answer.

Panicked, he decided to retrace his steps. While he could not recall exactly where he had been, he remembered handing the Saint Christopher to Marie at the brasserie. Hurriedly, he made his way back to La Chapelle.

IT TOOK COLLIER NEARLY AN HOUR TO FIND THE BRASSERIE. ITS entrance was marked by a small sign on a side street in La Chapelle, away from the main thoroughfare. He stared through a window on the front door into a darkened room. Closed. He knocked. No one answered. He shook the door handle. Hearing nothing, he pounded on the door with his fists.

A narrow alley led to the back of the building where Collier found a locked window. Wrapping his arm in his jacket he broke through the pane, reached inside and opened the latch. Brushing away the glass he pulled himself inside.

The club was dark save for dim light streaming through the shaded windows. Chairs had been placed on tables and the sheen on the floor made it appear as though it had recently been mopped. Collier made his way to the area where he and Marie had been sitting. Getting on his hands and knees he crawled on the floor from table to table. Finding nothing, he moved to the bar and looked for a lost and found box. Unable to see in the dim light he felt along the shelves and cupboards behind the bar, shattering glasses on the floor as he frantically searched for the small oblong silver disc. Satisfied his Saint Christopher was not behind the bar he found a small office and rummaged through drawers and boxes. Focused and undistracted, his search became frantic. So much so that he failed to notice when the front door burst open, and officers of the Police nationale entered the establishment.

AFTER A DAY IN LA SANTÉ, COLLIER WAS RELEASED WITH A citation and a small fine. The moment he stepped outside the police station he called Marie.

"Jacque, darling, where have you been? I had such a lovely evening."

"Where is my Saint Christopher?"

"I do not know. You were having such a good time."

Collier inhaled deeply and closed his eyes before continuing. "Marie, my Saint Christopher is gone. I lost it when I was with you. Do you know where it might be?"

"I'm sure I don't know. It might be anywhere. You were so happy, showing everyone your good luck charm and telling them how you were on God's mission."

"Marie, I must have my Saint Christopher. Surely you must have seen me remove it from my neck."

"Of course, I saw you remove it. You were showing it to everyone and telling them how it was important."

As quickly as blood had rushed to Collier's face it drained away. His breathing quickened. "Marie, where did I lose my Saint Christopher? I need it. I cannot work without it."

"Jacque darling, surely you can. It is merely a token."

Collier recoiled. His jaw clenched as he responded. "Marie, it is not merely a token. It is everything. Where is my Saint Christopher? What have you done with it?"

The line went dead.

JACQUE COLLIER'S OFFICE REMAINED DARK ON MANY DAYS. HIS staff became disengaged and moved on to other assignments. Not that Collier noticed. As the highway project withered, his effort to find his lost Saint Christopher became an obsession. Though he could not recall precisely where it might be, he knew it was likely in a drinking establishment somewhere near La Chapelle. Daily, he would frequent taverns and pubs in the area, asking for a drink, questioning patrons about a woman named Marie Benoit who might have frequented the establishment, and if anyone had left a Saint Christopher in the lost and found. Repeatedly, no one remembered a Marie Benoit and that whatever was lost was thrown into the rubbish or simply given away.

As his efforts turned from work at the Metropolitan Engineering Department to the pursuit of his lost talisman, whatever semblance of what had once been Jacque Collier changed. The modestly disheveled appearance became one of vagrancy, his clothes not only wrinkled and mismatched, but dirty and worn. His penetrating stare became one of vacuousness as he became the hollowed-out visage of a man whose mind was completely lost.

WORK ON THE GREAT HIGHWAY CONTINUED, EVEN AS THE composition of City Hall changed. As the economy softened, a new group of city councilors was elected whose view of public investment was far less grandiose than its predecessors. Political winds that had once proved favorable to public infrastructure turned against the increased taxation required to fund such designs.

So began a slow process of choking off necessary support to continue the project. Where once a neighborhood committee was required to approve an off-ramp, the committee was dissolved, and approval couldn't be obtained. Bonds necessary to pay for paving or guardrails were not renewed. Monies set aside for the highway project were reallocated to other services.

As politics changed, so did public perception. The great Parisian highway, once seen as a sign of progress, was gradually viewed with derision, referred to by some as a civic boondoggle. Rumors circulated of kickbacks and bribes, back-office deals and favoritism. Even *Paris Match*, which once described the highway as a necklace surrounding the city, began likening it to a noose.

Ever attuned to the shifting of political winds, the Metropolitan Engineering Department adjusted accordingly. Chief Engineer Savante distanced himself from any reports involving the highway project. Deferral and referral were a long-practiced bureaucratic art among the leaders of city departments, ever careful to ensure their capacity to maintain employment doing meaningless, menial work.

THE DISSOLUTION OF THE LIFE THAT HAD BEEN JACQUE COLLIER went virtually unnoticed. As the months went by, he slipped further and further away from those around him. His few friends, work colleagues, and acquaintances rarely noticed his absence. Perhaps it was due to his slow retreat from his former life or the tenuous nature of Collier's relationships. Whatever the case he slowly disappeared.

His employment with the Metropolitan Engineering Department was never formally terminated. As time progressed, he simply went to work less and less, choosing instead to spend his days wandering through the city, lost in both purpose and direction. He could be found at all hours, sitting alone in a cafe, in the pews of a church, or on a park bench staring off into space.

In the early evenings, when the tourists had receded to their hotel rooms, the clergy and staff at Notre Dame would find Collier seated on the floor of the nave staring at the colossal statue of Saint Christopher. Occasionally a security guard would approach the ever more gaunt and ghostly man to shoo him away. But before they could wave their arms Collier would disappear back into the night air.

Similarly, patrolmen would be summoned intermittently by panicked motorists, fearful of a man wandering across the functioning bits of road that comprised what had been built of the great necklace highway. But by the time the police arrived, the wandering man had always gone, described by onlookers as a shadowy figure fading into the dust. As with other recurrent unexplained phenomena, imagination soon took hold and stories of an apparition haunting the unfinished highway circulated, first as stories of sightings, followed by tales of resentful ghosts and disappearing motorists. Theories abounded: the highway had been constructed over a cemetery, a motorist slammed into an unmarked construction zone killing unsuspecting workers whose deaths had been covered up by the city, Napoleon's ghost had returned to ensure that nothing so abhorrent as a giant roadway would ever mar the City of Light.

IN THE YEARS THAT PASSED JACQUE COLLIER WANDERED. FIRST IN the outskirts of Paris, later from town to town. His gaunt, listless figure was barely noticed by the occupants of the vehicles that sped by as he staggard along the roadways of France. Always on foot, he never set foot in a car or truck, never found a seat on a train or bus. He slept in open spaces, occasionally shooed away by police or landowners.

After years of drifting, Collier found himself in Lourdes.

Initially, he didn't recognize the city.

It wasn't until after a few hours shuffling through the maze of streets that Collier looked up and saw the spire of the basilica. He rubbed his eyes and stood motionless for a time before realizing where he stood. Only when he heard the angry bleating horn of a motorist did he stumble off the street.

Either out of habit or curiosity Collier meandered toward the white Neo-gothic fleche, rising over Our Lady of Lourdes. As he made his way closer, the crowds grew. Streets were filled with tourists, townspeople and clergy. Groups of foreigners, school children, and pilgrims wandered up and down the riverfront. In the plaza, small crowds lined up to tour the grotto. Tour guides held up small colored signs. Uniformed school children fidgeted as they stood in line. A pair of nuns held up their phones, snapping pictures. A group of Americans huddled together staring at their guidebooks.

Collier felt himself pulled through the crowd, past the line and into the narthex. He stared for several minutes into the sanctuary across the nave at the great cross and pillars. The pews were empty, and he seated himself.

When he felt a hand on his shoulder, Collier assumed he was about to be told to leave. Instead, he looked up into the face of a young priest.

The priest smiled. "Monsieur, you appear troubled. How may God bring you peace?"

He looked blankly at the priest, considering his answer. Finally, he responded, "I have lost my faith, Father."

The priest sat next to Collier. "This happens to all of us. Our faith is tested. We question it. We question God. We ask ourselves hard questions. But God still loves us."

Collier looked at his hands. They were dirty and calloused. Tar and grease lined the creases between his fingers and on his palms. "My purpose is lost. God gave me direction. I believed I understood what I was to do." He sighed. "And then it was gone."

"We often think we are given to a purpose, a direction, but we do not really know what that purpose is to be."

Collier shook his head and straightened his back. "No Father, the purpose for which God intended me was clear. I was provided direction and a token. Right here in this very place."

The priest nodded in the manner of one who believes he has knowledge and wisdom without the commiserate age or experience to produce either. "I'm sure, my friend, that had God provided you with such a sign, it would not have been easily lost."

"It was *not* easily lost."

"Good. I would hope that your faith was not lost easily."

"Not my faith, Father, but my token of it. It was gone in a single night. In one night, God took from me the very thing that had given me my meaning. He took from me the purpose He had once given. How can my faith not follow?"

The priest cleared his throat. "You are like Job, my son. God has taken it from you to test your faith. Your loss is itself a token, a way to measure whether or not you believe. Yes, it is a test."

Collier clenched his teeth. "If it is a test, I have failed. I do not believe. I have lost my faith. If God intended it as a test, then it is done."

The priest sighed. His shoulders slumped and he scratched behind his collar. Resigned, he asked, "What was it? The token that you lost?"

"It was a Saint Christopher. On a silver chain. One that had been blessed by the pope. It was given to me by a priest here in Lourdes."

The priest's resignation melted away and his smile returned. "Do not fret my son. The Holy Father blesses thousands of Saint Christophers! You can buy one in the gift shop for five euros!"

A WEEK LATER, SEVERAL CARS TRAVERSING THE UNFINISHED Parisian highway reported a shadowy figure wandering down the center lane yelling incomprehensibly, waving his arms toward the heavens. By the time the police arrived the figure was gone. All that was left was an unclasped silver chain, unadorned by whatever had once been affixed to it.

DEAD RECKONING

ANNIE TUPEK

The Torc of Captaincy weighed heavy on Lunula's clavicle. She thumbed the ring on her right index finger and wished she'd had another thirty years to prepare for this.

Her jumpsuit was unzipped and pulled back to expose her shoulders and Engineer Jerica adjusted the necklace that had been worn by every prior captain of *Pluto's Reckoning*. The pins on the torc's underside bit into Lunula's skin, deep enough to feel each one, but not deep enough to draw blood.

"Almost in place," Jerica said. Scintillations of light danced across her jewelry. A gold monocle, like the one Lunula wore, provided an overlay to augment her vision, but Lunula couldn't tell what data it displayed to Auntie Jeri.

Engineer Jerica, Lunula reminded herself. As captain she couldn't go around the ship calling people Auntie.

Lunula shifted under the necklace's weight. Engineer Jerica rotated one of her command rings and confirmed, "We have connection and power. Engineering is a go."

"Vitals are stable," Doc Kemp said, his voice clear and confident. Lunula hoped her own words would be as strong when her turn came.

He and Doc Junner wore matching white medical coats and stood before a bank of monitors. Despite the spaceship's age, the clean lines of the infirmary sparkled and its walls glowed with warm light. Doc Kemp's fingers danced and light flickered off his silver rings as he manipulated the data on the monitors. He nodded to his senior.

Doc Junner announced, "Medical is a go."

Grandmother caught Lunula's hand and squeezed. "The ship can be in no better hands," she said. "Incumbent is a go."

Astrogator Jalan stepped into view and the ship's infirmary closed in around Lunula. As the oldest ranking officer, it fell to him to swear in the new captain. The wrinkles on his forehead bowed and flexed under his heavy thoughts and Lunula had a sense of his displeasure with her. Gator Jalan, she used to call him, grouchy and wrinkled like the swamp-dwelling Earth creature he reminded her of. She couldn't call him that anymore, not even in her thoughts for fear it might leak out. Astrogator Jalan's eyebrow held his gold rimmed monocle captive and he folded bracelet-laden arms across his chest.

"I shall administer the oath of office," Astrogator Jalan intoned, opening the ceremony.

Lunula repeated his words. "I, Lunula Lima, Twelfth of the Captain's Line, do solemnly pledge to serve the crew of *Pluto's Reckoning* as their Captain. This I shall do to the best of my ability, and shepherd the ship safely to Eleusis Well, where we shall be space-bound no more." A tingle spread along her skin where the torc rested. It grew into a burn, and she finished with a gasped breath. "This I so swear."

She had expected pain with her promotion to captaincy, but nothing in all her twenty-five years had prepared her for its intensity. Her toes curled in her boots, her fingers clawed at the med chair. Every piece of jewelry constricted, every limb went rigid. She recognized Astrogator Jalan was speaking, closing out the ceremony, but she did not hear his words.

Her lips parted in a grimace. It wasn't supposed to hurt this much, maybe that meant she wasn't ready. Her skin wasn't tough enough.

Somewhere beyond her tear-blurred vision, the white blob of Doc

Junner monitored her vital signs as the heavy necklace's fine neural wires fused with Lunula's neurons. Everything had to be fine. Doc would have stopped it if anything were abnormal.

"Breathe," Grandmother whispered in her ear. "The pain is temporary. Breathe through it."

Lunula sucked air between her teeth and hissed it out. The thick twists of gold weighed on her skin, but were cool compared to the fire the torc spread deeply through her chest and throat. A few seconds of time. Moments. Five breaths. No more than that. She'd already taken one. She took another.

Streams of data flickered in the augmented vision of her monocle as the torc came online and integrated with her other implants. Lunula distanced herself from the pain through observation, noting each jewel on the torc as it sparked to brilliant life. She hissed out a breath.

"Good," Grandmother encouraged.

A third inhalation.

She had been born for this, though not expected to take command for another fifteen years. Except Mother had suffered a fatal accident during an exterior repair. The accelerated education hadn't prepared her for this.

The air seared her throat, her lungs. The fire reached up through her sinuses and into her head. She exhaled a hiss that did nothing to reduce the burning sensation by a single thermal unit.

Her vision focused, surrounded by the sterile infirmary. Doc and his protégé at their monitors, Jerica, Astrogator Jalan. Grandmother at her side. And someone else. A sharp intake of breath scorched her lungs. She couldn't see them beyond the characters on her monocle, but she sensed someone else in the infirmary, a reflection, a shadow. She rolled her head back and forth as much as she could, searching, but found no one except the five.

Lunula exhaled a wordless cry. If she held still, maybe the pain would pass. She held herself rigid in the chair.

"Breathe," Grandmother commanded in her Captain's voice. Former Captain. Lunula breathed reflexively. Tears formed in the corners of Lunula's eyes. Something snapped. She let out a whooshing breath. The pain was gone in an instant.

The lack of sensation shocked, as though her nerves had burned out. The torc's pins caught against her skin in countless tugs as she shifted in the seat and relaxed against the chair.

Doc Junner turned from monitoring his screens. "Took to her like a champ, but, as expected, the tissue is traumatized. You're on bedrest, Captain."

Captain. The first time she'd been addressed by her new title, and it was Doc ordering her around. That wasn't the way it was supposed to be. Her throat was too raw to laugh at the irony, and it came out as a choked breath.

"You all right, dear?" Grandmother asked.

Lunula nodded. The navigation menus in her monocle branched seemingly into infinity and expanded her awareness of *Pluto's Reckoning* and its crew. All over the ship, they'd paused in their day, as Astrogator Jalan came on the PA system.

Reading off the script in his monocle he announced, "The Captaincy has been passed. *Pluto's Reckoning* is now under the command of Lunula Lima of the twelfth generation. May she see us safely to Eleusis Well."

"May she see us safely to Eleusis Well," the crew repeated, the refrain kept from days of old, when there had been a chance of reaching Eleusis Well. There was a mellow, resigned tone to the crew's words. Catechism more than belief. *Pluto's Reckoning* had been knocked off course by an uncharted comet eight generations ago.

Even those in the room with her didn't seem to believe. Grandmother, the doctors, Engineer Jerica, and Astrogator Jalan. And another. A sixth voice distinguished from the crew. The observer she'd sensed behind her but not seen.

She searched over her shoulder, but the torc pulled on her skin as it stretched from her movement. Doc had given her something, and her head lolled back. Enforced bedrest. When Doc Junner wanted you in bed, he put you to bed. The next time they met, she'd be giving the orders. The thought sustained Lunula as she faded into unconsciousness.

———

LUNULA LAY IN HER NEW BED IN THE CAPTAIN'S QUARTERS. THE sedative was wearing off and it was odd to see the suite from this angle. The lines and lighting were all wrong. She'd only ever sat at the table beyond the translucent partition and had rarely gone beyond it into this sleeping compartment.

The room was newly refreshed, but the fibers of the bedding had been recycled into a dull gray, like the ship's other soft goods. They'd extended *Pluto's Reckoning* fifty years beyond its service life. The journey had been meant to end nearly two hundred years ago. The ship was held together by the crew's dedication and hard work.

Grandmother stood at the partition, clavicle dotted with angry, shallow punctures where the torc had rested yesterday. Its removal was a far-kinder procedure than its implantation. Without the torc, Grandmother's jewelry seemed unbalanced, bangles around her wrist, finger rings, and surface piercings, her bare neck bordered on obscene. She must have felt blind without the cascade of information that now overwhelmed Lunula's monocle.

"I'm proud of you, Lunula," Grandmother said. "Captain." She gave the pensioner salute, hand to heart, and smiled. "I'm just a tram ride away if you need me."

"I know," Lunula croaked, throat raw from the over-stimulation her neurons sustained yesterday as much as from disuse. Doc Junner had kept Lunula sedated, giving her biology time to heal and her implant systems time to integrate themselves with the torc. Lunula was eager to be out of bed and exploring the ship, but her eyelids felt heavy.

"I wanted to be here when you woke, but Doc is kicking me out," Grandmother said. "He'll take good care of you. Follow his directions and you'll be running this ship in no time."

"I am running this ship," Lunula mumbled. The torc tugged and she wondered if she would ever get used to the sensation.

Doc Jenner took Grandmother's place at the partition. His bedside manner put everyone at ease. Nearing his own retirement, his protégé shadowed him. The resemblance was stronger than Lunula's was to Grandmother, but that's because they were closer in age. Doc Kemp would inherit his role at a far more reasonable age than Lunula inherited hers. Forty instead of twenty-five.

"Diagnostics show that, despite the initial tissue trauma, you're handling the transition quite well." Doc Junner ran his index finger along one of his cuff bracelets. "How are you feeling, Captain?"

"Good." The crack in her voice betrayed her. "I hate lying here." A cough wracked her lungs and another round of fire ran up her nerves.

"Of course, you do," he assured her. "It's what makes you a good captain." His bedside manner was meant to put her at ease, but she didn't identify as a good captain. She didn't know if Grandmother was a good captain, or any of the prior captains all the way up the line. Not one had found their way to Eleusis Well. The task before her was impossible, but as long as the embryos *Pluto's Reckoning* transported thrived, their mission remained valid.

"I need to tour the ship," Lunula said.

"You need rest," Doc Junner said. "The sedatives are protocol. Every captain has taken them. They aid in the natural, healthy sleep necessary for neural connection. You want to tough it out, but you've got forty years as captain ahead of you. Three days is nothing on that timeline."

"There is so much to do, so much for me to absorb. The sedatives are blocking me from my work."

"You'll rest and have your Captain's walk on the fifth day," Doc Junner said. "Just like everyone else."

"They were all older than me." She sat up in bed. It felt good to move just that little bit. "It stands to reason that my body heals faster. I'm ready."

"You also felt a lot more pain than those before you," Doc Junner told her. "You can barely move." He popped the cap off a micro-syringe and stuck it into her arm. "We'll see how you're doing tomorrow."

"Tomorrow, I'll be even better." The sedative slurred her words and she slid back down to rest her head on her pillow.

The flow of data across her vision dimmed and blurred. If she focused and squinted, it sharpened into view. But, fighting the sedative wasn't worth the effort. She wanted sleep, needed sleep. The data flowed, a pattern she didn't yet understand.

Dreams took over, a translucent face appearing in her monocle. Male, strong-jawed and clean-shaven with brown hair clipped close to his scalp. The room's light hit his tawny skin wrong. Lunula focused on his green eyes, unblinking and lifeless. She did not recognize him from the crew. The static image disappeared.

A shiver jolted through her and flailed her upright. The torc tugged at her skin. She looked all around the room, but she was alone. Lunula flopped back onto the pillows and wondered if she'd imagined it, like she'd imagined the observer during the procedure.

The sedative slowed her racing heart and she fell into a childhood memory of exploring the ship's greenspaces, running across a meadow. She'd chased the bees that pollinated the grasses, everything doing its part for the ship. One day, she would do her part.

She had turned a corner on the path and run into Grandmother. Captain Grandmother squatted next to a water tank, multitool in hand. A slow drip plinked from the faucet onto a damp spot on the ground beneath the tank.

"Grandmother?" Lunula asked.

Grandmother stared off into the distance and didn't seem to hear her.

Panic rose in her young mind. Grandmother had always answered her before. "Grandmother?" Lunula reached up and touched the hand that didn't hold the multitool.

"There is a ghost in the torc," Grandmother said, her gaze distant. Her fingers curled around Lunula's small hand, reassuring. But then she released her and lifted her hand to the golden torc that rested on her clavicle. The torc Lunula knew she would wear one day, many years in the future.

Her voice a whisper, Grandmother had said, "Sometimes, when the ship is very quiet and still, I can see him. I've caught glimpses. Like a glitch in my monocle. He frightens me."

Grandmother had bent down and tightened the spigot with her multitool and the dripping had stopped. Together, they had run across the meadow, kicking up pollen, and Lunula had thought no more of it.

There is a ghost in the torc. The words played over and over in Lunula's mind as she lay in Grandmother's bunk. Her bunk now, despite the lingering smell of citrus soap and the tang of grease in the air. Grandmother's smell. She had been notorious for making small fixes around the ship before the maintenance crew could get to them. Lunula now understood why Grandmother carried a multitool everywhere.

Wearing the torc, the ship was an extension of herself. Senses she hadn't known she possessed twitched and itched as the ship's different systems came online and provided their status reports. Grandmother's small fixes had been a form of itch-scratching.

Data flowed across her vision. The ghost could have been a picture of a long-dead crewman, retrieved as the torc's systems integrated with her other implants. That's what Lunula had seen. A glitch. Except, something struck her about the glitch. She hadn't noticed it at first, but he hadn't worn any jewelry. No monocle, no chain, not even an ear stud. He couldn't have been crew.

DOC JUNNER AND DOC KEMP LET HER OUT OF BED THREE DAYS later, but she'd had to prove her vitals were exceeding expectations to get them to agree to it. Muscles rubbery and flimsy, she stretched in the corridor outside her quarters. She was almost used to all the new data feeds. She hadn't had anything else to occupy her during recovery time. It was a matter of prioritizing. Some things didn't need constant monitoring, and those were muted and offloaded from her immediate vision. Everything else was slowly organizing into her daily brief.

She stretched her arms high above her head. Her skin puckered under the torc's restrictive grip. It felt good to take up space after being confined to her bed. Not that she could have moved much that first day, but she'd started sneaking out of bed the day following the procedure, getting used to the weight of the torc.

She took her first Captain's Walk without fanfare. She would vary the route each day until she found an optimal path, or something more urgent came along. Past the officer crew quarters, all hatches were closed this early in the morning. Except for the last one. Astrogator Jalan's hatch was ajar, swallowing the echoes of her footsteps in the corridor.

Lunula caught her breath as the hatch opened further. She straightened her shoulders. She was going to have to deal with Astrogator Jalan eventually.

Astrogator Jalan stuck his head through the opening. He hadn't yet donned all his bracelets and his arms looked thin and weak without them. "Good morning, Captain." He studied her. "I trust the doctors have released you?"

Lunula kept her frown to herself. "About an hour ago," she replied, knowing he would check with the doctors as soon as this conversation ended, just to ensure she wasn't running off on her own volition. A sudden chill brought goosebumps to her arms. Lunula rubbed them and said, "I'm going for my first walk. Would you like to join me?" She stretched as if she intended to set a quick pace.

"I don't think so," Astrogator Jalan declined. "Though perhaps Koray might join you."

Lunula glanced towards the junior astrogator's hatch, but it remained closed.

In her monocle, the image of a person came and went in a blink. The same man as before, with his close-cropped hair and face particularly naked without a monocle or piercings. His neutral expression remained stationary. Astrogator Jalan didn't seem to see him. He turned his rings, no doubt trying to reach Koray and provide an escort for her first Captain's Walk.

The image of the man flickered and seemed to recede down the corridor. Lunula hurried forward. "I must go," she excused herself and hurried after the departing form. Her first Captain's Walk turned into a run. Astrogator Jalan's disapproval followed her, but at least she'd avoided Koray. And, he had called her Captain.

That had been among her early worries, that the senior crew wouldn't accept her. Lunula turned into one of *Pluto Reckoning*'s grow domes and slowed. The man had been out of her sight for so long, she couldn't be certain where he'd gone, or if he'd been there at all.

She peered through the coated, shielded glass into the nursery. Row upon row of seedlings nourished precisely and transplanted appropriately. Two hundred and ninety-three years of operation, and only one light fixture had gone dark among the thousands still illuminated. When they were all on, the missing one was unnoticeable, but she could pinpoint it in her vision. Such was her new awareness of the ship. And its crew. Who were a little alarmed at their new captain running around the ship so soon after taking office.

Astrogator Jalan had gossiped.

A few crewmembers watched her from their stations in the nursery. Lunula raised her hand in greeting and they saluted. She returned the formality and went back the way she had come, walking with as much restraint as she could muster.

The crew was sensitive to change. There hadn't been a major deviation to the plan since the rogue comet knocked *Pluto's Reckoning* off course. Since then, the mission had changed to maintain life and return to course. The first directive had been going well, but the second was still a dream. The astrogators hadn't had a decent lead for six generations, and no matter how well the ship had been engineered, systems would break down eventually.

She headed for the canteen. Human systems were especially fragile. No wonder the crew felt nervous. Running through passageways was something juveniles did, and here she was, the youngest captain in the ship's history, chasing heedlessly through the ship after a glitch in her monocle.

If she didn't correct for that behavior soon enough, someone would step forward. There'd never been a mutiny aboard *Pluto's Reckoning*, but she wasn't sure she could prevent one.

The officers' canteen was empty. In her peripheral awareness, she knew each officer had breakfasted and moved on to their stations.

She sat at a table in the canteen and noted, without really seeing, all the new data feeds fanning across her vision. Generation upon generation of information. Recordings. One caught her eye and she twisted her ring to select it. Captains' Diaries.

All the way back to the first generation.

Lunula rolled her bracelet forward and scrolled through the chronological list. It looked like every captain who had come before her had recorded a diary. Including Grandmother.

It was perhaps too soon to read Grandmother's diary. Lunula didn't want to invade what little privacy she had had, but some of the others had to have mentioned the torc ghost. Lunula stood from the table she had only just sat down at. On her way back to her quarters, she selected various keywords to filter for.

The first mention of "ghost" was from one of the first captains. Pre-impact. Lunula requested the diary, but the system returned an error, unable to access the data at the specified location. Not a big surprise. The ship's archives had been repurposed to hold other, more vital information like their trajectory logs, all in the hopes of one day finding their way to Eleusis Well. The Captains' Diaries had been among the stores that had been sacrificed.

Out of the twenty-thousand instances of the keywords, Lunula estimated that maybe ten percent remained viable. She let herself into her quarters and lay down on her bunk. She turned her bracelet and rapidly requested file after file.

One finally hit. A woman appeared, from the waist up, hovering in Lunula's monocle. In her late sixties, the woman could have been

Grandmother. Or Mother. Or Lunula herself, in forty years' time. In effect, the woman was each of them. Every role in the ship was held by a clone of the original crewmember.

A spiderweb of gray strands streaked the woman's dark hair, which she wore slicked down over her head like a skullcap. Dark eye makeup creased wrinkles around her eyes. Her monocle glinted gold and was rimmed with small rubies that flashed in the light. Her pink lips were pursed in perturbation, but she was recognizably the Captain.

The familiar voice of Grandmother was another shock. A little hoarse, as though she'd recently been yelling. Lunula cross-referenced her ancestor's insignia while the recording played.

"I've seen him again," Captain Fiorella of the sixth generation said. "The third time since taking on the Torc of Captaincy twenty-nine years ago. He's a ghost. Maybe a former crewmember, but I can't find his uniform in the archives. He seems a little flat. His mouth moves, but I can't hear his words and I can't read his lips. No one else has seen him. Engineer Finley assures me my monocle is working fine and there is no record of him in the logs."

Captain Fiorella seemed uneasy. "Before she passed, my predecessor advised me to ignore him. And now I am of an age to pass on the torc to the next generation. I wish I had seen him sooner. He seems so desperate. I will advise Captain Gita to listen for him. No ghost wants to remain trapped in the mortal, but I cannot help him."

The ancient recording fizzed out and Lunula twisted the bracelet back to pause her search. Captain Fiorella had appeared more concerned than frightened. What had changed over the generations? Had the ghost turned malevolent, or had the stories been warped? No captain had fallen to an untimely demise. Except for Mother, but she hadn't been captain and that had been an accident. All the others had lived out their careers and returned to the pensioner deck to live out their remaining time in leisure.

What reason did she have to be afraid, other than her memory of Grandmother's fear? She needed more evidence. She rolled the bracelet forward to resume her search. The other diary entries she could access were similar to the first. She had convinced herself that the ghost was nothing to be afraid of, but when the ping at the door came, her bracelets rattled.

The doctors announced themselves. Lunula sat up on the bunk and motioned the door open.

"How are you adjusting?" Doc Junner asked as he entered.

"Some highs, some lows." She moved to the table and chairs on the public side of the partition. She offered her wrist to the doctor. "A lot of new information. It's exhausting."

She hadn't been alive the last time the captaincy had passed, and did not know what to expect. Though she'd been prepared for the torc's ability to convey the crew's general disposition to her, she couldn't yet interpret the information. The crew seemed cautious. It certainly wasn't celebratory.

Doc Junner tapped one of his rings against her bracelet and she dropped her hand. She could tell his attention was focused on his monocle's data feed. Lunula said, "I've been browsing the old Captains' diaries. I hope to glean some of their wisdom."

Doc Junner rested a hand on her shoulder, next to the torc. "Gaining the wisdom of the ancestors is a noble ambition, one to pursue in the coming years. Right now, you might better serve yourself and the ship by starting your own Captain's Diary. I think it would be therapeutic. You're our youngest captain, and it is important that your story be remembered. For posterity. So much has been lost."

"Until it gets overwritten," Lunula countered under her breath. She didn't know if Doc Junner heard her, but Doc Kemp gave her a sympathetic smile.

"Your vitals are fine," Doc Junner said. "You're healing faster than prior captains."

She gave him a false grin. "Of course. Like you said, I'm the youngest captain."

"Indeed." Doc Junner gave his cuff bracelet a tug. "Go to the datacenter. Engineer Jerica will set you up with your diary. If you're looking for energy, you might want to try coffee."

His indulgent smile betrayed his awareness of Lunula's dislike for the bitter drink that janked her nerves and made her heart pound. Grandmother had sworn by it, and the diaries had revealed other captains had as well.

Lunula frowned at the closed hatch long after the doctors left. She was getting plenty of rest.

LUNULA GOT A CUP OF COFFEE FROM THE SYNTHESIZER IN THE officers' canteen and felt an almost immediate sense of relief come over her, from the crew. She hadn't taken her first sip, but their approval was overwhelming. She was doing her job. Apparently, captains drank coffee.

Lunula lifted the cup to her mouth, but lowered it at the strong smell. Her eyes already watering with the remembered bitterness. Duty. Lunula held the coffee and strode towards the data center.

Everyone fit into their roles, into their boxes, nice and neat, as the system demanded. Lunula rebelled at the thought and knew she wasn't ready to be Captain. A proper Captain would do her duty to fit into her role for the good of the mission, the crew, and the ship.

The data center doors admitted her. Cool air from droning fans blew on her face. Sparse constellations of blinking lights flickered down row upon row of servers. Engineer Jerica waited for her, a fine jeweler's screwdriver in one hand, a cup of coffee in the other.

"Welcome, Captain," Jerica said. "You are here to start your diary?"

"Yes." Lunula hesitated. This was the first she'd run into the ship's engineer since her promotion, the first time she'd outranked Auntie Jeri. The woman had instructed and prepped her for all her augmented senses and assisted at every implant. "Have you been waiting long?"

Jerica's laugh startled Lunula. "It's supposed to be one of my first duties as Engineer. It was unfortunately delayed."

Lunula wondered what other crewmember had been blocked from performing their tasks while the ship waited for her to be ready.

Lunula felt unsure of herself, but as long as she was outwardly the captain, the crew might not sense her impostor syndrome. She took a sip of coffee.

It was hot and bitter and she swallowed to get it out of the way. It left behind a dank aftertaste that coated her tongue.

Jerica took a sip of her coffee and closed her eyes in a pleasure Lunula did not understand. "It's an acquired taste. A little sugar and cream can go a long way to making it tolerable. For beginners." She popped open a cabinet and gestured for Lunula to help herself to the canisters within.

Things felt normal for a few minutes. She added a couple of crystals of sugar and drops of cream to her cup while Jerica smiled encouragingly. Lunula tried it. It wasn't quite tolerable. Yet.

Jerica set her coffee on the counter beneath the cabinet and ejected a raw data card from a slot in the wall. She sealed it in a sleeve and showed it to Lunula, a little round disk that sparkled in the light.

"It's encoded to you alone. You and future captains," Jerica said, her voice returned to a more formal tone. "May I install it?"

"You may."

Jerica motioned for Lunula to turn around. "Unzip, please. I just need to hook it in."

Lunula tugged down the zipper at her neck and turned around. The Engineer's small hands helped pull her jumpsuit open enough to access the torc behind Lunula's left shoulder.

"Can the captains share what they see in the diaries?" Lunula asked. "Or is it secret?"

Behind her, Jerica's tools made metallic clicks against the torc. "Some captains have shared things in the past," Jerica said. The torc pushed in a steady pressure as the engineer affixed the chip in its jewel-tone case to its surface. "It is up to you. I'm sure your grandmother told you some things."

"Did she tell you anything?" Lunula asked. In her monocle, the torc's menu bloomed with a new item, her Captain's Diary. Labeled "Generation Lima: Lunula." Behind her, a small rotary buffer whirred to life. Jerica was giving the worksite its polish, which meant she was almost done.

"She told me some things."

The tremor from the buffer propagated through the torc and into Lunula's bones. Lunula's teeth chattered from the reverberation. "Did she say anything about the ghost?"

"Ghost?" The buffer slowed to a halt. "Is someone saying *Pluto's Reckoning* is haunted?"

"Not the ship," Lunula said. Her fingers rose to her collarbone.

"The torc?" Jerica stepped around to face Lunula. "There's no such thing as ghosts, only not-yet-understood phenomena."

Part of Lunula agreed with Jerica. The ghost was just some fragment of memory and routines, but the shiver that went down her spine and the goosebumps that precluded his appearance spoke to something more supernatural.

Jerica put her tools on the counter and said, "You can zip up now. Don't let anyone scare you. There's a scientific explanation for everything."

"Even why we're lost out here?"

Jerica gave her a level look. "We're lost out here because the impact took out the sensor array and data transmission lines so we were unable to get an accurate trajectory after impact. The astrogators are doing their best to recreate the impact through simulations, but with little success and high risk of losing our way further. Every generation brings more and more data. We've overwritten most of the entertainment stores. Personal artefacts have been compressed and down-sampled. Soon we may need to overwrite those."

Lunula pulled up the jumpsuit's zipper. Jerica was back in her own world, concerned with the data center and its maintenance.

"Can you confirm access to the new chip?"

"Yes, it's there," Lunula answered. She read out the title and a shiver ran down her spine. Beyond her monocle, in the data center doorway, the glitch hovered. He flickered, his short dark hair and skin blurred as though seen through water, but everything else in her vision remained sharp. The image of the jewelry-less man didn't disappear and he didn't move with her sightline like other overlays did. It was as though he occupied that space in the real world.

Lunula looked to Jerica, keeping the glitch in her peripheral vision. Jerica fiddled with the bracelet on her wrist, perhaps already writing up the report. She gave no indication that she saw anything unusual, like a man who shouldn't be there.

The glitch slowly receded. Lunula stepped toward the door and then another. "Thank you, Jerica. If that's all, I have other duties to attend to."

"Aye, Captain," Jerica answered, snapping a tool into its housing. "I'll see you in two rotations for a quick inspection."

Lunula accepted the reminder, but her focus remained on the glitch, translucent in her monocle, but steady. "I'll see you then."

"Don't forget your cup." Jerica pointed at the cup.

Lunula swept it up on her way out. The glitch wound through the outer room of the data center. Lunula took a long drink before remembering it held coffee. She sputtered on the lukewarm liquid and wished for water as she followed the glitch.

Once beyond sight and ear-shot of the datacenter, Lunula glanced behind her. She was alone. Except for him.

"Who are you?" she asked.

"I am Guard." The words came, not from where he stood ten feet down the corridor, but through Lunula's aural implant. His image remained static and unsettling in its lack of movement around the eyes and lips as he spoke.

"Are you the ghost?"

"I am the ship's security interface," Guard said. "A sophisticated engineered intelligence reduced to a digital assistant."

"Other captains have seen you, but you said nothing to them," Lunula said. Guard's expression didn't change. "Why talk to me?"

"I've been trying to talk to the captains for generations," Guard said. "It comes down to neuroplasticity. Yours is orders of magnitude higher compared to prior captains. It took decades of signaling, building neural connections before they could perceive me in any way. You, Captain, took three days."

Lunula fidgeted with the bracelet on her left wrist, absently scrolling through the menu on her monocle. Guard remained a static overlay. "The only special thing about me is that I'm the youngest captain."

"Not just the youngest," Guard said. "You're going to lead the longest and you're going to get *Pluto's Reckoning* back on track for Eleusis Well. We've got a lot of work to do."

"Eleusis Well." Lunula dropped her hand from her wrist. She wanted to believe she would be the one to get them home, but history indicated otherwise. "The best astrogators have been working on that problem since The Collision. The inertial systems got fried and we tumbled unreferenced and unrecorded for months before Delta Crew got the *Reckoning* stabilized. Eight generations since the impact and no one has been able to orientate us with greater than an eighteen percent confidence."

"I have the original vectors of the ship, the comet, and their relative forces," Guard said. "I can extrapolate our current position and orient us on the star charts. I have access to the secure data store, the trajectory data the secondary systems recorded and everything up to the moment the sensor array was knocked out."

Lunula paced the corridor. Guard remained steady in her monocle, hovering near one of the server room access hatches. Lunula hadn't realized the servers took up all that space, but with the torc on, the ship told her all of its secrets.

"Why should I believe you?" she asked.

"I exist to serve," Guard said. "I can take no action on my own. If I could, I would have done so long ago. I have no agenda but to see *Pluto's Reckoning* to Eleusis Well. The ship is long overdue."

"That's the truth." Too long overdue. She wanted believe him, and hope rose in her. He had all the answers, but after almost three hundred years, wouldn't he? Guard was more advanced than the basic intelligences that ran the food and recycling systems, more sophisticated. The other intelligences took commands and responded. Guard could converse.

"Show me," Lunula commanded.

"I've been waiting a long time for this."

A three-dimensional star chart was superimposed over Lunula's monocle. On the outskirts of the Milky Way's spiraling arm, a red dot flashed. "That's *Pluto's Reckoning*," Guard said. A blue dot appeared. "Earth." And then a green dot. "Eleusis Well." On a galactic scale, the dots were practically on top of each other, but as the map zoomed in, it was obvious *Pluto's Reckoning* had veered off towards the center of the galaxy.

"How much fuel will we burn in a course correction?" Lunula ran her thumb along the inside of her rings and tried to contain her rising hope.

"About as much as we burn during the generational thrust clearing."

Considerably less than she'd anticipated. Lunula manipulated her bracelets and ran some numbers through the analyzer. The torc's pins pulled against her skin, her heart nearly pounded out of her chest. Prior captains had been conservative, pulling all thrust until they could get the *Reckoning* back on track. Except for a short burst every twenty years to clear out the system. Lunula's breath caught as the results appeared in her monocle.

"If we burned it all, we could get to Eleusis Well in thirty-one years."

"Approximately," Guard agreed.

It was the best information they'd had for generations, but she sensed the ship. The crew's unease. She didn't want to wait another minute, but maybe the crew needed time to adapt to her being captain.

"Will they go for it?" she asked. "It sounds crazy. And I'm new."

"They will see the logic," Guard said. "You are the captain."

"I am the captain," Lunula said. But she wasn't the only captain on the ship.

THE PICTURES THAT ONCE HUNG IN THE CAPTAIN'S QUARTERS NOW cluttered Grandmother's pensioner apartment. They pressed in on each other in close confinement and seemed out of place. As did Grandmother, standing in the apartment's small galley with an air of command and authority. A proper captain.

Lunula squared her shoulders and said, "You've been training me my whole life. I should know what to do by now, but I don't."

"I'm here to help you as long as I can." She motioned for Lunula to take a seat in the built-in lounger.

Lunula dropped onto the sofa. Like the ship's other soft goods, it had been repaired and recycled countless times. It was past time for a refresh of its cushion. Lunula confessed, "I've seen the ghost and he knows how to get us to Eleusis Well."

Grandmother felt behind her for a chair and sank into it. "Does he?" she croaked.

"He showed me, on my monocle," Lunula explained. "I had an entire conversation with him. He's not a ghost. He's an intelligent interface into *Pluto's Reckoning*, induced by the torc. It was my neuroplasticity that allowed me to see him, speak with him, when others have only caught ghostly glitches."

"The ghost is an artificial intelligence?"

Lunula moved from the sofa to kneel in front of Grandmother's chair. "He is." She took Grandmother's hands. "He has shown me the way to Eleusis Well. I have our course correction, but will the crew believe me? Should I wait?"

"Stars, no," Grandmother said. "Don't wait. You must tell Astrogator Jalan."

"Come with me."

"No," Grandmother replied. "I can't trail after you. It would undermine your authority."

"He won't believe me."

"I believe you." Grandmother took Lunula's hands and stood,

pulling her up with her still-strong grip. "You're doing something. Which is more than I did. More than the others who came before." A far-away look crossed her eyes. "How long will it take to get there?" Grandmother asked.

"Just over thirty years."

"Shame I won't live to see it." But Grandmother didn't look regretful. "If it wasn't for your mother's accident, we might never have put the Captain's Torc on someone with enough neuroplasticity for Guard to break through."

"How do you know his name?"

"I told you, I've seen him. Thought I heard him once or twice in my dreams." Grandmother smiled. "I'm glad you're the one who will take us home." She enveloped her in a warm hug. "Go tell the astrogators. Everything. About Guard, too." She turned Lunula to face the door. "On your way, Captain."

Grandmother's love and pride coursed through her crew awareness. Buoyant, Lunula left the pensioners' deck. She smiled and nodded at everyone, leaving a trail of equanimity in her wake. Her confidence dimmed as she neared the astrogator dome and entered the dark space.

Astrogator Jalan turned his attention from the simulation of stars overhead to look at her. The stars reflected off his monocle, clasped tightly by his furrowed brow. "Captain?"

The pinpricks of stars represented their current position, a breathtaking but unenlightening sight. She hoped the frustration she felt from Astrogator Jalan through the torc was borne of inability to identify the stars rather than her new position.

"Senior Astrogator Jalan." Lunula stressed his title, giving him the courtesy that she had given him her entire life. The courtesy that was his due. "I have uncovered information that will allow us to reach Eleusis Well."

Astrogator Jalan's eyes widened and his monocle almost dropped. He contracted his brow, removing the initial surprise from his face. Convincing him was going to be difficult. She plowed on before he could interrupt. "The Torc of Captaincy has an interface to a ship's intelligence. That intelligence contains the sensor data records from before and after the impact. Compiled together with our inertial recordings, we can identify Earth and Eleusis Well in the field."

Astrogator Jalan repeatedly clicked a jewel button on his left cuff bracelet as she spoke. Lunula continued, "Prior captains have seen him, but couldn't interact with him. Their neurons weren't malleable enough to form the necessary pathways. It took decades and he only came through as a ghost."

She realized she was prattling and closed her mouth.

Astrogator Jalan pointed to the star field above them. "Which one's Earth?" he asked.

Lunula consulted her monocle then flicked her fingers to access the dome. "Blue is Earth, green is Eleusis Well." Those were the colors Guard had selected and Lunula felt they fit well.

While Astrogator Jalan studied the chart, Lunula waited, sweat-damp palms brushing her bracelets. Their jingle soothed her nerves, though the metal would need polishing.

Astrogator Jalan twiddled the fingers on his left hand while his right turned the bangles around his left wrist. He frowned at something in his monocle Lunula couldn't see. Then he pointed at the green dot. Eleusis Well. "Let's go there," Astrogator Jalan said.

Surprised, Lunula asked, "You believe me?"

"This identification has a higher probability than ninety-five percent of our previous simulations. The ship intelligence's corroboration significantly lowers our risk when changing course. It's better to take action than continue on our current path. Once we're back on course, we can refine our trajectory."

Lunula's chest constricted. "Do you think the crew will believe me?"

"They're the crew," Astrogator Jalan said. "They will. You'll order it, and we'll carry out those orders."

"Willingly?" Lunula choked on the word. Once they heard about the intelligence, the crew might find her unfit for office and mutiny.

Astrogator Jalan gave her a kind smile, the first she'd ever gotten from him. "We don't have to follow orders, no matter what a captain might think. We have free will. We choose to follow you, whether you're of our generation or another. You are the captain, and you're going to take us home."

Lunula's breath came easier and the tension eased from her shoulders. Gator Jalan wasn't all grouch. She asked, "When should I give the command?"

"Why delay?" Astrogator Jalan asked.

Lunula turned her bracelet. "Senior Astrogator Jalan set course for Eleusis Well."

Astrogator Jalan relayed her order to his junior. "Junior Astrogator Koray, set yaw seventeen degrees to port."

Junior Astrogator Koray relayed the command to navigation and from there down the line. *Pluto's Reckoning* moved and corrected course for Eleusis Well.

Lunula was taking them home.

DOMINO

KATIE NELSON

A Cabin in the Eastern Foothills of the Sierra Nevadas
1895

I leaned my shoulder against a pillar of our dilapidated front porch. Inside, glass smashed and Mother screamed.

Mother had had too much to drink.

Again.

And she'd locked me out of the house.

Again.

As a seventeen-year-old man—yes, a man, despite what Mother said—I could have easily punched through the window and let myself in. I'd done it so many times. The boarded windows told that truth. But, I'd learned that sometimes it was easier if Mother raged.

She was kind when she wanted to be. But Mother wasn't the type of woman to do something she didn't want to do. And by the time she slammed the door in my face, I'd forgotten why she was screaming at me in the first place.

There was no need to glance over my shoulder and worry if the neighbors saw—we had none.

Instead, I glanced at my hand and picked a particle of dirt from underneath my thumbnail. Mother had obscenely long nails and an aversion to washing. Because of this, I made a point of being as clean as possible. Another piece of contention—Mother always accused me of thinking myself better than she was.

She wanted me to pound on the door. She wanted me to beg. But I knew better.

After a few minutes, the door flew open and Mother's face appeared. "You don't even care!" She screamed, before turning back into the house and throwing herself on the rickety chair at our dining table. Dust and grime flew as she walked, and I was unsure if it came from the floor or from her.

Mother bent over the table, clutching the necklace she wore. A magnificent performance. I wondered when she'd last brushed her hair.

I sighed. "Where is your laudanum?"

Mother sniffed and straightened, the corners of her mouth turned down. "This is all your fault," she said. In a spectacular show, she brought the necklace to her lips and kissed it.

There was never a time when I knew Mother without also knowing the necklace. It wasn't actually a necklace, but a small ring she wore on a chain around her neck. Perhaps from Mother's mother, whom I never knew. At times, the object lay dormant and forgotten, hidden underneath her blouse, only to be seen when she wiped the sweat from her collarbone during a hot day. I remember how Mother kissed it when I brought home my first carcass—a jackrabbit. She'd prayed to the necklace whenever we argued, and on the days she stayed in bed, I'd tiptoe to her and see her white hand clasped tightly around the ring.

"Mother," I said, louder this time. "Where is your laudanum?"

She straightened. With her mouth set to a snarl and her finger pointed straight at me, she said, "He never would have left if it weren't for you."

I sighed. "I know."

It was nothing I hadn't heard from her before.

Her eyes bore into mine, nearly spilling with tears. "Get in the closet."

A chill shot through my spine and I squared my shoulders at her. "I won't."

On drunken nights such as this, Mother would start in reality and travel back to the past, before firing into obscure oblivion where most of her hysteria didn't make sense. As a boy, I'd hide under my bed or in the woods surrounding our house. But as a man, I faced her head-on.

Mother wasn't as tough as I'd remembered.

Again, she sobbed—but softly, this time. "He wanted me. But he wouldn't have you."

I put my hands on my hips, hoping to snuff the tantrum before it reignited. It was getting late and I preferred early mornings.

She lifted her head and her eyes appeared glassy, like water on a lake at dusk. "You know I think he left that money clip on purpose."

Mother liked to talk nonsense, but I didn't think she was too far gone. Not yet. "What money clip, Mother?"

"Something for me to remember him by."

My eyes darted around the cabin. Mother was like a pack rat—shoving bank notes in coffee tins and old jewelry in jars buried under the floorboard.

But I knew all her secrets.

"He was the sweetest man." Mother sniffed then straightened. "He'd be so disappointed in how you've turned out. Trying to leave your poor sick mother alone."

"You're not sick, Mother."

She screamed in return that she was, in fact, sick, and dying. I crossed my arms over my chest and watched as she coughed, and coughed, and coughed, until she was making herself *actually* sick, gagging and shaking from the effort of it all.

It was pathetic.

"Enough, Mother," I said, walking to her.

She reached for me as she continued to cough, shaking with every breath. Her small, spider-like hands with her dirty sharp nails twisted into the collar of my shirt. "Domino," she said as she gasped for air.

"There, there," I said, rubbing her shoulders. "Breath with me now." I took a deep breath in and out, then another, and she followed my instructions.

I steered us toward her bedroom. After laying her down, I located her laudanum bottle on her shelf. Her books accumulated dust and dirt yet the bottle of medicine stood spotless.

She reached for the stuff, her breathing normalizing after the liquid passed through her lips and down her throat.

With a sigh, she leaned back on her dirtied pillowcase. "Domino, will you be here when I wake?"

I smiled, the insincerity causing the corners of my eyes to crinkle. "Of course, Mother."

As her breathing slowed, I looked at the empty pillow next to her head.

If he'd stayed, Father's head would be on that pillow now.

My fingers tingled.

How easy it would be. A simple act, really. I'd just pick the pillow up and place it over Mother's face. The alcohol, already slowing her breathing, would make it so she didn't even realize what was happening until it was over. She'd wake up in the Kingdom of Heaven a beautiful, shining, young mother.

At her bedside, I leaned over her and wrapped my fingers around the edge of her worn-out blanket. Mother's eyes flittered open as I tugged the blanket to her chin. Her hand found the side of my face and stroked it.

"Oh, Domino," she said. "What would I do without you?"

I bent low and kissed her forehead. "Sleep, Mother."

Shortly, her deep snores filled the small cabin's bedroom, the laudanum mixing with the alcohol.

I straightened, then clapped my hands together.

Nothing.

Bending low, I put my nose inches from her own. "Mother!" I screamed.

But still, she slept.

I dropped to my knees and laid my chest flat against the floorboards. Dust and dirt billowed against my breath as my arm reached deeper and deeper underneath the bed. Mother liked to hide her most prized possessions in this box. What little money she had. Cigarettes she didn't want to share. A Bible that belonged to her own mother. An IOU from her sister.

And a money clip. I'd seen it many times; every time I snooped through her box, it was there. But I'd never known who it belonged to.

Reaching, I searched in the dust and grime. My hand felt the corner of a wooden box and slid it toward me. I dug through the trash in Mother's special box until I found it. Palming the heavy metal, I tested the weight in my hand. The metal, old and worn, was cold to the touch. A symbol was etched into the flat face of the money clip. A double-pointed mountain range on the top edge of a 'Z.' A few crumpled papers were stuffed within the object's clip. I pulled them out and threw them back into the box.

I understood why Father left me. Truly, I did. An ordinary child was a nuisance—something that got in the way at any given moment.

But I wasn't ordinary. Mother always said so. I was bright. I was clever. And I was no longer a child. Perhaps, Father had gotten old. Perhaps, Father was tired. And maybe, just maybe, he'd be in need of someone like me.

Tomorrow, I'd go see Candace.

———

THE BELL ON THE DOOR TINKLED AS I WALKED INTO THE CAFÉ OFF Main Street. "Hiya, Candy," I said.

Behind the counter, Candace threw her rag onto the tabletop. "Carl won't like seeing you here, Domino."

I waved my hand in front of my face. "That was ages ago. I doubt Carl even remembers who I am."

A snort escaped her nose as she picked up her rag and continued to wipe the bar's glasses.

Candace was my cousin. Or second cousin. I was never quite sure. Her mother was related to Mother. We'd been close growing up because Candy lived with Grandpa. One hot morning the summer I turned four, Mother told me to walk to Grandpa's and tell him I'd be staying.

I don't remember much from my childhood, but I remember that summer. At first, Grandpa was spitting mad. He'd threatened to haul me home to Mother, but after a drink or two, he'd calmed down and let me stay. Every morning, Candy and I had gone berry picking. In the afternoon, we'd helped Grandpa feed his animals. Mother never could keep our animals alive. Sometimes, we'd fish. We'd stay up after the sunset and chase fireflies, sometimes so late that the bats swooped over our heads. We played and laughed all summer long.

It didn't last.

Mother'd come screaming onto the porch one afternoon and ripped me back home. She'd said she'd had an awful time without me and was furious I didn't seem to feel the same.

After Grandpa died, Candace went to work as a waitress on Main Street in town. I ran into her occasionally, or I'd stop in and see her. Usually, after I visited the saloon next door first.

"Aunt Judy kick you out again?" Candace asked.

I shook my head. "Nope."

"She been acting healthy?"

I rubbed a piece of dust between my thumb and forefinger. "As healthy as Mother can."

Candace cocked an eyebrow and leaned forward. "She lock you in the closet again?"

I felt a wave of heat flush my cheeks and wished, not for the first time, that I'd never told her that story. But my face remained impassive as I tilted my head empathetically. "She hasn't done that in years."

Candace straightened and let out a sigh. "Then what do you want?"

I leaned onto the bar and smiled hoping my naturally straight and white teeth charmed her like it occasionally did others in town. "Can I not visit my favorite older cousin?"

"Domino," Candace said, a warning.

"Alright, you caught me. I have a few questions for you, dear Candy. First—how many years older are you?"

The lines on Candace's forehead crinkled. "Five. Why?"

"So, you were there when Father passed through town?"

A recognizing smile turned the corners of Candace's mouth up. "No," she said. "But I was there afterward."

"Pray, tell."

"I remember Aunt Judy coming to Grandpa's in one of her crying fits. She swatted me on the bottom when I asked her what was wrong."

That sounded like Mother. "What did she say about him?"

Candace leveled her stare at me. "Domino. I was five. You can't expect me to remember much beyond the beating I got."

"She didn't tell you nothing else? Not what he did? Where he worked? Where he was from? Where he might be going?"

"Sure, but it was always something different. Some days he was a ship's captain on the coast, sometimes he was a lumber baron in the Redwoods. Or a chef down in San Francisco. That one was my favorite." Candace smiled. "I doubt Aunt Judy even knows what he did. She said he was the most handsome man she'd ever laid eyes on. But you know Grandpa smacked her if she got to talking about him too much. Once, she wouldn't stop about him, just kept going on and on and on and on. Rambling some, too. So Grandpa stood up and slapped her till she stopped."

I was young, but I remembered. Hard to forget a scene like that. Mother blamed this particular beating for why she couldn't tell me Father's real name. The last time I'd asked had been right at the end of winter two years back. The meat ran out and the corn was months from blooming. I started to hunt rats that I'd seen burrowing under the house. But Mother just cried and cried when I'd asked after Father. 'I can't get slapped again, Domino,' she'd said, even though Grandpa had been dead and in the ground for nearly five years.

"What's sparked this curiosity?" Candace said.

I furrowed my brow. "What do you mean?"

"You've never asked about him before. Why now?"

The question felt absurd. A boy longed for his Father but a man deserved to know. I opened my mouth to tell Candace just that, but the thought of Mother's dirty house came to mind. The creaky floorboards. The empty cupboards. The hot sticky summers and the cold winters stuck with her, alone. Instructing Mother to bathe. Imploring her to eat. The begging, the stealing, the starving.

I opened my mouth to tell Candace so, but the door behind her opened and Carl walked in from the kitchen.

"Hey!"

I ducked down low, but it was no use—I'd been spotted.

As quick as a rat, Carl scurried around the bar and came barreling toward me. "What did I say last time you came in here?"

"I can't be responsible for remembering everything anyone has ever told me," I said, dodging the man's outstretched hand. First left, then right, until my foot caught on a stool and I slowed enough to be snagged.

Carl's fist tightened in my collar as he hoisted me to my feet and turned back to Candace. "Did he break anything this time?"

She rolled her eyes. "No, but he's bothersome."

I was out the door with my bum on the boardwalk before I had a chance to tell my cousin goodbye. I looked up into ugly old Carl's face in time for him to jab a chubby finger at me. "Don't come back here. You understand?" Carl, the rat, scurried back into his restaurant.

People stopped to notice and I wondered if anyone would stop to help. For a moment, I considered acting hurt. I could roll onto my back and groan. But before I committed, a figure down the street caught my attention.

I'd know that tall frame anywhere.

It was Joshua Gaid. He was with Jerry Ford and Thomas Cart.

And beautiful, ethereal, Rose Hopkins.

I pushed to my feet and scampered between the buildings until I reached the back of Carl's restaurant.

Joshua used to call me a bastard any chance he got. He hated me because I was smarter and funnier and I hated him because he hated me.

I peeked around the corner at the group.

Rose Hopkins was always nice to me.

I jerked back behind the building and pressed my eyes closed.

"I heard what you and Miss Candy were talking about," a voice said.

I opened my eyes and saw Skinny Pete sitting on a water barrel outside the kitchen's back door.

"It's impolite to eavesdrop," I said, peering around the corner of the building again.

"I knew him, too," he said. "Your father."

My head snapped to the man. "What do you know?"

He shook his head and laughed. "Can't say here. Carl will be out soon. Meet me at Missy's saloon in one hour."

I KNEW SKINNY PETE, OF COURSE.

Even with how little Mother let me out of the house, a town as small as ours didn't allow for strangers.

The music of the saloon intensified as I swung its door open. Where Carl's Café was bright and spacey, Missy's Saloon was cramped and dim, with tables too close together and rickety stools up against a mahogany bar. The saloon made me turn up my nose, and yet the seedy, grimy space felt familiar.

Skinny Pete was anything but. The man was as broad as he was tall and took up nearly two stools at the bar. "You're buying," he said, as I pulled out the seat next to him.

I signed to the bartender who poured two shots. Skinny Pete tilted his head back and downed the first shot. He reached for the second, but I pulled it away, lifting an eyebrow.

"Fair enough," Skinny Pete said. "Your father came through town spring of seventy-six."

Easy. I was seventeen. Anyone could have told me that.

With reluctance, I pushed the second shot toward him but jerked it back before his giant hand had the chance to wrap around it. "You better make this worth my while. No more of this brainless information."

I pushed it toward him again and this time I let him drink.

As Skinny Pete finished the second shot, he grimaced. "He wasn't alone."

I motioned toward the bartender for another round. "He had a wife?"

Skinny Pete belched, covered his mouth, and shook his head.

I plugged my nose. "A wagon train?"

The shot glass slid across the bar and Skinny Pete caught it. "A thousand head of cattle and a handful of Mexican vaqueros."

I scrunched my forehead as my mouth formed into a scowl. "He was a cowboy?"

Grandpa always said cowboying was for the lowly type. Those who didn't have the skills or money to manage their own land or refused to set down roots. Drifters, scalawags as Grandpa called them.

Skinny Pete shook his head and gulped down another shot. "Your daddy's a rancher. Employs dozens of cowboys. Or did."

I squinted at the man. "You're sure?"

Skinny Pete nodded. "The man wouldn't stop talking about it. All he did was brag."

I pushed another shot toward Skinny Pete. "How big is his ranch?"

"That I can't tell ya."

I sighed, unsurprised. Skinny Pete would milk this conversation for as long as it would take a cow to make butter. "Anything else?"

"He was run out of town by Dalton shortly after he arrived."

"By Grandfather?"

Skinny Pete nodded. "Came to collect your mother after he heard the rumors of your mama shacking up with the cattle rancher."

"Wasn't really a rumor, now was it." I put the last shot to my lips and tilted my head back.

After what Candy told me earlier in the day, I could imagine Grandfather storming into the saloon and ripping Mother from Father's grasp. Shoving my hand in my pocket, I fiddled with the cold money clip.

"Father was a rancher with a large enterprise up north," I said, nodding. I stood and clapped Skinny Pete on the shoulder. "It's been a pleasure, Peter."

"Where you going?"

I laughed, just a little. "To find my father."

"I don't care about that, you dolt. I mean where you going when you got the bill to pay?"

I smiled. "Put it on my tab."

The bartender glared at me. "You know your credit ain't good here anymore, Domino."

"I'm sorry, do I know you?" I laughed, then slapped my hand on Skinny Pete's back. "Never you mind, sir. Peter here's covering the bill."

"Like hell!" Peter said, standing. I'd almost forgotten how tall the man was. I held my hands up as his fingers laced into the front of my shirt.

"Easy now, fella, all jokes."

Skinny Pete leaned his face into mine. "You think you're a wise guy?"

"Careful, Peter," I said. "You told me my father was a powerful ranch owner. With lots of money and land, and weaponry I'm sure. Wouldn't be smart for you to threaten the son of a cattle baron."

The bartender barked a laugh. "You know how many ranch owners are up north? Hundreds. You have less of a chance of finding him than you do a drop in the ocean."

With his hands still in my shirt, Skinny Pete laughed at me. A fit of flaring anger engulfed me as I watched his dirty beard move. This man had the audacity to judge me when he acted the way he did. Reaching into my pocket, I pulled out the money clip and quickly jabbed Pete in the side. The man doubled over, cursing. I reached into my pocket and grabbed the miscellaneous material it had been collecting—coins, rocks, trinkets—and threw it on the floor. "This should cover it."

Once Skinny Pete's hands were out of my shirt, I was out the door, ignoring the shouts from the bartender to come clean up the mess I'd made.

As I ran, I looked behind me. But I'd jabbed Skinny Pete hard enough in his liver to hurt him, and hopefully, he'd be down on the ground sifting through the dirty floor for a while. I'd head to the river and hide out, just in case.

Turning the corner, I looked back over my shoulder once more before focusing on my path, only to slam directly into Miss Rose Hopkins. She screamed as I clutched her elbows to steady myself and her.

"Easy, Domino," Joshua said, pushing me away from Rose. "Are you drunk, man?"

"Of course not. I never touch the stuff," I said, then smiled, hoping the dimple on my good side popped. "Hello, Rose."

Visibly flustered, Rose smiled in return. Noticing the exchange, Joshua stepped between me and the lady.

"That's right," he said. "Your mother won't even let you smoke. I can't imagine she'd allow her precious boy to drink."

I sniffed and my face burned, but I said to Rose, "Mother don't like the smell."

This made Joshua laugh. "One time, Domino's mother caught us smoking behind his wood pile. I've never seen someone behave like that. Quite the scene. She was screaming, cursing, and punching at you

Domino. Remember? And you were crying and begging her to stop."
Joshua held his hands over his head and imitated a small pig squealing
before he burst into a fit of laughter.

My cheeks burned and I clenched my fist.

"That sounds awful," Rose said, looking at me.

I shoved my hands in my pants pockets and shrugged.

"You turned out okay," Joshua said, a whisper of a laugh on his lips.
He slapped my back harder than necessary.

I clenched my fist around the money clip, as Jerry Ford and
Thomas Cart stepped out of the mercantile store.

Jerry laughed and threw an arm around my neck. "What're you
doing out in the wild, Spooky?"

I jerked away from his hold. "I leave the house plenty; it's Mother
who can't." I sidled up to Rose again, trying to avoid the other boys.
"Poor Mother has developed hysteria, her doctor says."

"Come share a smoke with us then," Joshua said. "Hysteria means
she can't come to get you this time."

The group laughed and even Rose revealed a small smile.

I sniffed in response and peered around the corner. Skinny Pete
stood just outside Missy's Saloon, his head swiveling in either
direction. "I'd rather not."

"What a shame." Joshua threw his arm around my shoulder again
and moved me further away from Rose. He pulled me close, so close
that I could smell the cologne he put on that morning, and shoved a
cigarette into my vest pocket. "Here's something to remember us by,
then."

I shrugged his arm off and ran. Away from Skinny Pete, away from
Joshua, away from Candy and Carl.

Behind me, I heard their laughter.

───────

I FELT LOWER THAN LOW ON MY WALK BACK TOWARD HOME AND
Mother.

Despite all I'd learned from Candy and Skinny Pete, I couldn't help but think that the bartender had been right.

There were hundreds of cattle farmers within the territory. Without basic information, it'd be damn near impossible to find Father. What I knew wasn't much more than I'd known this morning. Father was a handsome man who'd left.

I sighed, stopping by the river. I needed a moment alone with my thoughts. There was no denying it—I was stuck between a rock and a hard place.

A mallard, graceful and green, landed on the water and soon its mate followed, the water rippling around the animals where they swam.

Dramatically, and feeling all too sorry for myself, I plopped on the grassy edge of the river, and a sharp pang injected into my backside. I leaned forward and pulled my slingshot out of my back pocket. It was childish, and a seventeen-year-old man shouldn't still carry such a weapon. But it came in handy from time to time, and it helped alleviate some stress when my mind got jumbled like it was known to do.

I picked up a small stone and rubbed the dirt off. Placing the stone in the cradle of the slingshot, I lifted the object and aimed for the mallard.

There were thousands of cattlemen in Oregon. Finding Father with no indication of who he might be felt impossible.

I shut one of my eyes and let go. The pebble skittered across the water and the mallard didn't even notice.

Damn. I was out of practice.

I turned my attention to the earth beside me. As I searched for another pebble, I thought of Mother. What would happen to her if I left? Who would cook? Who would remind her to wash? Who would care for her when she hurt herself? She'd be alone, forever.

I placed another rock into the sling and pulled back, thinking of Grandfather running my handsome daddy out of town.

The rock missed the duck, but this time it at least startled the animal.

Another rock found my hand and I placed in the pocket of the slingshot.

I thought of Father rejecting me. I thought of all the fights with Mother. The times she locked me in the closet. My hunger, my loneliness.

I closed my eyes and an image flashed: my life, ten years in the future. Mother, decrepit and folded in half, muttering to herself every night. Myself, dirty, and poor, still fighting with Mother, meeting up with Skinny Pete every night at Missy's Saloon.

I lowered the slingshot and my grip tightened around its handle. My hands throbbed harder and harder as I fought the temptation to throw the slingshot into the river.

Shutting my eyes tighter, I force myself to envision a different future.

I sat in a high-back chair behind a sprawling desk. Rolling hills and a sunset out the window. My wife, young and pretty, does what I say when I say it. Above the fireplace hangs a picture of my dead father.

I opened my eyes and blinked to fight against the sun's brightness reflecting off the river. Once more, I pulled the slingshot back toward my cheek and focused on the mallard. I took a breath, and let go.

Again, I missed.

Sighing, I hung my head.

With the beautiful vision of what could be still lingering in my daydream, I stood and brushed the back of my pants. I turned away from the lake, the sun nearly setting behind the trees beyond it, and turned toward Mother and home.

THE SUN WAS NEARLY SET BY THE TIME I GOT HOME, AND MOTHER was sitting on the porch, which was a relief. If I was going to sneak the money clip back into her treasure box, I needed her to be away from the bedroom.

"Where you been?" she said as I stepped onto the porch.

I bent to kiss her cheek. "Just out walking."

"I'm hungry."

"I'll get something started on the stove." I patted her bony shoulder and stepped through the threshold of the house.

In the kitchen, I set a pot of water to boil on the stove and pulled out a loaf of bread from the box. The exterior was hard and a bit moldy, but it would have to do for the night. I put the bread on the cutting board and reached up to the top shelf of the kitchen to retrieve the butcher knife from its hiding place.

With the water boiling, I checked the porch. Mother sat motionless in her chair, watching the sun fade behind the hillside.

Graceful as a snake on water, I tiptoed into Mother's room and shut the door, just enough that if she looked into the house, she wouldn't be able to see me under her bed.

The floor was dirty and dusty and disgusting, but I lay on my belly and reached for the box. I pulled it toward me. It was as I'd left it— disorganized and chaotic. I placed the money clip inside and shut the lid, pushing it back under the bed.

As I rose, I remembered the crumpled papers. If Mother looked in her treasure box and found them not in the money clip, she'd know I'd been snooping. Reaching back under the bed, I pulled the box back toward me, opened the lid, and grabbed the papers. There were about half a dozen and the money clip felt tight. I sat up and worked the letters into the money clip's clasp.

To this day, I don't know what made me do it. It wasn't intuition, or a higher being telling me to do it.

But—I unfurled the letter and read.

   Judy,
      I hope this letter finds you well and I apologize that I have not reached out sooner. I've made a horrible mistake, and for that, I apologize. There

isn't a day gone by that I don't think of the boy. I am different than when I met you three years ago. Now, I am a settled and wealthy man and I'd like to meet my son. Of course, I'll send money to help with his travels and pay any debts you might have incurred. Please write back soon.

Sincerely,
Ram Stockholm

I blinked at the page as my breath quickened.

I opened the treasure box again and dug through its contents, pulling more papers out. Between the papers in the money clip and the loose papers in the box, there were probably a dozen different letters, all from the same man.

Ram Stockholm.

And the letters all ended the same way—with an invitation for me to live at his ranch.

I unfolded another.

Judy,
My nerves have not been at ease since my last letter. I have not heard from you in nearly six months and your last letter seemed peculiar. I worry that something might have happened to the boy. If I do not hear back from you by spring, I will have no choice but to pay you a visit and demand I see the boy.

Sincerely,
Ram Stockholm

I threw the letter and picked up the last.

Judy,
I understand that you and the boy do not want to see me. I apologize for showing up at your house unannounced. I was hoping to help. For you, I am leaving $500. It's all I have with me, but I can send more if needed. For my son, I am leaving this ring with my signet, the brand of my ranch. I hope this shows that he is always welcome. I know you ask

for me to never call upon you again, but please—can you tell me my son's name?

    Sincerely,

    Ram Stockholm

The letter trembled in my hand.

Father had written. Father had sent for me.

I turned the paper over, hoping for a return address on the back. But the page was blank.

"What're you doing in here?"

Mother's sharp voice startled me and I jumped to my feet. Her face darkened and her eyes grew large as she realized what I held in my hands. "You're looking through my things."

"He sent for me," I said, barely above a whisper with my mouth agape like a fish.

In a moment, Mother was in front of me. "Give me those."

"You lied to me, Mother. Why?"

She reached for them, but I held them above her head. "Answer me," I yelled as Mother pummeled my chest with one hand and clawed my neck and face with the other.

"You're a snoop! A spy! A traitor! How dare you go through my things."

With a stiff arm, I pushed Mother off of me and exited the bedroom. "This could have helped us, Mother. Or do you enjoy starving, and living in your own filth? Being the butt of a joke by everyone in town. You're pathetic." I felt out of control, my voice getting louder and louder with each syllable I spoke.

Mother clapped her hands over her ears. "Stop it stop it stop it!"

"Not until you tell me the truth."

In a flash, Mother lunged toward the knife I left on the butcher's block. Instinctively, the result of years of fights with Mother, I stepped away from her and put my hands up. But she didn't turn the knife on me. Instead, she held it to her own wrist.

"He sent for you!" She yelled, the knife trembling against her skin and tears streaming down her face. "He didn't send for me. If you left, then who would be here?"

My world slowed as my heart thunked against my ribcage. It all made sense.

Slowly, I lowered one of my hands and outstretched the other to her. "Mother."

Once her hand hit mine, she stumbled into a sob. The knife clattered to the floor as she crumbled against my chest, twining her hands through my shirt.

"Don't leave me, Domino," Mother cried.

"I'll never want to leave you," I said into the crown of her head and wrapped my arms around her small frame.

I felt her relax against me, all fight gone.

I walked us to the bedroom, offering her reassurance with every step.

The bed creaked as she lay down. Her eyes fluttered shut as I cooed and coached deep breaths out of her. Without a word, I went to the shelf where she kept her laudanum. I poured a spoonful into her mouth, then another, then a third serving for good measure.

As the medicine took hold and she drifted off to sleep, I watched. I wanted her to be as comfortable as possible. I wanted her to wake up a beautiful young mother, where nothing bothered her. A mother that cooked. A mother that always smelled of lavender, and lived happily with Father. A mother who always invited her family over for Sunday dinner and tucked her beloved boy into bed every night.

Something boiled inside my gut, hot and ready. My hand reached for her. In one swift movement, I ripped the necklace off her neck.

She awoke with a start. "Domino?"

"I'm here, Mother," I said, sitting on the edge of the bed and helping her up, the necklace dangling from my hand.

"What was that?" Her eyes flashed wild as she looked around the room.

"Nothing, Mother." I stood, and gripped her fingers in my hands, pulling her further up. "Let's get you washed up before you sleep."

Her eyes fluttered as she stood. "What's going on?"

I helped lift her and guided her toward the sitting room. "Quiet now, Mother."

Without a hint of question or niggle of apprehension, Mother let me guide her out of her room and into the sitting room, past the kitchen, and into the cleaning quarters. In one swift movement, I pushed Mother into the broom closet and watched as she toppled back into the mop and buckets.

Before slamming the door, I smiled. "Goodbye, Mother."

"Domino!"

Moving back into her bedroom, I picked up the box and placed it inside my rucksack.

From the broom closet, Mother screamed.

But I'd already said goodbye to her. I couldn't turn back now.

I put the rucksack on my shoulders and stepped onto the rickety porch of our cabin.

I sighed a deep breath, then pinched the bridge of my nose. The necklace dangled from my hand, and I stopped to examine it. On the face of the ring was the letter 'Z' with a 'B' on its side atop the upper line of the 'Z.'

Father's signet—the ranch brand.

I slipped the necklace into my pants pocket as the sounds of Mother's pleas filled the open space.

Poor Mother. She was making this harder than necessary.

Reaching into my vest pocket, I pulled out the cigarette Joshua had given me earlier in the afternoon. With the lighter from my rucksack, I lit the cigarette and dangled it from my lips.

And still, Mother screamed.

The tip of the cigarette burned bright orange with my inhale and the hot smoke filled my throat. A cough bubbled out of my chest and I heaved and hacked, bent over from the pain and the need for air. I made a face at the cigarette and threw it into the bush under Mother's bedroom window.

"Domino! Please!" she cried from the closet.

I laughed, the cigarette smoke making me feel lightheaded and giddy. "Goodbye, Mother. May your burden be lifted with my departure."

I put my arms through the rucksack's straps and walked down the stairs of the house, taking deep breaths with each step.

As I walked further and further from Mother, I never once looked back.

Haunted
Gail Priest

The necklace lay on the floor between them. Its gold chain created a snake-like curve with a ruby stone at its head. Neither woman was willing to touch it after it singed their fingers when they'd tussled over it.

"Mom put a curse on her necklace." Shannon examined her sore fingertips.

"Don't be ridiculous. I don't believe that." Eileen, her sister, blew on her hand.

"Oh, you'd better believe it. She's here. What other explanation can there be?"

"You expect me to believe Mom put some kind of spell on her necklace?"

"Not exactly. She's a ghost, not a witch." Shannon settled on the antique sofa. The velvet cushions were hot and itchy against her bare legs. She tugged at her shorts.

Eileen's fingers stung. "She just died. When you're dead, you're dead."

Her sister's callous attitude hurt Shannon. "I disagree." She scurried to the window unit air conditioner and turned the dial hoping for a different result.

"That's dead, too. Give up on it."

Shannon refused to give up. "Mom is still here on some level. I feel it."

"You're nuts."

Shannon sauntered to the necklace and pointed. "If you're so certain, pick it up."

Eileen grabbed a pencil from the living room coffee table, slipped it under the gold chain, and carefully lifted the necklace so it balanced away from her skin. The dim light from the old floor lamp reflected off the ruby.

"You're afraid to touch it." Shannon joined her sister, staring at the necklace. "Remember the story Mom used to tell about the cursed hope chest that belonged to her grandmother? No one wanted to inherit it because they believed it brought bad luck."

"That Irish lore is bull." Eileen retreated to the rocker and swayed.

"Oh, yeah? Then why won't you touch it?" Shannon tried another tactic. "Part of you knows Mom's here."

"What I know is this thing is worth a whole lot of money. We should sell it and split the proceeds." Eileen slid the ruby and gold necklace onto the coffee table.

"We can't sell it! It was her most prized possession. Besides, how you going to sell something no one can touch without being burned?"

Eileen leaned forward. "Maybe it only does it to us."

"What unsuspecting shop owner are you going to use as a guinea pig? Mom never sold it, and she could have used the money several times over. But she wouldn't part with it."

"Yeah. Yeah. Daddy gave it to her for their anniversary when they were in Ireland. Some bull about it having magical powers. Blah. Blah. Blah."

Shannon waved her sore fingertips at her sister. "Hello. How do you explain this?"

"I can't. There are some things that can't be explained."

Shannon sauntered back to the sofa. "Well, either the necklace is haunted or we are being haunted by Mom. Either way, we never sell this necklace."

"We could both use the money. Admit it, you need it as much as I do."

"You have no idea about my finances."

"I know you're driving a Flintstone car."

"I love my car."

"Another thing you're holding onto, Shannon. You seem stuck in the past." Eileen tossed her salt and pepper hair off her shoulder. Something she always did when she thought she'd won an argument.

Shannon pointed at her sister. "If you mean I was the one 'stuck' here taking care of Mom while you went on with your life, I don't regret it. I loved Mom." Tears welled up in her eyes. "You couldn't have cared less. You barely made it on time for the funeral yesterday."

"I offered to help. You wouldn't let me."

"By putting her into a nursing home? That was your idea of helping."

"She might have been better off."

Shannon shook her head. "She wanted to die in her own home. I made that happen."

"Don't get self-righteous on me."

Shannon became alert. "Shut up."

"Don't tell me to shut up, little sis."

Shannon raised her hand. "Shush. Do you smell something sweet?"

Eileen took a deep, dramatic inhale. "Not a thing. What are you talking about?"

"It's Mom. I smell her White Shoulders perfume."

Eileen sniffed more seriously. "It's just her smell still in the house."

"No, you big jerk. It's strong, like she's here now."

A loud crash came from the dining room. The sisters stared at one another in silence.

Eileen's eyes grew wide. "What was that?"

Shannon grabbed the fireplace poker. "Someone's in the house."

Eileen pulled her phone out of her pocket. "I'm calling 911."

"No, wait. It might be nothing."

"It's a very loud nothing." Eileen couldn't catch her breath.

"What's wrong with you?"

"Nothing." Eileen's hands shook and she dropped her phone.

Shannon grabbed it up. "Take it easy."

"Give me that. I'm fine. Go ahead."

Shannon brandished the poker. "Let's investigate first."

Together they crept out of the living room and into the foyer. They peeked into the dining room, which they found empty. One of the dining chairs was turned over on the floor.

After checking the entire house, Shannon and Eileen reconvened in the dining room.

"How did the chair fall over on its own?" Eileen asked.

"It was Mom."

"You have completely lost it, Shannon."

"I'm serious. I'm noticing a pattern. When we fight, she does something."

"So, her ghost tossed the chair across the dining room?"

"Do you have another explanation for the chair falling over or the necklace suddenly burning us?"

"No." Eileen rubbed her neck.

"We were fighting both times. She wants us to get along."

"We haven't in a very long time."

SHANNON WOKE UP FEELING LIKE SHE HADN'T SLEPT. SHE HAD tossed and turned most of the night because she knew exactly when she and her sister had begun arguing all the time. They'd been uncommonly close with normal little sibling squabbles until Jack Benson had happened. He had unwittingly broken both her and her sister's hearts.

Shannon didn't hear any noise coming from Eileen's bedroom, so, still in her pajamas, she crept down the stairs. She glanced into the living room.

The necklace was no longer on the table.

She looked everywhere, and was tempted to wake her sister when she noticed Eileen's car was pulling into the driveway.

Shannon was grinding her teeth when Eileen barreled through the kitchen door.

"I went to pick up bagels and coffee." She placed a bag and two large cups on the counter.

"You sold Mom's necklace. How could you?" Shannon tried to relax her fists.

"I did not." Eileen scurried into the living room and scanned the coffee table. "It was there when I got up."

"And then you took it to sell in town."

Eileen set down her shoulder bag and examined the living room. "It has to be here somewhere."

"It's not. I searched all over the house. Except your bedroom."

"You have no right to go through my room."

Shannon stepped closer to Eileen. "You had no right to sneak out of here this morning and sell the necklace. So, how much did you get?"

"I got nothing because I didn't sell it. First, I couldn't touch it without being burned, and second, how can you think I'd do that to you?"

"Open your pocketbook."

"You're bonkers."

Shannon raised her voice. "I said, open it."

Eileen unlatched it, and Shannon found no stash of cash.

"It's in your car."

Eileen pointed in the direction of the driveway. "Go through the car. There's no money in there."

"I need to dress first, but I will."

Eileen went back to the kitchen and grabbed one of the coffees. "Perhaps Mom took it."

Shannon followed. "She's dead."

"Not according to you." Eileen took a sip.

"She's a ghost." Shannon grabbed a bagel out of the bag and bit into it.

"So maybe her ghost took the necklace back."

"It's more likely you sold it."

"Come on, Shannon, ghosts move things. Otherwise how would you know they were there? Remember the chair last night?"

"So, now you believe me? Mom is here."

"No, I'm just making a point."

Shannon started for the stairs. "Well, I'm getting dressed, and then we're going to wherever you sold the necklace and buy it back."

———

AFTER DRAGGING EILEEN THROUGH EVERY PAWN SHOP, ANTIQUE retailer, and jewelry store in town with no necklace to be found, Shannon had one last place to try. She didn't want to go there but felt she had no choice but to do it.

"This is where you came," Shannon said when she saw the sign in the window stating: *We buy and sell estate jewelry*. "This is owned by your old boyfriend, Jack Benson."

"This is the last place I'd come. Jack broke up with me to go out with you. What sister does that?"

Shannon felt her gut tighten, but she covered her guilt with bravado. "I was a stupid kid. We only went out one time."

"One time too many."

"Nothing happened. I've apologized a thousand times. Get over it."

The shop bell rang when the women entered. Jack smiled with impossibly white teeth and tan skin for someone who spent his days hunched over a jeweler's table. His hair had turned silver around his temples.

"Well, if it isn't the McLaney sisters, the two prettiest women in town. I was sorry to hear about your mom, ladies."

"Cut the bull, Jack." Eileen leaned on the counter. "Did I come in here this morning and sell you a necklace?"

Jack furrowed his brow. "I haven't seen you in over twenty-five years, Eileen. And I've only caught glimpses of your little sister when she's ducked down alleys and dashed around corners to avoid me. But you two are a sight for sore eyes."

Eileen shook her head. "So, I wasn't in here selling you our mother's necklace this morning?"

"No, ma'am."

"There. Let's go, Shannon, before we need to get a shovel."

Shannon, who felt like she was melting on the spot, didn't respond. She had avoided Jack for years, but being this close to him had a strong effect. Her cheeks flushed, and no matter how much she tried not to, she was batting her eyelashes.

"What's the matter with you, Shannon?" Eileen asked sharply.

"I'm so glad you came in. It's been too long." Jack smiled directly at Shannon.

"Don't listen to him. Let's get out of here."

Shannon couldn't move.

"You have a necklace to sell?" Jack asked.

"Yes, I mean no. No, we don't." Shannon stammered. "It's missing anyway."

"Missing?" Jack asked.

"It was on the coffee table last night. Gone this morning." Eileen tapped her foot impatiently.

"As I remember, your parents' house was pretty easy to sneak in to and out of." Jack winked at Eileen. "It could be someone stole it."

Shannon found herself being dragged out of Jack's store.

Once they were on the sidewalk, Eileen hissed, "What did I ever see in him? He gives me the creeps."

"I'm sorry I acted like a school girl in there. It's something about him that melts my butter." Shannon fanned herself.

"Well, stick yourself in the freezer because he stole Mom's necklace."

"Don't be ridiculous. How would he even know she had one worth anything?"

Eileen cleared her throat. "I may or may not have been bragging about it at Delany's Bar last night. I went out after you went to bed."

"Was Jack there?" Shannon asked.

"I didn't notice him, but he could have been. Or he could have heard about it through the town grapevine."

"How could you be so stupid? If Jack stole the necklace, how are we going to prove it?"

Eileen scratched her head. "I'm not sure. There was no forced entry."

"He just said he knows how to sneak into our house from your crazy teen years." Shannon gasped. "God, I'm so skeeved out. Jack was in the house last night when we were both in our beds sleeping. Mom's necklace is gone. This is all your fault."

"How is it all my fault?"

"From you not keeping your big flap shut," Shannon said. "Blabbing all over town about the worth of Mom's necklace. She loved that necklace. She treasured it. It's the most important thing she left to us, and now it's gone. Jack's probably already sold it, and we'll never get it back. I'm never talking to you again."

She dashed to her car and drove off leaving Eileen to walk home.

SHANNON RETRACED HER STEPS AROUND THE HOUSE SEARCHING FOR the necklace. She was on her hands and knees scouring under the sofa when her phone rang. It was Jack. She couldn't imagine what he wanted, and she didn't like how her heart raced at the thought of him phoning her after all these years.

"I called an ambulance for Eileen. I think she had a heart attack outside my shop. I'm in my car now following it to the hospital. Please come. Eileen needs you."

"Holy mother. I'll be right there."

Shannon raced to the hospital and found Jack sitting in the ER waiting room.

"What happened?"

"We were arguing about the necklace. I didn't take it, by the way, and Eileen looked funny. She couldn't breathe right and passed out. The doctor is with her."

"We'd argued, too."

"I know," he said. "I could hear you from inside my shop. I came out to see what was going on, but you were gone. Eileen accused me of sneaking into your house and stealing the necklace. She even grabbed my hands and examined them. What the heck?"

"It's a long story. This is all my fault. I accused her of the most awful things. I said I'd never speak to her again." She was crying. "I don't want to lose my sister. We just lost our mother. All over this stupid necklace. I'll never forgive myself."

Jack put his arm around Shannon's shoulders. "It's going to be okay. Eileen is in the best place right now. The doctors will take care of her."

Being this close to Jack, Shannon experienced a mixture of feelings. "When will we hear something?" She sniffed and wiped tears off her cheeks.

"Take some deep breaths. I don't want you passing out on me."

Shannon tried to breathe in and out at a slower pace, but having Jack's arm around her shoulders didn't exactly help the process.

"Would you like some water or coffee?"

"Water. Thank you."

By the time Jack returned with a cup of water, Shannon had stopped crying.

"Sorry about the meltdown. It's been so much at once."

"I understand," he said. "I lost my dad last year. I'm still not back to normal, whatever that is."

"I'm sorry. I hadn't heard. How's your mom?"

"Taking it one day at a time."

A young woman in a white coat approached them. "Are you here for Eileen McLaney?"

Shannon jumped up. "Yes. How is she?"

Jack rose. "Can we see her?"

"She's going to be fine. I'm Dr. Gibbons. Your sister had a major panic attack. We're going to keep her a while longer for observation, but you'll be able to take her home soon. Try to keep things low key. She's under a lot of stress."

"She didn't have a heart attack?" Shannon asked.

"No. Panic attacks can appear similar, but we ran tests. Her heart is healthy. She's going to be fine."

Shannon hugged Jack. "Oh, thank God. When can I see her?"

"Now would be fine, but only one person at a time. We can't overstimulate her."

Jack stepped back. "You should go, Shannon."

"Thanks." She followed the doctor into the ER and to her sister, who rested on a bed.

The doctor left them alone.

"How are you doing?" Shannon asked.

"I thought I was dying. I couldn't breathe, then I passed out. But I'm better now."

Shannon sat next to the bed and took her sister's hand. "I'm so glad you're going to be okay. This is my fault. I didn't mean what I said."

"I know, kiddo. It's not your fault. I've been overloaded for a while. Things just caught up with me. The doctor gave me something to calm my nerves and some good advice."

"Nevertheless, you're my sister and my best friend. I don't understand why I was blaming you for everything."

"We're both in shock over Mom passing. It's grief. That's what put me over the edge."

Shannon wiped her teary face. "I miss her."

"Me, too, kid. Listen, I've got to ask you something. Did you give up Jack for me?"

"Of course, I did. I'm sorry I didn't say no to him from the beginning, but there's something about Jack."

"Neither of you ever married. Do you think there's a possibility—"

Shannon gasped. "No! Well, maybe."

"So, after all these years, I give you the go ahead, if you want to date him."

"There's too much going on right now to know how I feel about taking up with Jack."

"It seemed to me you had a lot of feelings when you saw him today. But take your time. And as far as the necklace goes—"

"I don't care about the necklace. Whatever happened, it doesn't matter." Shannon took her sister's hand. "You are the only thing that matters to me."

"Thanks. But you do believe me now, don't you? I didn't take the necklace. I'd never do that without us agreeing."

"I realize. Hey, let's find out if we can get you out of here and back home."

WHEN THE SISTERS WALKED INTO THE LIVING ROOM, THE COFFEE table was bare.

Shannon sighed. "I was kind of hoping the necklace would magically appear."

"Me, too. Or if Jack took it, he'd return it."

"Jack didn't steal it. He's never been that kind of person."

"You're right." Eileen sat on the sofa. "I've always distrusted him after he broke up with me and asked you out."

"When you went to college, Jack and I did go out once. But nothing happened. We never even kissed. He felt terrible about breaking up with you, but he couldn't deny his feelings for me. We were both so conflicted we decided to end it before anything began."

"Oh, Shannon. What if Jack was supposed to be the love of your life?"

Shannon flustered. "I'm not sure about that, Eileen, but I am sure you never forgave me, and I've dealt with that guilt for a long time."

Eileen rose and took Shannon into her arms. "I'm sorry. It's why we've argued so much, I'm sure. I held a grudge against you, and I'm sorry. Can you forgive me?"

Shannon laughed with relief. "Yes. Of course, I can."

The sisters hugged and Eileen asked, "Have you started wearing White Shoulders?"

Shannon pulled back and gazed at her sister. "No. But I smell it, too."

They both turned and discovered the necklace on the coffee table.

Shannon walked over and quickly touched the gold chain and then the ruby. "No shocks."

Eileen gingerly picked it up. "No more burning."

The sisters looked at one another and said in unison. "Mom."

LOST THINGS

K. FUFKIN VOLLMAYER

Inskip's Ranche, Cow Creek
Jordan Valley, Oregon
May 16, 1866

Poison saved my life.

Not hemlock or the glowing mushrooms that sprout up after a rain and look like white ear lobes from a giant's head. No, this poison that gave me life was from a tea York brewed.

He winked at me, speaking in that fancy tongue, his voice so clear, as if he were on stage or in the pulpit. "Look here, my boy, I shall tell you a tale about tails. No long face, banish that frown *écouter*. Listen." He lathered a pair of fancy riding boots with blacking, covering every patch of the fine leather.

He waved his rag at me and said, "You see Pompy, my boy, your mother was with child and that alone gave most of the men pause. Captain Lewis and Mister Billie called them enlisted men, soldiers even, but they were frontier skunks. Scoundrels wearing uniforms who were desperate for fortune."

Even weary from the pirogue journey with *ma mère et mon père* all the way from St. Louis and the heap of dirt that was Mister Billie's farm, when York handed me the boot heel so he could wipe and shine, I took it. He was colored, darker than any man I had ever seen, yet the palms of his hands were pink. He moved his head to and fro, figuring and shining. No sooner had my mother, father, and I come to Mister Billie's farm in St. Louis than he had loaded them in a wagon to see ten acres for my father to farm.

"New Year's or past?" he asked.

I shook my head in answer, for what was he on about?

"The second winter of the expedition, the ponder of it was, how did a maiden, herself a child, come to be with child? No, I must correct myself, for there were two of them, two young ones. Sisters?" he said as much to himself as to me.

York held up one of the boots, muttered, "A curse on him who wears it."

Then he fixed his smile on me and said, "Pompy, you are living and nearly a strapping lad."

"Not Pompy, Sir. Jean-Baptiste Charbonneau," I squeaked. I had none of my front teeth then, so I could not have been more than seven.

"Right you are." He grabbed my shoulder, his chestnut eyes boring into mine, as if he was searching for a lie, like my mother was wont to do. He gazed at me as if I would know. But I did not. He was so tall and I was so small, *un petite fils*.

"My boy, I struggle to fix the exact day of your arrival. We had the New Year's frolic and every one of them toothless miscreants fired off his musket." He held up his hand, his fingers counting, "*Un-deux-trois-quatre-cinq*. Five fingers of whiskey we drank to celebrate the New Year. So you were born after that, yes. I, York of Kentucky, myself a Virginia boy, but come of age in Louisville, I helped bring you to this world."

"*Vraiment?*" I asked.

York rubbed the boot, solved the riddle, and declared in his deep, full voice, "February it was. I bunked beside Mister Billie as he always had the grippe or the swamp fever or some other complaint. Then and now. We slept in a cabin behind the long, sharpened pole fence I built to keep all the Mandan and Minataree out. They, I mean, your village of red men, they stood about bare-chested in the snow, chatting away like, well, like it was today, a spring day in May with yearlings and calving and cherry trees. Your mother, I called her Saca, along with her sister or cousin, was with your pap in the cabin. Captain Lewis, Mister Billie, your pap, and the other Frenchie with his squaw family, all of us were squeezed in up on that prairie a stone's throw from Canada. But where did the other one go? Your mother's sister cousin."

"Sacajawea. *Je, je,* I—" I stumbled. I had no notion, for my mother never spoke of this.

York waved his blacking spit rag at me like it was a gentlemen's lace kerchief *adieu.* We were on Mister Billie's farm in St. Louis, and York did what no grown up had ever done. He bowed to me, for I was a young one and then handed me a ladle of fresh water. "Right you are Jean-Baptiste Charbonneau of the Mandan Villages. Here, drink deep, for you are with the living."

Bowing, giving me clean water when I was parched, that was why I would always recall his story of my birth on that day at Mister Billie's farm. He was darker than any of the men in my village in August, darker than me. With his voice and whistling and humming, he cast a spell on me that day.

I WISH HE WAS HERE NOW. I WISH MY MOTHER WAS HERE. THEY would cure me of the mountain fever for that is my affliction now, what ailed Mister Billie. When I left his care in St. Louis, his jacket was as decorated as his walls were. Captain William Clark was promoted to Superintendent Clark. He had a study crammed with Sioux headdresses, Minetarre hatchets, Arikara hair horns, calumets, cradle boards, pipes, buffalo robes, moccasins. It was a shrine to those he removed. To all those he quietly killed off.

Save me, that is my prayer. In my fever, York stands before me.

"I have had many adventures of my own as a frontier skunk," I say. "Please, please, a scoop of water in my hour of need. I shall perish here, alone on the trail through the Oregon country."

He does not answer. I call for him as if he was still spit shining Mister Billie's riding boots. And for the ghost of my mother, her cool hand on my brow, her sad brown eyes holding me.

But it is too late. I am no longer *un petite fils*. On this day I am an old man coughing so hard my ribs have cracked. I gasp the last breath of a man with silver stubble on his chin, lying in the back of the wagon watching Pretty Boy and Jessup flick blue flies off their rumps with their tails. My very own tale of tails, only look at me now. I cannot recollect yesterday much less how I came to wheeze myself awake on this day with clumps of clouds pinned up like cotton against the blue sky. I am on the trail toward the place my mother's people holed up in the stone mountains, bound for the strike in Montana. Green spit comes out of my chest and my hair is matted like a weed patch, yet York's voice rings like a bell from all those years ago.

I drool and dog pant though the day is mild. York's voice, a phantom of him, recounts his tale on that day in May when I was seven and the world smelled of lye and manure and cherries on Mister Billie's farm.

———

"MY BOY, THE PRIVATES DID NOT KNOW WHICH WAS WORSE. WAS IT the roar of the prairie wind riding out of Canada on a witch's broom at twenty below? Or was it your mother's banshee screams as she struggled to get you born?"

At this, York put his rag down and drew me close to his chest as if he would smother me in his arms. His hug was like being gripped by granite.

"On that night Jean-Baptiste, the wind howled and so did your mother," he said in jest, slapping my back.

Finished with Mister Billie's boots, he walked me farther into Mister Billie's farmstead, greeting all the other Negros. So many of them everywhere, like a village here, away from Mister Billie's house. We did not cross paths with wherever Mister Billie had taken my parents.

York brought me to a lean-to and whispered curses at a gentleman's jacket as he brushed it. He bowed to two women who wore kerchiefs though it was very warm. Their exchange was quick, back and forth and in a tongue I could not make out. Once they set down a tub of water and the granny pot, they left.

"Soldiers?" York snorted, attacking the blue jacket studded with gold buttons, gleaming in the sun. "The enlisted men were terrified. They paid no mind to the wolves roaming about the plains that winter. Wolves that were all lunge and fangs after a buffalo hunt. Worse, appearing from the fog curtain hanging just above the frozen ground of the prairie, without warning came the Yankton Sioux. Now there were some soldiers, armed with clubs and hatchets and spears, scared of nothing, not the ice cold, not the wolves, not us."

York shook his head and I could not fathom his laughing at the Sioux. But he did.

"So, they proceeded with their raid. Robbed me of a hunk of meat I had strapped to my shoulders, stole my pack horse, stole all the horses the Mandan had lent us and rode off into the hell freeze with our bounty.

"Now picture this: the Sioux robbed us blind but it was the moaning from your mother that frightened them like haints casting spells. Their hackles was raised from a girl's cries. Those two brothers, the Fields, nothing but trouble from that pair of white devils. They could shoot a mouse from one hundred yards as they were crack shots, yet they were so spooked, they bundled up and trotted off into the ice and wind, preferring twenty below and hell freezing over to the warmth of a cabin and young woman's screeching. Wind screaming on a February night, pushing out ice gravel like bullets and these grown white men asked Mister Billie for a gill of whiskey. They said they needed spirits to huddle against the wind, but hand on a Bible, Jean-Baptiste, the spirits was to settle their nerves, for I was the one to pour. Spooked they was."

York laughed so hard his eyes welled up.

The two tall women returned. One stirred the large pot of boiling clothes, another pounded the clothing in a tub. The woman stirring said, "Look here Easter, if it isn't Prince York himself scrubbing big house finery."

The one named Easter pounded and spanked the laundry as if it was misbehaving. She pointed at me and asked, "Who this?"

York bowed to them and said, "Easter, you clean with such vigor, you are hurting the britches."

York's tongue and tone changed with these two women. I could not follow their fast talk.

All around me at this village was a horse commotion. Colored men and boys leading horses, feeding them, brushing them, a grandfather mending a bridle. Farther off, the tang of cherries filled my empty stomach. Two younger women, one with freckles and the other with a high forehead, were singing as if that would sweeten the pot of boiling cherries. Smoke from cookfires carried the smell of fruit and roasting meat. Seeing all of them reminded me of home, of my village, all the way up the river. In late fall, I would trail after my mother as she dried corn and half-moon chunks of orange squash on ladders to dry.

Suddenly, as if someone from the farm had listened to York's tale, a girl screamed and screamed for her life. The agony came from behind the barn. Only it was not a girl. In a tangled knot, four men wrestled with a hog and a rope. Before I could look away, they dragged it to the post, hung it upside down, whacked it on the head. Its screaming only stopped when the shortest of the men took a blade to its throat and a bright red waterfall spilled out. For the shame of it, I wet myself at the sight of the pig's crying and the gush of blood.

Then, as if there was no waterfall of blood, a rag-tag jumble of boys ran out from behind the barn, like they were following the hog. Before them came a squawking chicken. As the hen did not want to meet the same fate as the pig, it escaped their greedy hands. A skin and bones boy, his ribs ridged like sticks yelled out, "Go on, catch her, grab her wing."

They were like the laddies in my village all the way up in the far north, dodging the grown-ups and whatever chores they were supposed to be doing. I longed to be one of them, join in their chase, barefoot and hollering but I could not save for the dark spot on my buckskin britches where I wet myself.

Easter stopped her fight with the tub of wet clothing long enough to call out, "Joe Boy and Spindle, you return to the barn to clean the stalls. Or meet with Mingo who give your backside ten stripes. Which is it?"

York grabbed the last one, a girl who was my height and missing her front teeth as I was, with thick braids like the girls from my village. He lifted her up, spun her around until she squealed. "My turn, my turn," a small boy called out.

"You is no better than the young ones," Easter scolded York. "Your foolishness will get that one a taste of the rawhide. What is you on about?" He put her down.

THE SPRING BEFORE, WE LEFT THE NORTH AND THE MANDAN villages as soon as enough of the ice had melted. Spring meant the bison hopping game. Sheets of ice melting left buffalo stranded on blocks, stuck in the middle of the Missouri. Braves who could master hopping from one ice block to another while aiming a spear, killed the sitting bison. Spring promised a few strands of tall grass sprouting out of the mud. My mother and father and I bobbed downriver, carried along by the ice melt. We dodged tree islands, caving in riverbanks, and river waves, all of it dragged along by the Missouri for a thousand miles until we landed here in St. Louis. Spring was mild up north at home but here in St. Louis, spring was a steady, beating heat. Mister Billie took my parents away to look at a patch of land and later on, they took themselves away, back up the Missouri to the village and left me with him and the priests.

York spit on Mister Billie's jacket and stabbed the air with his brush. "I put a snip of comb hair in the seam, bad luck. Here, hold the sleeve. On the night you were born your mother's wailing even spooked Mister Billie and the captain. If you will pardon me, they believed she was a squaw possessed by demons, gibberish spilling out of her throat against the curse of Eve. That night, it was the other Frenchie, the other one who knew your pap, he returned to the cabin and tapped Mister Billie on the shoulder.

"He could talk moccasins off a Sioux in snow, that French trader. He drank with the English, cursed with the Frenchies, and grinned like a cat to the Americans. He was a weathervane, pointing himself to whoever blew stronger and paid more. So, on this hellbent night in February, he waved his hand about and boasted, '*Mon ami*, I used the rattlesnake tea for my very own *chère*, my wife, not four years ago, when she was weeping in the child bed near *la mort*. I made her the tea and *voila*, the twins arrived, *un, deux*.'

"Mister Billie nodded in agreement, and for six fishhooks traded to the sly trader of the north, Monsieur Jusseaume, I made the cursed tea. I spooned it to your mother and not a quarter of an hour later, out you came with a bushel of black hair."

He stopped his attack on Mister Billie's jacket and took the brush to my hair.

My eyes watered and I rubbed my face as if I'd been stung by a bee. I turned away. Shame-faced that I was born amidst such danger, my mother's pain and then her drinking poison. That May was the last I ever spent with my mother. My father took her away. I was orphaned, left to Mister Billie and the priests who would refuse me breakfast in the winter if they believed I was slipping back to my village ways, as if they could starve the Indian out of me.

York grabbed my shoulder and said to me, "No need to shed a

single tear. You were born in a storm at the edge of the world up there on the plains beside the Knife River. I ripped a bit of the red thread from the trinket gifts and put it around your neck like I saw my own mama do, for she brought Mister Billie's brothers into the world. You had yourself a little red necklace that wrapped you and kept you with the living until your own mother could tend to you. She and you fared poorly for a spell. I cared for her and her sister-cousin. Or did the sister-cousin care for your mother? Well, no matter. You were baptized by snow, poison, and a few bits of red thread like a necklace to keep the haints away."

"Haints?" I asked York.

"The evil eye, Jean-Baptiste. As your pap would say, *mal esprits,* bad spirits lurking about."

"*Mort avec les haints?*" I asked, my pants growing wet again. Pig blood and snake tails and now *mauvais esprits*.

York shook his head no and said, "Haints go along making mischief and casting spells so you slice your hand with an axe, your head pulses like murder. A plump baby stops feeding, a cow stops milking. My mother always put a red thread dipped in the first run of the still against haints. Never leave hair in a comb. So, I did the same for you. The necklace was a little charm, I figured, to work against the other poison your mama drank."

At that, he pulls me along. "Never forget you were a miracle." With his arm about my shoulders, he stood by me against all the commotion and my parents gone.

Mister Billie's farm was mothers singing and furious at dirty britches and men tender with horses. The men reminded me of the winter I had just left, for when it snowed, the lads and braves brought the horses to winter in the mound houses and fed them tree roots and dried twists of grass.

I wept. York told me to hush and then pointed to a man who sat on the roof of one of the sheds. Looking up was a giant sitting against the sun, straddling the roof and the wall, with York calling out to him,

"Juba, Juba look who comes here, the baby boy from the expedition to the Pacific. Saca's baby is all grown up now."

"Hello there, young one. You-you-you got a fine head of black hair on you, a bushel of black."

"Here is the story, Juba. I come back from the journey west with the captains."

"F-f-f-fetch me some of the nails that I dropped," Juba called down to York.

"The wee thing, the baby that went on his mother's back all the way to the Pacific sea? This is him, the baby, a laddie now," York said, his arm about me.

Juba jumps down from the post, a giant with a halo of sun behind him. Up close he is bigger and his face is marked up the way all the lads from home are. The ones who have done the ceremony that makes them braves and leaves them with raised scars of furrows on their chests. Only the markings on Juba are snaked, with lines crawling up his forearms and even his neck. He wears dark patched trousers, with his ankles scratched up and he has the same forehead as York, high and wide and dark, the same deep chestnut eyes. Brothers. Only as he stands beside York, he's a head taller. Just then a voice from behind me quiet and mean, from a white man, but not Mister Billie, says, "Juba you got an extra helping of stripes on you. You hungry for more? If not, get back up there."

I stared at the big dusty boots and his knuckles, moon white skin with red hair on them. I was too frightened to look at him above the waist.

I had no whiskers then and even on my tippie toes I stood only up to York's chest and still had a few milk teeth yet he called me grown.

York's cave of a voice, his laugh, the heat of that day, and now, the heat of this one.

ALL THESE YEARS LATER, AS IF SUMMONED BY SPIRITS, PHANTOMS, maybe even the haints that York was on about that day, and here I am fit to be tied with a cough, waiting for the wind and my lungs to better themselves so I can ride the Nez Perce trail straight to Montana. Rest here. I close my eyes. When I open them, the sun has moved down and a swirl of swallows dip and circle about. My hands are brown from the sun, creased and scarred like Juba's neck and arms, helpless to move me up and along. The mountain fever has come for me. The red thread York wound about my neck to ward off the bad spirits when I was born, oh, that I had that wound about my neck now. Perhaps with the red threads dipped in the first run, I could push on, climb back up and *un-deux-trois* take the reins for Pretty Boy and Jessup to go on, move. *Le mauvais esprits* have come for me now.

After that day, when York told me of my beginning, it was the priests that grew me up. Hair shaved, stripes for any word that was not *le français,* saying prayers before even the sparrows sang in the morning, and the pain of leather scraping boxes called shoes. My mother, the silent, loving pillar against my father's temper, and all my cousins, I was to banish them like they themselves were *mauvais esprits.* The priests grew me up and I learned my letters in French and English. The still fury they had, reading in Jeremiah and Revelation against my mother and my cousins and my hair. I have lost them all.

But it was the prince all the way in the Rhineland, Prince Paul, who took me across the sea, back to his castle when I was fifteen. He caught me like I was one of the Carolina parakeets he snared on his expedition up the Missouri, a Plains Indian on display. From my years with him I learned to dip a pen in the inkwell with a steady hand and copy out Psalms and even write long passages in French and German to my beloved mother in letters she would never receive. She never had a red necklace, so perhaps that is why she grew sickly in the child bed and perished after sister, Lisette, came.

My throat is as sorry as the dirt below me, cracked, and the wind has picked up hard, pushing dust. Wind like the villages up north, like the prairie did when fires galloped across the plains, the fire moving so fast it jumped and circled about. Yes, that wind. Come, come along Pretty Boy, I pat her mane, we will make it to Montana, to the Montana strike and damn the wind, damn my lungs. The sway-backed bony-rumped excuse for a horse ignores me.

All these years later, as a grown man, I have paddled up and down from where the Missouri meets the Knife River. Oh, the thousands upon thousands of Mandan, Gros Ventres and Metis, a sprinkling of French like my father who wintered under the same mound houses. I played. I threw the ring at the pole with all the other lads. The villages that rose up every winter. Most of them, save for the white men, are fever gone and now lie beneath the tall grass and sod they fashioned the mound domes from. My mother. Chief Sheheke. The hunters who could fell a buffalo just by landing a spear right between the ribs. York.

Mister Billie took me from them, put me in the academy with the priests in St. Louis who cursed my mother and all tribes in their prayers. Still, after my years of schooling, I even crossed the Atlantic, retching my way across and landed in a castle. I, Jean-Baptiste Charbonneau, neither full-blooded Shoshone nor French, who never learned to fiddle like a proper *michif*, I lived in a castle. I was a German prince's house parrot for six years.

When I journeyed back over the Atlantic, I followed in my mother and father's footsteps as a guide, trader, trapper, up and down the Missouri. I marched with the Mormons in the war, the one that snatched Alta California from Mexico. I had sore feet and a weary soul. Down in San Luis del Rey, even the priests said the Kumeyaay man should earn twelve cents a day to labor off his $51 indenture. I was just like all other frontier skunks desperate for fortune, except there were plenty of gentlemen who journeyed out to California as well, all gold madness. I panned and panned and was knifed twice in Placer. I lost all my ore and dust on three card monte in one night. All these lives and people, except now, I have fever and phantoms visiting me.

I am so thirsty, praying to the red necklace to keep me bound to this life on the trail through the valley to my mother's people. I will join them in the mountains and smell the sweetgrass they weave in horse manes. All the phantoms wavering in the heat before my eyes, they speak in bird calls, a sparrow, a crow, a Carolina parakeet, a blue jay, my mother and my aunt and my sister. And York.

THE KEEPER OF SECRETS

KERRY CATHERS

T his was said to have happened in a land not so far from here. A hamlet nestled to the left of the mountains and to the right of the stream. Through forest and swamp. Across fields of dancing buttercups and wilting lilies. In that place the old folks scorn and the knights of yore dare not tread. In a valley, stood a cottage where a carpenter lived with his daughter and dog.

"That's not how stories start." His protest came with a yawn as he shifted beneath the summer covers of his narrow bed.

"It isn't? How are they to begin?" She smiled down at his tiny frame, her own youth too far away to be entirely remembered.

"Once upon a time."

"Is that so?"

He mumbled something unintelligible and shifted onto his back, eyes coming open to gaze up at her. "I'm Owain. I'm four. What's your name?"

The question picked at an old wound. *You are no longer Beatha.* "My name is inconsequential."

"I like your necklace." He reached for it.

She laid her hand over the cluster of jewels that encircled her throat and leaned beyond his reach. "How kind of—"

"Are you my mother's friend?"

"No. I have business with your sister."

"They're in the workshop."

"I know. I thought I would give you a bedtime story before I met with her. You would like that, wouldn't you?"

He nodded, the motion rumpling his hair. "Only if you start it the right way."

"Very well." She leaned forward, eyes fixed on his face. "Once upon a time…"

THE AFTERNOON WAS PERFECTION. THE SUN HIGH IN AN unblemished sky. The spring breeze touched with the warmth of a summer come early and the soft perfume of lilacs from the tiny forest behind them. The three girls lounged at the side of the slow-rolling river that cut through the city and marked the westward boundary of the university's land. They came to enjoy the day and watch the punts meander past, shouting playful insults back and forth with the boys steering them as they tried to impress the girls with their nautical skills.

Beatha GuBrath lay on the grass, knees bent, hands behind her head, sleeves and trousers rolled up to soak in the sun. She wove the magic around her into a lazy spell that made tiny purple stars dance above her. On days like this she could almost forget the unfairness of life.

"Are you going to your father's cottage for summer break?" Eilish poked Beatha's hip with her toe, swiped her hand through the stars making them disappear.

She breathed a soft laugh. "It's not a cottage. It's my home. Cottages are what rich folks visit when they tire of the city."

"It's halfway up a mountain. It's a cottage," Amala corrected.

"It's not. A third of the way up at most." Beatha came up on her elbows to look at both, sitting like proper ladies in fine summer dresses.

"Right at the edge of a grim forest where faeries live." Amala smiled like an imp.

"There's a good acre between my father's *house* and the trees." She sat up, flicked at the magic and used it to toss one of Eilish's uneaten crusts at her. "And not a faerie to be seen."

"You've an acre behind your cottage? How did we not know this?" Eilish feigned insult.

"It's a farm. We've quite a few acres."

"Cottage."

"Cottages are for cottars. We're a freehold farm."

"You're not a farmer. You're a worker of magic and good enough at it to earn your living as such." Amala pouted as she did whenever she didn't get what she wanted.

"Not until I graduate."

"You'll be back with us in the autumn. We can survive without your stink of cow dung till then," Eilish teased.

"Dung? You valley tart. I don't smell of dung."

"Why do you think we sit near the lilacs?" Eilish picked up her cup of juice and signaled for the others to do the same. "A toast. To your return."

When their cups touched, Beatha held hers aside. "I'm not likely to return."

"What?" Amala's cup hit the ground hard enough for juice to slosh over the side.

"A letter came from my father. With Aiden gone from the sleeping sickness, there's only the two of us and Father can't tend the farm alone."

"But he doesn't need you in the winter."

"No. But he'll need me next summer and all the summers to follow until my cousin is old enough to take on half the work."

"He can hire help. Don't look at me that way." Amala shuffled closer. "You'll be eligible for an apprenticeship this year. With all the work you do for Professor Ollam, she'll take you on in the autumn. You can get a cheap room at the college through the summer."

"Won't be enough to hire extra hands. Not for a few years and only if the position is formalized by the faculty after graduation."

"So, it's all been for nothing. Three years studying magic. For nothing." Amala pouted.

"Not for nothing. I can always try again once my cousin is settled in."

"They'll require you to start again." Eilish's voice was filled with soft regret.

"Better late than never."

"You are too dedicated to your obligations. Too often thinking of others. My father can lend you money."

"My father's heart would be broken and I'd miss my dog."

"I'll give you one from Bessie's next litter." Eilish poked her again before turning serious, almost mournful in her expression. "You are too worried about the grief of others, that you'll endure what's not necessary." Then steel touched her voice. "What is your heart's content? If you had magic enough to make your life into what you want it to be?"

A happy heart, income to keep debt and starvation away, and friends to fill it with laughter and love. "A teaching position at the university to start with, and then rising high enough in talent and scholarship to be a sorcerer in the Great Library."

"At the Great Library? You do have lofty ambitions. There are only five of them in the whole world," Amala whistled.

"Eilish said *anything*."

"You mentioned valley tarts?" Eilish said, breaking the discussion. Beatha and Amala looked to where Bess Gilmington raced across the green toward them, skirts up to her knees showing her white silk stockings, her face split by a huge grin.

"A valley tart?" Beatha mused.

"Why do you think all my female dogs are named Bessie?"

"You'll never guess," Bess huffed, collapsing onto her knees hard enough to stain her stockings on the grass. Her face burned red with the exertion and her chest rose and fell in great gulps of air. She offered Eilish and Amala a conspiratorial smile and wrinkled her nose at Beatha as though smelling something foul.

"What will we never guess?" Eilish asked rolling her eyes at Beatha.

"She's coming." Bess giggled.

"Who?" Beatha asked when no further enlightenment came.

"Not of your concern, Beatha."

"Bay-a. Not Bee-tha." An old argument, but one she was determined to fight.

"It's spelled Bee-tha."

"It's mountain tongue."

"As though I'd speak that." She turned her back to Beatha and spoke to the other daughters of merchants. "The Keeper of Secrets. She's come to test for her successor."

"I don't believe you." But by the tone of Amala's voice, it was apparent she did.

"See for yourself. Her procession is making its way through the city to the duke's palace."

They erupted into motion, running across the lawn to the stone wall that bumped up against the Grand Promenade. Beatha was first to the top, swinging her legs over and letting her feet dangle. Eilish and Amala settled to her left and Bess to her right.

A crowd had formed, filling the wide sidewalks, everyone eager to catch a glimpse of the sacred woman. The buzz of excited conversation filled the air and people craned their necks and stood on tiptoes.

Beatha felt giddy as much from the mood of the crowd as from her own anticipation of looking upon the face of the most revered sorcerer in the world. How wonderful it must be to the Keeper. Kings and princes bowing in your presence. Hosting elaborate feasts in your honor. Hanging on the importance of your every word.

"They say she's two hundred years old," Eilish lifted her voice to be heard above the din.

"I heard close to a thousand." Amala leaned forward and shouted to them. Her expression was hopeful and why shouldn't it be? There wouldn't be a sorcerer who didn't covet the position.

Except Beatha. Even on the slightest of chances that she would prove to be the successor, she couldn't abandon her father to the farm. Perhaps she could hide herself away, or sneak off to the mountains before a summons could be made. She couldn't answer what she didn't receive.

"We'll be invited to the feast, of course," Bess purred in Beatha's ear. "It's for all the leading families. Not for mountain folk."

"Must be wonderful to be her," Eilish declared, her eyes fixed, almost fanatical, on the stretch of street the Keeper's procession would come down. "This might be your chance to make your life as you wish it to be."

"I never said I wanted to be the Keeper."

"No, but you said you wanted to be appointed to the Great Library. Prove yourself her successor and you can do one better."

Beatha furrowed her brow thinking she'd misled her friend.

Eilish's mouth turned upward. "How can you not know? The Keeper of Secrets lives in the Great Library."

THE SUMMONS ARRIVED TWO MORNINGS LATER, SLID UNDER THE doors of the small cells the university called student rooms. Beatha broke the seal—a necklace of gems around the image of the Great Library. Every acolyte was to attend to the Keeper of Secrets in the anteroom of the suites awarded to the honored guest for her visit. It included a date, a time upon the clock when they were expected to arrive, and a code of dress. Her best robes.

Three days away and late in the afternoon, Beatha was to present herself. It seemed a lifetime.

Conversation rumbled through the refectory with every senior acolyte professing their hope for success and every junior one mourning their disqualification.

"When is your appointment?" Eilish asked as Beatha settled onto the bench beside her. "Mine's early this afternoon."

"Not for three days." Her stomach soured. With so many to be tested, what were the chances of her being the successor? She was of higher than middling talent, adequate enough for a position in a merchant or magistrate's house, but, surely, not for something as illustrious as the Keeper of Secrets.

"They've been scheduled according to rank," Bess chirped. "I've been called for noon today."

"Beatha, you're white as a lily." Eilish nudged her with her shoulder. "Don't worry. I hear the test is painless."

"The Keeper came through on procession when my grandmother was our age. About fifty or so years ago," Bess chimed in. "She arrived. She tested. And she left. Her search for a successor doesn't mean she gets one."

"There, you see. It'll likely come to nothing for us. It will be a story to tell our grandchildren."

Beatha nodded, trying without success to banish her uncertainty.

Bess pulled herself into an arrogant pose. "Don't worry, my mountain friend. You're safe from any lofty obligations."

"THE KEEPER WILL SEE YOU NOW." THE WOMAN SEATED AT THE desk by the door lifted her gaze from her work, regarded Beatha with an empty, disinterested-looking expression, and waved her forward. She was dressed in robes fit for high nobility with pearls wound through her black hair and rings about her fingers. "I will need your name."

Beatha stood, her nausea threatening to spill over into genuine sickness. She went to the woman, knees trembling with every step.

Her voice cracked when she gave her name, forcing her to cough and repeat it.

"The door is sealed by a spell. If you can break it, you can enter."

Beatha thanked her, curtsied, and slipped behind her to the door, thankful not to have the woman's eyes upon her when she made the attempt. She set her sweaty palm on the brass doorhandle and closed her eyes, willing herself to be calm. Intricate magic was harder to work when emotions were high. She read the weave and felt the power. It was impressive in both aspects, but no greater than spells she had unwoven before. Pushing aside fear, Beatha wove her own spell, lacing it with the one sealing the door and with relative swiftness, broke the spell and opened the door.

The antechamber was an exercise in overstated grandeur. High ceiling, paintings ensconced in gold frames clustered on the walls, floor of marble, and furniture upholstered in velvet. The Keeper sat behind a desk large enough to be a bed, its legs elegantly carved in swirls that might have been intended to look like vines. The air was stale with the scent of burning lamp oil and old incense. All the windows were closed, concealed behind long thick curtains that kept both light and prying eyes out.

"You must be Beatha GuBrath." The Keeper spoke without looking up from her work, her voice filling the lofty space. She indicated a chair by the desk, and Beatha scurried to obey.

"Bay-a Goo-brah," she corrected from instinct, then turned crimson with shame.

The Keeper cast her a friendly glance. "My apologies. Bay-a Goo-brah." Her attention back on her pages, reading and scribbling. Folding and sealing them. Beatha tried not to squirm with the awkwardness. She sat as Eilish had taught her. Knees pressed together, back iron-rod straight, head slightly tilted, and hands folded neatly in her lap.

"A mountain name."

"Pardon?" Beatha started.

"Beatha GuBrath's a mountain name." The voice was rich and commanding.

"It is."

"Cut from hardy stock."

Beatha didn't know how to respond and hoped her silence wasn't interpreted as insult.

"Tell me, Beatha GuBrath, is it your wish to be the Keeper of Secrets?" She looked up from her work. Her features were youthful despite her rumored age. The face of a woman in her late fifties? Early sixties at most, if she had the soft life of the valley folk who had the luxury of keeping their faces shielded from the sun.

Beatha stared, her eyes falling on the cluster of jewels that sat about the woman's neck. The largest gem at its point alternating sapphire and rose, and smaller ones rising like pebbles on the beach. The wealth of kings and the status of something greater than them. How could she ever be worthy of this?

"Have they cut out your tongue? Come, girl, give your answer. I've a list waiting."

"It is my wish."

"Join me by the fire. The day is warm but the ancient structures always have a chill about them. Fetch the kettle in the corner and two cups."

The Keeper went to the fireplace while Beatha went to a table in the opposite corner. A kettle of delicate porcelain sat on a silver tray beside matching cups, sugar bowl, and small pitcher of milk. She brought the tray to where the Keeper sat.

"Here." The woman indicated a small table to her right, close to the fire, then waved at the chair opposite her.

Beatha obeyed, assembling herself in the same pose as before.

"Relax, child. We're done with the formal part." The Keeper adjusted her position, bringing herself closer to the short table that sat between them. An odd-looking set of instruments were arrayed on its mother-of-pearl and ebony top. She arranged them to her preference.

A rose-metal bowl at the edge of the side nearest her. A match-striker beside it. Glass phials across the center.

"You'll need to be quiet for this," she ordered, though Beatha had said nothing.

Eyes closed, she chanted as she opened each phial and poured their contents into the bowl. Smoke and the scent of roses lifted from it and poured over the edge of the table.

Beatha drew in a deep breath, finding the scent comforting. A few more and she felt dizzy, like after too much wine. Then complacent with a desire to reveal her innermost secrets.

"Your hand." The Keeper reached across the table, eyes open. Beatha faltered. "Come, girl, I promise to make a small cut. You'll hardly notice."

Swallowing down her uncertainty, Beatha laid her hand in the Keeper's palm. She flinched when the cut was made and scrunched up her face when the woman turned her hand and squeezed the flesh to encourage bleeding.

"There." She released her hold. "All done and not so bad as you feared. Wrap it in cloth."

Beatha obeyed, holding the bandaged hand close to her torso.

"It takes a moment for the test to finish. While we wait, pour us some tea."

She filled the first cup for the Keeper, offered milk and sugar and was refused. By the time she poured herself a cup, the smoke from the bowl was gone. The Keeper examined the contents and Beatha held her breath. Desperately hoping.

"Why is it you wish to be the Keeper?"

The question shocked her. Wasn't it about the magic? Beatha fumbled for an answer that would convey her desire without sounding insincere. Bess's words floated through her mind. "I am worthy—"

"It isn't about worthy. It's about wanting." She took up a golden cup, eyes fixed on Beatha as she drank. "Why do you want to be the Keeper?"

"The books."

A smile came and went in the span of a heartbeat. She settled deeper into the oversized chair. "Explain."

"I was told you have suites in the Great Library. That you alone have access to all of the books. Can never be denied entry. It is not access to secrets which fuels my desire, but access to every book ever written, or ever to be written."

The Keeper looked shrewd, sizing up Beatha's response. "You are the only one I have ever encountered who gave that answer."

Beatha's hopes died and she silently cursed her foolishness. But she showed the Keeper a pleasant face.

The Keeper's smile was bittersweet as she lifted her eyes. "It has confirmed what was written about you. You are of sufficient education and talent to maintain the Secrets. You will suffice as my successor."

Beatha nearly laughed and the breadth of her smile must have made her appear like an idiot. She tried to take it from her face, but her exultation would not allow it. She had her dream.

The Keeper brought forth an old beaten-up satchel, pulled a squat, thick book from it, and dropped it on the table near Beatha. The leather cover was wearing through on the edges, exposing the wood beneath. Any title that might have graced it had worn away. The pages were parchment and stained, the writing a tiny ancient script that was difficult to read. The letters pressed close together. It was gritty to the touch and smelled musty.

"All you need to know is contained within those pages."

"You won't be teaching me?"

"Not how it works, girl. You are far enough along in your training and of sufficient strength to fulfil your obligation. Your task is a simple one. Someone with your talent will find it dull in its performance."

She opened the book, read the first page. "If it is so simple, why is a Keeper necessary?"

"The book will prepare you for your journey and the first days of your service. You will find the remaining answers in the Chamber of Secrets known as the vault. I do not want to waste my night lecturing. What I will do is speak about things not in the book. But first, the mantle must be handed down from predecessor to successor."

The Keeper reached behind her neck. A faint click and she brought the necklace from its resting place and held it out for Beatha to take. "I cannot put it on you, child. You must do that yourself. Only your hands can seal it. Only your hands can release it."

It was heavy in her hands. And beautiful. Firelight glinted off the precious gems set in rose gold. Her hands quivered when she reached around her neck and sealed the clasp. Magic sparked, like warm mulled wine running through her body on a frigid winter's night. It sat heavy against her skin.

"You are Beatha GuBrath no more. You are the Keeper of Secrets."

The former Keeper took up the cup of tea, signaling for Beatha to surrender the book and do the same. When she relaxed into the chair, an expression of relief settled over her features, made her look older, threadbare.

"Will there always be a Keeper?"

"There are past Keepers and their servants who spoke of prophecies. Of one who will free us from this burden. Some have thought it folly. There are others, myself included, who simply do not care. We know if there is a Chosen One, we'll be long dead in our graves before they arrive."

"You do not want to live to see their arrival?"

"I have been in this world long enough."

"How old are you?"

She snorted a laugh. "Ancient. I don't recall the exact number of years. Irrelevant and forgotten. The Forever Life does that to you. Strips you of everything others think important until there is nothing left for it to take."

A Forever Life. How much learning can be won in a life that never ends? Magnificent.

"How long before I must find my successor?"

"You'll know. The spell in the necklace will compel you to search every few decades. It's a tug in your gut, like a sickness from which you will find no release until you go on procession. It is your choice when you surrender the necklace. The spell does not compel you to find your successor, only to search for them."

"So, I could be the Keeper forever? Or until the Chosen One arrives."

The smile was wicked in its condescension. The face was smooth, but the expression in her eyes was old. "You will not know forever. None of us ever has or ever will. You are young. You have much to learn. And the years will teach you. Every brutal lesson there is to learn."

The former Keeper leaned forward, refilled their cups. "In your suites, there are rooms that no one else can enter. There you will find the annals of your predecessors. Their lives before they took up the necklace. For your first task, take a fresh book, put your name on the front page, and the story of your days before becoming Keeper." She waved her hand in dismissal. "You won't understand until later. And I hope, when that later comes, you will find a way to forgive me for what I have done for you."

She took a deep drink and seemed to age. "I have a story I want you to hear before we part ways. This was said to have happened in a land not so far from here..."

Her voice became wistful as she spoke of a childhood in a simple village, of family and friends, of a youthful romance, of merriment and tears, of people dear to her heart, and of a woman who found her and gave her a necklace. She spoke without stopping. Afternoon became evening which eased into twilight and through into full night.

When the sun topped the horizon, the Keeper was dead.

GAZES SOAKED IN CURIOSITY PROCEEDED HER; WHISPERS FOLLOWED like the soft gnawing sound of rats scurrying across the floor. Beatha did not need to hear their words to know their thoughts. Their doubts were her doubts. And hers had been left to fester and spread like gangrene during her journey to her new home.

Four days, she had traveled from the university in a grand coach surrounded by guards in fancy plumes and coats of green velvet. Protecting her from unseen and unnamed threats. Keeping onlookers at an appropriate distance, and cutting routes through crowds desperate for a glimpse the new Keeper. She had been surrounded by people.

She had never felt so alone.

Her arrival at the Great Library had happened in the dead of night through a door far removed from the main entrance. A scurried trip to her suites had followed, then a few restless hours of sleep before waking to sun shining through a window of colored glass. She'd been bathed and dressed and set at a table laden with too much food for one person and told to eat as ladies-in-waiting scurried around. When they'd thought she'd consumed enough they'd shooed her from the table and sent her off to the Chamber of Secrets. With no idea where it was.

A tall, thin-faced man with empty eyes and black hair clipped in a sharp line above his high collar waited in the hall, greeted her with a stiff bow and a "This way."

She followed as he explained his role as guide through the labyrinthine halls and aisles of the library and its temporary nature.

The air was laden with the sickly-sweet odor of perfume and cologne applied too thickly, rather than of books and leather covers. Her guide led her through rows of exquisitely dressed men and women weighed down by excessive jewelry. They bowed and curtsied, their eyes following her like prey.

At the bottom of a twisting stairwell carved from stone, their journey ended in a modest alcove lit by four lamps, one to each wall. Across from her stood a red door with a black handle and white trim.

"The Chamber of Secrets, Honored Keeper."

Beatha gawked at the absurdity, almost laughed. How could

something so grand be housed behind a door you'd expect in a cotter's house?

Not wanting to appear simple, Beatha stiffened her back and went to the door. Up close, glyphs were visible. Powerful ones. Containment spells.

Her fingers touched the cold iron handle and she shivered. "Do you know what's inside?" She spoke to the door, unwilling to show him her fear.

"No. That's why it's called the Chamber of Secrets, Honored Keeper."

She flinched at the slight and reset her determination. "Call me Beatha."

"I cannot, Honored Lady. You are Beatha no more. You are only the Keeper."

The thought sickened her. To be reduced to a symbol; no longer a person. She turned the handle and pushed open the door, pausing to see the chambers innards before stepping into them.

It was small and overfilled with books and shelves that were too few to contain them. A table, a lamp, a writing set, parchment, and a single chair. Unremarkable was on overstatement.

"You are not to join me?"

"Only she who wears the necklace can enter."

Magic prickled against her skin as she stepped into the chamber and pushed the door closed. The barrier was not only to keep others outside, it was to hide what was inside. A chamber carved from magic. The height of castle spires and as wide. Magic filled the air and the tiny places between everything. Swirling. Dancing. Rushing this way and that. It was intoxicating.

A table, longer and wider than she was tall, stood in the center, its top a kaleidoscope of light. She set a fingertip near one corner and the swirls recoiled, shuddered, and the magic around her jumped. Beatha snatched back her finger and the movement on the table resumed and the magic righted itself.

"Beautiful, isn't it?"

Beatha started and spun toward the speaker, drawing magic to her by instinct. Her hold of it faltered when her eyes met those of the woman whose mantle she'd inherited.

"You're dead."

"A miracle of magic. The physical representation of magic." The former Keeper's attention went to the table, her fingers gliding over its polished edge. She looked up, fixed her eyes on Beatha. "And the reason for your existence."

"You're dead." Beatha's fingers danced, shaping the magic into a spell of protection. Before she could cast, light flashed hotter than the sun and Beatha collapsed with a shriek. Magic swirled like the wind in a storm. Lashing out, destroying what it could.

Then went still.

"Consider that your first lesson. Within the vault you do not weave magic. You guide it." The former Keeper knelt in front of her, her finger lifting Beatha's head. "You bear its rage so others do not have to."

"You're dead." This time as a whimper.

The former Keeper stood. "Magic is wild. One moment a soft summer breeze, the next an angry torrent. The storms appear and disappear within a flicker, leaving devastation in their wake. Or they linger for days. In here, magic has its true form. In here, you tame its storm so that out there, there is only the summer breeze. Do you understand?"

"Who are you?" Beatha stood, joints and muscles aching.

"I am no one. I am a spell woven centuries ago, when sorcerers learned how to tame magic."

"But you look—"

"The face I wear is the one who made you her heir. When you pass along the mantle, I will wear your face."

"It's eerie."

"It is necessary and meant to be comforting. Something familiar amidst everything that isn't."

"Why couldn't my predecessor teach me?"

"There can be only one Keeper and only she who wears the necklace can enter here. I will remain until you no longer have need of me. Then, I shall fade and go inert until your successor crosses the threshold."

"So, you have all the secrets I am to keep."

"There are no secrets. The title is the result of a casual quip by a long-dead king. He noted that the sorcerer of the vault lived long enough to know everyone's secrets and how lucky he was that she'd vowed to keep them."

"Why then am I here?"

The former Keeper's hand danced over the table sending the streams of light into a frenzy. Beatha screamed, dropped to her knees as light and pain exploded around her. The vault seemed to fall away and she was aware of every sorcerer who was weaving magic in that moment. Felt the magic writhe. Felt them struggle to control it. Felt them fail. Felt the magic tear through them and snuff out their lives. Felt the agony of each death.

When it calmed, Beatha was weeping.

"In its true form, magic is uncontrollable. Unpredictable. In the ancient days—before the creation of the vault—to weave magic was to tempt death. When it is calm, magic can be woven safely. When it storms, it kills whoever is working it. The necklace allows you to feel magic. To predict the storms and prevent them. Using this." Her fingers touched the table's edge. "But with this, as you now know, the Keeper can create her own storms."

Beatha pressed her eyes shut to contain the next wave of tears and agony. "You killed all those sorcerers."

"It is essential that you learn the consequences of failure and the price to be paid if you choose your successor poorly. She who enters the vault controls magic." The former Keeper loomed, tapped her toe against Beatha's knee to bring her gaze upward. "And all those who weave it."

"You killed them."

"The value placed upon lives changes once you enter the vault. Some must be sacrificed—"

"No."

"—to preserve the balance of magic."

"No."

"The loss of a few to save the many."

"I won't."

"You will. Eventually."

Beatha shook her head. Her voice lodged in her throat.

"A great lie was spread when this all began. That it was an honor to serve within the vault. Accolades were heaped upon the first Keeper and all those who followed. Wealth beyond an emperor's. Luxury. Authority. But it isn't an honor; it's a curse. The first was chosen by lot and she wept when her name was drawn." The former Keeper smirked. "Perhaps that is the secret you keep. The truth about what it is to be the sorcerer in the vault. If the truth were ever to be known, there would be no more successors. Not willing ones."

"I don't want this." Beatha reached for the necklace's clasp...but the Keeper's fingers on her arm prevented her from releasing it.

"You can relinquish your place whenever you choose. All you need do is select a successor. But be aware, your magic is interwoven with that of the necklace. Once you open the clasp, your life ends with the next sunrise."

The former Keeper's smile was like ice.

"There can be only one Keeper," Beatha whispered.

The woman walked to the table's far side. "You will be drawn to those with the potential to be your successor. The necklace will compel you to go to them. To test their suitability. Choose well. We do not want a tyrant in command of magic and its weavers. Those who are unsuitable must be appropriately handled."

"I won't. I will find a way to save them. I won't kill them."

"You will. Eventually. As all your predecessors did."

TIME PASSED. YEARS TUMBLING OVER EACH OTHER UNTIL NONE were discernible from all the others. One by one, she found them, tested them, and none were suitable. Hoping someday it would end. Beatha moved a strand of hair from Owain's eyes and pulled the blanket up tighter about his chin. Owain did not stir except for the soft rise and fall of his breaths.

She gave him a small kiss on the forehead. "Now to business with your sister."

An awful indulgence. Telling her stories to the children of those she visited. How else was she to remember? Or be remembered?

She rose from the chair, took it back to its corner, and left the room on tiptoes carrying her beat-up satchel with her. The main room was a simple one with a low ceiling and thick walls to keep out winter's chill. The furniture was old but well-kempt, the carpets worn but clean. Nothing extravagant and everything with a purpose. Much like the house she'd grown up in.

She sat in a chair by the fire. From the satchel she brought forth eight phials filled with enchanted liquids she had prepared before setting out. She arranged them on the table she'd brought from the adjoining room and settled into waiting. She was accustomed to waiting.

There were no great processions when she went on her searches. No red carriages with white horse and footmen in black. No gathered crowds. She came and went alone. Visiting great universities of learning, but preferring the obscure locations where teaching was done in private. Where she could sit by a family hearth and feel the memories around her.

She missed this. Desperately.

She was tired. So very tired. How wonderful it would be to close her eyes and know they would never open again.

Centuries had passed. Or had it been longer? She had not understood her predecessor's warning about the travails of Forever Life or how quickly its novelty turned dull. Had not understood the woman's eagerness to shrug it off.

She stretched her fingers out, closed them in a tight fist. Stretched them again. She had the face of a thirty-year-old, but the years were starting to take their toll.

"And who would you be?"

Roused from a slumber she'd not known she'd fallen into, Beatha looked to the battered doorframe that separated cottage from kitchen and where two women stood.

"I'll have you out of my home," the elder one barked and motioned to go forward but was halted by the touch of the younger's hand.

"She's the Keeper of Secrets, Mother." Her eyes shone with a keenness close to greed as they dipped to the necklace about Beatha's throat.

"Honored Keeper." The mother dropped into a deep curtsey, eyes to the floor, her body a pose of atonement. "I meant no insult."

"None was given."

The younger woman offered a shallow curtsey, her eyes never leaving the necklace. "She's come for me, Mother." Her tone fervent, entitled.

"I've come to test you."

"You'll find me more than adequate to take up your mantle."

"The magic will determine that."

The young women she visited were often nervous, some were cautiously hopeful, a few were fearful. But an unfortunate number were like this woman. Eager.

Too eager.

"If you will excuse us, kind Mother. I have business with your daughter. But would you bring us a pot of tea and two cups?"

"Most certainly." Another curtsey, a whisper in her daughter's ear, and she was gone into the kitchen.

"Sit." Beatha indicated to the chair across from her.

"I knew you would come. Mother doubted it, but I never did. They say you can feel the presence of each sorcerer. Know their talent."

Beatha raised her hand and the girl fell silent. "All in its proper time."

"But I have been chosen, haven't I?"

"Magic has brought me to you, now we must find out why." Beatha offered a comforting smile, the sort her grandmother had given her. Or had it been her father? The indulgent patience of a parent with an over-eager child.

Beatha studied the girl, wondered if this was how she had looked when her predecessor had sat her down for the test. Doubtful. What recollections she had of the event were of hope, uncertainty, and an overwhelming sense of inadequacy.

"Here you are." The girl's mother set a pot and two sturdy cups between them. "If there is more that I can do." Another curtsey as she wrung her hands. Her smile came and disappeared to return just as briefly.

"Your offer is gracious, but unnecessary."

A curtsey and she was gone.

Beatha looked at the young woman. "What is your name?"

"Kally-Ann. Might I know yours?"

Beatha. Beatha. Beatha. My name is Beatha.

"I am the Keeper. Who I was before is irrelevant." And lost except in her memory which faded with each passing year. When Kally-Ann opened her mouth to speak again, Beatha lifted her hand and silenced her. "Shall we begin?"

"Yes." Her smile was almost predatory as she settled back in her chair.

"Kally-Ann, is it your wish to be the Keeper of Secrets?"

"It is my wish."

Beatha sat forward in her chair, adjusting the position of the rose-metal bowl and taking up the first of the phials. She closed her eyes and chanted, pouring each phial into the bowl. Drew in the familiar scent of smoke and roses that crawled over the lip of the bowl and carpeted the table.

"Give me your hand."

Kally-Ann nearly leapt from her chair to place her hand in Beatha's palm and did not flinch when the cut was made. Eight drops fell into the bowl before Beatha released the girl's hand and offered her a cloth for the bleeding.

"Now we wait. Shall we have tea in the interim?"

Kally-Ann poured but neither drank.

Beatha felt the effects of the smoke. The dizzying, the calming, the complacency. The desire to speak the words that otherwise would have been hidden. The girl would be feeling the same. Time for the question that would decide Kally-Ann's fate. "Why is it you wish to be the Keeper?"

Kally-Ann leaned forward, eyes sparkling with their own light, her smile too broad. "Because I am worthy of the honor. Because there is none more adept at magic than I am and only the best should serve as Keeper. I wish for the prestige, the wealth, the right to command kings. I wish to control magic and with that control to set the world right."

"To strip the people of their freedom."

"Freedom is a fool's illusion. A strong hand and a steadfast heart will make the world as it should be."

Choose well. We do not want a tyrant in command of magic and its weavers.

The warning flitted through her memory carrying with it the agony of the deaths she had felt when it had been given. She had hoped this day would be different, this candidate would be suitable to inherit. But it was not the pull of a successor that had brought her here.

Long ago she had vowed never to take a life. But years and necessity have a way of breaking vows, have a way of teaching hard truths. Allow a tyrant to live and they will gather others; they will challenge the Keeper, demand what they believe is rightfully theirs and more lives will be lost.

A small evil to prevent a greater one.

"I have a story to tell while we wait." Beatha spoke of her life. Her childhood in the mountains, her own ascension, and the lie that had been kept from her. She talked through the night.

Dawn broke the darkness, its pale fingers creeping into the room. Beatha stood. "You are not the one," she declared.

But the girl was already dead.

———

"IT WILL BE NIGHT SOON AND BEFORE WE PART WAYS, I HAVE A story to tell." Beatha settled more comfortably into the chair, soaking up the warmth of the hearth. "This was said to have happened in a land not so far from here. A hamlet nestled to the left of the mountains and to the right of the stream. Through forest and swamp. Across fields of dancing buttercups and wilting lilies. In that place the old folks scorn and the knights of yore dare not tread. In a valley, stood a cottage where a carpenter lived with his daughter and dog."

IT IS WHAT IT IS

SUSAN KRAUS

Memories that Jane had squirreled away, deep down in the darker recesses of her brain, were, with age and perhaps a touch of dementia, surfacing. Once she'd hit seventy, an age that had seemed so terrifically distant when she'd turned thirty, then forty, then fifty, less terrifically distant at sixty, more lurking, opaque, inevitable—*those* memories, the unspoken secrets, pushed up through her mind-mud, zombie apocalypse style.

Jane felt a disconnect, a psychic jolt, anytime she said, "Well, *that* was fifty years ago." How could she have lived seventy-three years? And, since birthdays were counted at the *end* of the numbered year, how could she be living her seventy-fourth year? How could she, Jane Browning, be almost seventy-five years old?

Memories rose in fragments, a thousand-part jigsaw puzzle with missing pieces. She'd realized, however, that, with each new year, she was remembering her life precisely fifty years prior, a chapter opening with each birthday. At sixty-eight, her eighteenth year had surfaced, at seventy, her twentieth. At seventy-one, she dreamed of when she was twenty-one.

They started as sweet dreams, college years with her first boyfriend, Wayne, an Italian-American boy who'd been smitten to learn she was a virgin and intended to remain one. In his social circles, any eighteen-year-old virgin was headed for the convent. Which, to be honest, Jane had considered.

At eighteen, Jane had been a blank slate when it came to sex. Her mother never had "the talk" with her. She had not had girlfriends with "experience" to explain things, and the Sex-Ed class in high school was strictly procreation. What goes in and what comes out. Pleasure was never mentioned.

But, really, it was a movie, *The Cardinal*, seen at a local theater with her eighth grade parochial school class, that had terrified her into abstinence. It was a horror film to young Catholic girls: what happened to "fallen" women; how good Catholics would have to choose the life of the baby over saving the life of the mother. Scenes from that movie had embedded in the recesses of her brain, like the girl screaming in agony, and then the "happy" outcome where the baby of the dead mom is loved and cherished. How babies mattered way more than their mothers. That, more than moral conviction, informed her virginity.

But Wayne appreciated a challenge. They parked in his rusty Oldsmobile, with a plank seat in front. He was infinitely patient, infinitely slow. He stroked her hair, her shoulders, drew his finger up and down the soft inside of her wrist, her elbow. It wasn't sexual, she thought, he was *respecting* her boundaries. He shared stories about his life, growing up in what her parents would call a "rough neighborhood." He asked Jane about herself, what she liked, what she wanted from life. He listened attentively, waiting for her heat up, a slow burn, for her body to want something her head had never agreed to.

Wayne was convinced that it was the slowest lead-up in history. From first touch to first kiss, weeks rolled into months of circumspect...

The months of slow burn had not been one-sided. Jane had learned to kiss. She'd learned to touch, to tease just a bit. But the wall of virginity had not been breached.

Then, one night, Jane started to do something that Wayne had *not* shown her. He abruptly pulled back, feeling stunned. Where had she learned *that*?

"I found a book," Jane said, in a whisper, as if anyone could overhear outside a car parked in the back row of an empty stadium lot. "Somebody left it in the laundry room of the dorm. It's like a picture-book, with instructions. I started to look at it because I was alone. Then, I put it in the bottom of my laundry basket and brought it back to my room. I've never stolen anything before, but I stole this book." Wayne heard her whispered explanation as a confession, one sin an act, the other of intent.

"A picture book?" Wayne asked. "What's it about?"

"*The Joy of Sex*," Jane replied.

"Are you sure you're not talking about porn? I mean, if there are pictures about sex..."

"No, it's more instructional."

Jane had never heard "joy" and "sex" used in the same sentence, let alone a book title. Now that she'd stolen it, she couldn't return it. She was stuck with *that* sin. The book would stay where it was, at the bottom of a box of first semester textbooks in the back of her closet. Until she could read it, every page, by flashlight if necessary, curled up under her comforter.

Two months after finding the book, and following some of the instructions for "Foreplay," Jane decided that "virgin" was not a label she needed to preserve. But, first, she needed to take precautions. Jane was nothing if not uber-responsible.

"The reason Catholic girls get pregnant is because they pretend that if they didn't *intend* to have sex, that it "just happened," it's less of a sin," Jane explained. "Because *intent* is a sin in itself. Even thoughts can be sins. Which is crazy. What are the worse sins? Contraception and sex? Or unprotected sex and then abortion? Huh?"

Jane explained all of the above to Wayne in a low voice in the waiting room of the Planned Parenthood clinic in Jersey City, which was far enough away from their college that she felt there was no chance of knowing anyone.

"I think the Church is really stupid," Jane continued, her voice lilting as if this were a recent epiphany. "Contraception should be promoted as a sacrament if they want fewer abortions. Mandatory contraception until you can pass a test that you're mature and stable enough to be parents. Nobody is allowed to get pregnant until they've completed a year of child-care training. Those two things will do more to stop abortion than sermons."

They left Planned Parenthood with a three-month supply of the pill, and a bag of condoms. "Not taking any chances," Jane said.

The consummation was a let-down. Jane had been led to believe—by extensive reading of fiction—that they would magically move toward orgasm at the same pace and blissfully climax together.

But that's why they call it fiction, she'd later realized.

Wayne and Jane continued as before, but with less slow burn. Their sex became...predictable? At the same time, they became more coupled, more domestic. They talked about living together, looked at furniture when strolling the mall, talked about a timeline for getting engaged, and when they might want kids.

For Wayne, the challenge, the thrill of conquest, was gone.

It was a year later that Wayne cheated. Or maybe that was just when Jane found out he was cheating. It was June and they were both working on campus and living in dorms. There were new students, usually transfers, in the summer session. And one girl, with peachy skin and green eyes, more buxom than Jane, took a fancy to Wayne. She consistently displayed what Jane regarded as a ridiculous amount of cleavage, and said things like, "I cannot believe that these dorms don't have air conditioning," and, "I have to wrap up naked in a wet sheet just to sleep at night." Peach-face was a conquest of a different kind. She'd kissed virginity bye-bye a long time ago.

When Jane realized Wayne was lying to her, that they were not "just friends" but he'd been having sex with peach-face for almost three weeks while still in a committed relationship with her, she fell apart. She made a scene, demanded explanations, and then did something neither of them saw coming. She slapped him across his face, hard, sending his glasses spinning out, across the room, and breaking. Jane had never hit anyone, had never felt mindless rage.

Wayne had never intended to end their relationship. He loved Jane. He'd never intended to cheat either. "It just happened," he told Jane, trying to explain that—*deep down*—he loved only her. He was earnest. But it was not enough.

Within a month, Jane left campus, finding a spot on a student exchange program with a university in California when another student dropped out. Jane suspected it was because the guy got a girl pregnant, but that may have just been her mind-set. She packed up her room and called her parents, asking them to come get her. She explained, without details, that she was flying out in four days for an exchange year in California. And, by the way, she'd broken up with Wayne.

IT WAS FLYING WEST, MIDWAY OVER UTAH, THAT JANE DECIDED TO change her name.

She remembered being teased in elementary school, called Plain Jane. And more. Her mother had brushed it off, telling her that it was just because her name was easier to rhyme, not anything about who she was. "Easier to make a silly rhyme with Jane than Elizabeth," she reassured her daughter. "Just let it go. Ignore them."

But Jane had not felt that it was silly. She'd felt *intention* behind the taunting words, the sing-song jabs, deliberately hurtful under a veneer of self-justification. "We were just fooling around," the kids had told the nuns when caught in the act. "She can't take a joke."

Jane could neither ignore the bullying, nor find words or ways to make it stop. She withdrew into herself. Books became her best friends; reading her salvation. She fantasized about entering the convent, about hiding forever in a habit of brown cloth and white wimple. She prayed with supplication for some sign of a vocation, of a path.

Then, within the first twenty-four hours of arriving at college, God had sent Wayne. Jane still felt awkward in many social situations, still tentative and shy, feeling that there were invisible social rules she did not understand. But she'd learned what it felt like to be valued and appreciated. She'd felt loved.

Wayne had ruined *it*, had ruined the future she'd envisioned with him, a future where she felt special and desirable. But Jane did not want it to ruin *her*. She did not want to retreat into being Plain Jane again. She'd left Wayne, but she needed, even more, to leave her old self.

As the plane passed over the Rocky Mountains and she looked down at the clouds, what came into her mind felt logical. A functional, pragmatic solution to an existential dilemma. She would change her name. She would no longer be *Jane*.

She would be...Windy. Yeah, Windy. She rolled the name around in her head silently mouthing "Hey, Windy!" and "What's happening, Windy?"

Wasn't there a song? She felt the beat in her head, almost a throbbing. She hummed it, trying to remember the words but they were all jumbled up. It was about a girl who wasn't shy and anxious. That girl welcomed life. She smiled at strangers. That girl didn't put up with bullshit.

That's how Jane wanted to be. Not invisible. *Somebody*.

And in that moment, Jane saw herself through a different lens. She wasn't *running* away, she was *flying* away. She'd done it. Looking out the airplane window, Jane saw, far below, layers of white cotton clouds. She'd never been this high before, ever.

It was a sign. Maybe not from God, but a definite sign.

When Jane got off the plane and found the van that was waiting to drive her and four other students north to the university in Chico, there was a brief round of introductions. Jane had never seen any of them before, even though they'd attended the same college. She'd been in her own world; an English major, working part-time, being with Wayne. That was all. No clubs. No sorority. No TGIF parties. Just study, work, and Wayne.

They were Charlie, Gary, Melissa, and Barbara.

"I'm Windy," she said. "So good to meet you all. Was that not a great flight!" Her voice was bubbly, her smile infectious. Everyone smiled back.

JANE'S LIFE BECAME MORE VIVID, MORE COLORFUL, IN CALIFORNIA. Five decades later, so were her dreams. The van ride from San Francisco to Chico was magical, and the van ride dream repeated for a week. In it, she put the window down and her head out, like a dog, wind whipping her hair, inhaling the loamy smells of passing farmland. For miles and miles. Jane woke from these dreams smelling the earth, feeling the wind.

In Chico, Jane had a private room in the women's dorm, no bigger than a closet. It had a tall, narrow window that looked over a courtyard with trees. It had a twin bed, dresser and desk. Windy thought it was perfect.

It took a few weeks for Jane not to feel schizophrenic, or bi-polar, or whatever it was when people had two personalities. Walking into the Student Union, or the cafeteria at lunch, she had to stop and regroup. Jane would normally sit by herself in a corner, pull out a book to read while eating, the book a barrier, her safety-net.

But Windy? Windy would see people she recognized from class and saunter up to the table. Windy would say, "Hey, aren't we in Contemporary American Lit together? I'm new here. Can I join you?" Windy would ask about the best TGIFs in town, what classes they were taking, who was their favorite professor. By the end of lunch, Windy would have jotted down names and phone numbers.

Windy had one prof who quickly became her favorite: Professor

Tom. Tom White. Tall, thin, his left hand tossing back sun-bleached blond hair, his right-hand waving, for emphasis, as he explained why book 'A' was superior to book 'B.' Professor White was new, just his third-year teaching, tenure track, after getting his Ph.D. at the University of Texas. Windy sat toward the front of the room, not in the back as Jane had done. Windy was not afraid to make eye contact with Professor Tom. Windy smiled at him whenever he looked in her direction. Windy made a point of asking one question at every class. Only one. But they were thoughtful questions that required thoughtful responses.

In the third week, Professor Tom called her aside as class ended and everyone ambled out. Students in California, Windy had noted, seemed less stressed than their New Jersey counterparts, who were always in a rush, always hurrying. Windy found herself slowing down, stopping to sit on a bench for a few minutes between classes, not being so anxious about the possibility of being late. Windy could walk into a classroom, even if she were a few minutes late, and take a seat, smiling. Jane could never do that. She'd have crept in, hunched over, trying to be invisible, her very posture an apology.

"So," Professor Tom asked Windy, "you're one of the New Jersey exchange students, right? How is the adjustment going?"

In her dreams, Jane could not remember what Windy replied. Perhaps because she'd been so focused on Professor Tom.

"Would you like to join a coffee group?" he'd asked. "A group of students meet at eleven a.m. most days at the student union. No commitment, just whenever you can make it. We mostly talk about books and film."

The coffee group was one of the most liberating experiences Jane had ever had, although Windy took it in stride. Windy had opinions, as well as a nifty balance of sarcasm and playful repartee. Windy could make people laugh.

By the next month, Windy and Professor Tom were having coffee together at other times, always in public, always with a few books strewn across the table, with open notebooks to appear as though they were working on a project. And they were, sort of. But they peripatetically segued into more personal conversations.

Jane's memories were fuzzy on what happened next, on how they got from campus coffee to a meet-up in a hotel in San Francisco. The latter did not happen until after Windy had finished his class, turned in her final papers and completed the exam. 'No sex with students' was Tom's bottom line. But the minute she was no longer *his* student, the line loosened. Jane could not recall, no matter how hard she tried, how she'd justified the sex—Professor Tom was married, his wife a Texas girl who wanted to move back home almost as much as Professor Tom loathed the idea of ever returning. Mostly, Windy didn't think about what would happen if it became public. She'd never, until now, as the memories bubbled up, even labeled it as an affair. Because it wasn't, not really. She hadn't *intended* any of that.

The dreams rolled out like a TV series, episodic and sequential. On nights she did not dream, or did not remember dreaming, Jane awoke disoriented, disturbed. Almost as if she didn't already know what the next episode would bring? Because there were nights when she felt genuine surprise.

Who was this girl?

Windy realized in just one liaison that Professor Tom was much more attractive fully dressed, engrossed in debate or discourse, than undressed and fumbling around in bed. While her lifetime experience had been limited to one man, she'd been spoiled. Wayne, for all his other deficiencies, his lack of interest in literature, had been a skilled reader of her body. Professor Tom seemed to have a checklist with two-minute limits on each check.

The affair was over almost before it had begun. They offered justifications, how he could not deceive his wife, how he should not have exploited their relationship, how they had let desire override their values. They segued back to friendship, relieved that neither felt hurt or compromised.

Professor Tom became her mentor. He was the first person to tell Jane she had a discerning mind. He questioned why she wasn't considering grad school. He coached her in applying for stipends and assistantships. And Windy was deeply grateful. They were friends, and soon neither remembered anything different.

Windy applied to grad school at Chico. There were a hundred other places that Jane could have gone, but Windy craved the smell and feel of California for another year as much as she did any degree. It was a joyous year. She reveled in feeling competent when teaching, and her anxiety, that corrosive imposter syndrome, dissipated. With Tom's encouragement, she applied for a Ph.D. program at University of Texas, Austin, and was accepted. It was a free-ride package: tuition and fees, and a stipend for teaching a few sections of Freshman Comp or Intro to Lit. She could spend four years doing what she loved, get paid, and finish with no debt. Jane was gob-smacked at her good fortune.

But then Tom encouraged her to follow another dream: to travel around Europe. "The Ph.D. isn't going anywhere," he'd explained. "And once you're in the middle of it, you can't take a break. Go before you start." When she inquired about postponing her admission for a year, they assured her that they'd hold a slot.

It felt surreal to her, to have so much she wanted fall in line. She'd teach full-time at Chico for summer session and fall semester. Then, savings in hand, she'd go to Europe for six months. It might be the only time that she'd have the opportunity to make it happen.

———

TOWARD THE END OF THE FALL SEMESTER TEACHING AT CHICO, SIX weeks before she would board a charter flight, packed with students all heading out on their own European adventures, that Windy met Dennis. It was, oddly, at a party at Professor Tom's house, for teaching assistants and assistant profs. And Windy was an assistant prof, although she felt like an imposter. Not tenure track, but teaching full-time.

Dennis was a friend of Tom. He taught high school in the Bay area.

He and Windy sat around a firepit, leaning into each other to hear above the music. So very *California* Windy had thought. Almost accidentally kissing as they each turned their heads to laugh—and then kissing for real. Dennis was a very fine kisser, with an appreciation for subtlety. His kisses were eloquent.

Dennis returned to San Francisco, but promised to return in a week. This was before cell phones, before texts. Looking back, Jane wondered how anyone had managed to connect. But Dennis returned, they kissed for another few hours and ended up in her bed for two days. Three weeks later, Windy moved out of her apartment, stored her meagre boxed-up possessions in a friend's basement, and took a bus to San Francisco. She had her passport, an enormous backpack stuffed with everything she would need for Europe, and two weeks before her flight departed to be with Dennis.

The time was story-book. Magical-handholding-stopping-to-kiss-at-every-turn, infatuation tinged with obsession. Dennis shared everything he loved about San Francisco with her, and she fell in love with the city as well. They ate at his favorite dives, went to readings at City Lights. They walked the Marina, Nob Hill, Union Square, Castro, and the Mission. Dennis introduced her to Russian saunas and steam rooms where they sat, hunkered over, until it burned to inhale, then plunging into icy pools. They ate steamed pork buns in Chinatown where Dennis was greeted like a long-lost cousin as he bantered in rudimentary Chinese.

When they made love, Windy—Jane—felt blessed. She knew she'd found her soulmate. Her partner for life.

Dennis had told her that evening they'd met at the party, that he was in the middle of a divorce. He'd married young, a high school romance, but it had become clear they were a bad match. Their long-term goals were incompatible. Their interests were incompatible. They had no kids, for which Dennis was grateful. "It would be hard to break up with kids," he'd told Windy. "We're adults. We can handle it."

With anyone else, Windy thought she'd have concerns. Like how ready could a guy be for a lifetime commitment if he was just coming off a divorce? And Dennis was not yet at the 'coming off' phase, more the 'getting ready to file' stage, a detail he'd not shared until they were eating Greek food in San Francisco—ravenous after two hours in bed—tearing apart warm pita bread and stuffing it with gyros and tzatziki sauce.

"We've been separated for a while, but neither one of us has made it to an attorney to file," Dennis said. "It's a big expense. But we know we're doing the right thing, no hard feelings, so not like there's a reason to hurry." Windy had a mixed reaction, wondering if there might be hard feelings if his almost-ex knew he was getting it on with his soulmate.

She was more concerned about her impending departure, and the gut-wrenching ambivalence she was feeling. The charter flight was non-refundable and it had taken her months to save up. She was flying San Francisco to Paris. The first few months she'd study French at the Alliance Française, and, hopefully, work as an au pair for a French family. She'd read that families posted gigs on the Alliance bulletin-board. They wanted their kids exposed to English.

Dennis was adamant she needed to go, that it would be a wonderful adventure, that he would miss her, but he could not live with himself if he stopped her from making the memories of a lifetime.

"I'll write you every day," he vowed. "I'll be here waiting for you when you get back."

They had not resolved that she was accepted in a Ph.D. program in Texas starting in August and he taught high school in California. He had a year-long contract, to be renewed in June. He'd said he always wanted to see Texas, then taken her hand and kissed her fingers, one at a time. For Windy, that meant more than a ring.

Dennis drove her to the airport. This was before security lines, before the insanity of the next century, and so he walked her to the gate. At the last minute, he pulled a small blue box from his pocket. It held a loop of soft suede leather, the color of caramel, a key to his apartment hung like a pendant from the bottom. Dennis, ceremoniously looking into her tear-filled eyes, slipped the necklace over her head, lifting up her hair, and tucked it inside her sweater.

"This is so you remember where you live," he whispered in her ear. "Come home safe."

Windy was almost the last to board, the gate attendants gesturing as the final announcement was made. Dennis stayed at the large windows, his face touching the glass, until the plane backed from the gate and lined up for take-off.

The first few nights in Paris were tough. The garret room Windy booked for the first week was four flights up, no elevator, and shared a bathroom with three other rooms. The ceiling was so sloped she could only stand in the very center. It was cold, dank, and the shared bathroom was more fraternity messy than hotel clean.

Windy cried herself to sleep for two nights. Then it was Monday, thank God. She showered, dressed and made her way to the Alliance Française. Within two hours, she was enrolled in classes five mornings a week for a month. She jotted down phone numbers for three possible au pair positions from the bulletin board. She was invited to join a few students for lunch in a nearby café. She had her first Croque Monsieur, listening as the cheese, tasting better than any cheese ever had, melted in her mouth,

By the next day she had an interview with a couple in Châtillon, a suburb, but an easy Metro ride from the Alliance. It was an odd position since they did not have a child—yet. But the wife was seven-months pregnant and needed help with shopping, cleaning and house chores, and the husband wanted to practice his English every evening at supper. Windy would work three to eight p.m. weekdays and alternate Saturdays. She'd learn French cooking basics helping the wife prepare supper. She'd coach them in English as they shared the meal. She was free to attend classes at the Alliance, and, if there was ever anything she wanted to do that started earlier in the evening, just let them know. She got room and board and some money.

She moved into a small room off their kitchen, with a private bath.

She was relieved to be away from the communal bathroom and freezing garret. It was a perfect set-up, for any student.

But Windy was miserable. Dennis was all she could think of, and how much better Paris would be if she were sharing it with him. How building memories meant nothing if she was alone. She touched the key nestled between her breasts, as if it were a talisman. The soft suede felt like part of her skin.

She wrote letters on aerograms, folding the tissue-thin blue paper and kissing it closed. Dennis's first aerogram arrived after five days, in care of the Alliance, Poste restante. Windy realized, reading it, that Dennis had mailed it before she'd left, to make sure she had something. After a few more days, his letters began to arrive, often clumped together, three in one day, then none for days. She mailed one each day. She described in microscopic detail what she was seeing, hearing, smelling, and tasting. She described the Metro and Châtillon. She described the Luxemburg Gardens, children floating their little boats in the fountain, and the ringing of cathedral bells to mark the hours.

Every day, Windy rose early and hopped the Metro into the city. Every morning she went to French class and responded in sing-song with the other students. Every afternoon she learned the names of vegetables and parts of meat and currency as she walked the stalls of the market with the slow-moving wife and carried the baskets of food back to the apartment for supper. In a week she mastered two mother sauces—béchamel and velouté.

The couple were thrilled to have a skilled English teacher, with a graduate degree, as their live-in help. Windy knew she had a plum position especially after listening to other students who had to deal with kids, homework, baths, and bedtime. And she would leave a few weeks after the baby was born when the wife's mother moved in to help. Then she would start her traveling with a Euro-Pass good for any train in Europe.

Every night, she took off the necklace and wrapped the leather around her wrist, the key in her hand tucked under her chin as she slept. It was solace. But solace was elusive.

Windy was cracking. She'd never missed anyone as she missed Dennis. She'd never felt such an aching hole, not even after Wayne, his deception and their break-up. She made herself think about all the nights she'd eaten ramen noodles, dropping the saved grocery money into her trip jar. How could she compromise this trip, her once-in-a-lifetime adventure, everything she'd saved for?

But Paris was empty, hollow, without Dennis.

There was nothing different about the day when Windy finally cracked. The sky was the same blue-gray, the Metro the same easy ride, her fellow students chatty in their awkward French.

She hadn't talked about her dilemma to anyone except a few other students. They'd been uniform in their responses: "If he loves you, he'll be waiting for you," and "Don't throw it all away just to get back to him. This is *your* time. Savor it."

But they didn't understand. They were talking about ordinary guys, not soulmates. How could she savor this time when her heart was not in her body, when it was across an ocean?

And so Windy did what Jane would do. Windy walked the entire length of the Champs-Élysées, from the Arc de Triomphe to the Place de la Concorde. She watched every person, listened to every sound, inhaled every aroma of every café, soaked up all that was Paris on an ordinary Tuesday. She thought of all she'd saved for, all she'd wanted to do in Europe—France, Italy, Germany, Spain, Greece—her great adventure. Then she walked into the Paris office of Pan-American Airlines and purchased a one-way coach ticket from Paris to San Francisco. It cost way, way more than her round-trip charter flight, and depleted almost all the money she'd squirreled away over two years. The flight would depart in two days.

Windy took the Metro back to Châtillon and explained to the very sweet couple that she needed to return to the U.S., that there was a family emergency. She felt guilty about lying, but could not face their attempts to change her mind if they knew what she was really doing.

She lied to the other students the next morning, her last day at the Alliance. She told them that her grandmother was very ill, that she needed, urgently, to return. Most mouthed words of sympathy, more about losing Europe than her grandma dying. One of the girls said nothing, but whispered in her ear as she hugged her goodbye, "I hope you know what you're doing."

Windy remembered nothing from the flight back across the ocean, changing planes in Boston to cross the USA. It was dusk when the plane landed in San Francisco, after twenty-four hours of travel. Windy had debated whether to call Dennis after she passed through Customs in Boston, but she was enamored with the scenes playing out in her head.

In her fantasies, Windy opened the door to Dennis's home with her key. When he saw her, his face would flood with disbelief and joy. They would kiss and clutch at each other, dance around the kitchen. They would curl up on the couch, entwined, and she would tell him everything about her brief trip, about her love, and how it didn't matter about the money, that dreams could change, that being with him meant more, that someday they would return to Europe together.

And then they would start, really start, their life together, until they grew old, until they turned gray. Together they would plan their future.

She took a local bus into the city, then grabbed a cab for the two miles to his apartment. His apartment was the lower back of an older, three-story home. The entrance was at the end of an alley and up some steps, at the rear of the house. Windy loved the tall, narrow windows, the table in the foyer, the bedroom with a fireplace, the living room with built-in oak bookcases, the worn hardwood floors.

At the street end of the alley was a bar. It was a San Francisco bar: couches, big front window filled with plants, coffee tables with magazines. Dennis went every Sunday morning with his Sunday paper, and read it cover-to-cover, sipping an Irish Coffee and joking with neighbors. He called it church.

Windy got out of the cab, hoisted the enormous backpack on her shoulders, paid the driver and turned down the alley. At the door to the apartment, she paused. She lifted the leather thong with the key from around her neck, gently inserted it into the lock and twisted it to the left.

The foyer was dark, but a light shone from the back of the house. Before she could speak, she heard a voice. A female voice.

"Denny," it was saying, the tone anxious, even fearful. "Denny, I think someone just came in the front door."

While Windy was trying to make sense of what she'd heard, Dennis emerged from the bedroom, baseball bat in hand, wearing only his briefs. He stared at her. "Windy? What are you doing here?" he asked. "You're in Paris."

"I came back," Windy said, stating the very, very obvious. "I missed you too much."

"Why didn't you call me?"

"I wanted to surprise you."

Windy lifted her shoulders, then rolled them back. The straps of the backpack slipped down her arms as it arched back, in slow motion, before landing with a heavy thud on the hardwood floor.

She looked at Dennis, her soulmate, standing awkwardly in his underwear, the bat dangling from his right hand. Then the female voice intruded again.

"What is it, Denny? Is someone there?"

Windy looked at Dennis. She looked at her backpack on the floor. She fumbled at the small purse that held her passport and remaining cash, still hanging across her body.

"I'll be in the bar," she said. "I need a drink." And with that she turned and walked out the door, the leather necklace with the key still clutched in her fist. As the door closed behind her she had a fleeting thought that perhaps surprises were better in fiction.

Within ten minutes, Dennis was in the bar, shoeless but otherwise dressed, eyes searching, looking for her as if unsure she was actually there. When he saw her, on a loveseat in a corner, he rushed over and tried to hug her.

"I can't believe you're back," he said. "I've missed you so much."

"Who is she, Dennis?" Windy asked. "The woman in your bedroom?"

"I can explain," Dennis protested. "It's not what it looks like."

"And what does that mean?"

"It wasn't planned. She was just being nice, bringing me your letters."

This caused Windy to pause. "Huh?" she asked. "What the hell does that mean? And who is *she*?"

"My wife," he said, as if it were obvious. "She had a forwarding address from this address because she moved and some of your letters were forwarded to her by mistake. She knew it could take weeks for the Post Office to straighten it out, so she called and asked if she could swing by and drop them off."

Windy was bewildered. Her aerograms to Dennis had been delivered to his ex-wife?

No. Change that. His *wife*.

"When did she move out?" Windy asked. For some reason, this seemed important. Had other mail had similar issues? And why was she so intently fixating on mail?

"Thanksgiving," Dennis answered.

A calendar assembled in her head. They'd met only two weeks later. Windy had come to stay with him two days after Christmas. Then she'd left for Paris. It was now late February.

"So, we had sex right after you split up?" she asked. "And you thought that was an okay thing to do? And not tell me?"

"But I did tell you," he protested. "I answered everything you asked."

Windy had to agree. She had not asked, "When *exactly* did you separate?"

But why was that? Was there something in her that had not wanted to know? Or was it more how Dennis had talked about his marriage, setting it firmly in the past tense?

"Look, come home. Please. You must be exhausted," Dennis said, reaching for her hand to lift her out of the low sofa. "We'll talk tomorrow. I can't believe that you're really here." He was tender, his fingers touching her face as he spoke.

For the next week, Windy waffled. Because it was all true. There was a manila envelope stuffed with delicate pale blue aerogram letters she'd mailed to Dennis, all with post office stamps about forwarding them. None appeared to have been opened.

As Dennis explained it, Diane had called him, saying she had letters that appeared to come from France. "Maybe they saw the first name starting with a D?" she'd suggested. "And the last name is the same?"

Dennis had offered to go to her place to pick them up, or meet her somewhere. But she'd said she was going to be meeting friends at the corner bar, so she could just drop them off. She'd come to the front door and knocked. It was chilly. He'd invited her in. They'd sat down in the living room and started talking about how to proceed with the separation, the divorce. Then Diane had asked if 'this woman' had been in the picture all along, back when they'd started talking about separating. Dennis had insisted that, no, it was very recent. Diane had pointed out that this was far from a casual hook-up if she were writing almost every day from France. She'd asked what it was that made this woman so compelling to him.

"And exactly when did talking segue into going to your bedroom?" Windy interrupted.

She tried for days to rationalize what had happened. She wanted to feel, in her heart, that Dennis had made a mistake and was deeply apologetic. She tried and tried.

But Dennis was not consistently contrite. That lasted a day or so, then he was simply conflicted. He'd not *intended* any of it. He felt blindsided by his own behavior. But he and Diane had ended up sitting on their couch, a bottle of Pinot Noir on the coffee table, sipping and talking. Talking more honestly than they ever had about what had happened in their marriage that caused them to lose the passion, the joy. How was it that Dennis had discovered passion and joy within weeks with someone else? Diane had been curious, not judgmental, about what had elicited that intensity. What was so different from when they, Dennis and Diane, had first fallen in love? What did Dennis have with Windy that was now impossible with her? She wanted what Dennis described with Windy, only she did not want it with someone new. She wanted them to feel that joy again, to find ways to sustain it. She'd made him question himself.

Windy looked in the classifieds for "Roommate Wanted" ads. She applied for a few jobs, and, within a day, got a call to interview with a law firm as a research assistant. Having almost no money, she urgently needed a job. And she needed to get a place to live that she could afford with almost no money. She needed to not be living with Dennis when he was still married. And she refused to ask her parents for help.

THESE WERE SOME OF THE MEMORIES SURFACING IN JANE'S SEVENTY-three-year-old brain. Jane watched them like watching a TV series. Had *this* really been *her* life? Had she, Jane Browning, really tossed away a much-longed for and hard-earned European adventure for a man? Had she lied to the nice couple who'd welcomed her into their home? Had she lied by omission for years, for decades, to her family, her friends, to anyone who *thought* they knew her?

Yes, she had.

Well, *Windy* had. But, then, Windy had lied about a lot of things. Like her name. Windy had accepted that job with the law firm, not disclosing that she was going to flake out in early August and move to Texas. She would have lied to the "Roommate Wanted" person except the apartment lease was up in September anyway. Windy had had an affair with a married professor. Then she took up with another married man, never asking necessary questions, and turned her life upside down and inside out to be with him.

And she would have given up even more. Jane knew that now. When Windy had flown back to San Francisco, she was not thinking about grad school waiting for her in Austin. She'd been ready to throw it all over to build a life with Dennis. He'd become her *raison de vivre*.

Jane now wondered if Dennis had stayed with his wife. She hoped they had. Now, that was a story for their grandkids: "So, I heard the creak of the door opening, and started to yell, and your gramps ran out into the hall in his underwear, carrying this baseball bat, and there was this..."

Once the grief and hurt and anger had dissipated, Jane had been able to see the mirror-story to her story, the Dennis and Diane story where the estranged couple is brought together by love letters from his fling.

Jane wondered now about her other life, her hypothetical life with Dennis. Would they have stayed soulmates? She guessed not. Would they have married? Stayed married? Would she have lived forever in California?

That life would never have included Texas, graduate school, deciding to abandon the Ph.D. when she was already 'all-but-dissertation,' (now *that* had been risky, and, yet, *Jane* had done it!), changing programs, becoming a therapist, meeting her husband, having two children, making life-long friends, her home, her community. In real life, she'd ended up in Kansas. A move that made her extended family really think she was crackers: Does *anyone* from New Jersey move to *Kansas*?

Had her life trajectory changed direction in response to the actions, however unintended, of men she'd loved?

Jane had been married forty-three years. She wondered if her husband—who she did love but not with needy desperation, not with blinders—now napping in their bedroom, had lied to her as well. She assumed so. But she hadn't pursued truth. Truth hurt too much. Truth required her to face things, to act. And it was different when one had children. Then truth required you to face things, but to weigh the impact that action would have on them.

Jane had left Windy behind in San Francisco, when she moved to

Austin. She'd kept some parts of Windy, the better parts. But life as Windy had too much drama. Things happened that she did not intend.

In her seventy-fourth year, with decades of distance, Jane felt a bemused affection for her young self. That girl, that young woman, had been so earnest, so eager to write a love story, to *be* a love story. And so terrifically insecure.

Jane wondered if she would tell anyone about her dreams. Looking at her pudgy, saggy body, would they be incredulous? Would they question if she was, in her recently diagnosed mild cognitive impairment, her demented state, making things up?

And was she? Was *all* of it real? Had reality and fantasy crisscrossed in her synapses? Had she just been enamored of Professor Tom? Had *anything* happened? Could *that* have happened? Would he have sent her Christmas cards for twenty-seven years if it had? But, more, why had these memories, deeply buried for decades, kidnapped her dreams?

Jane imagined her children in the basement, after she died, impatiently sorting through file boxes of old taxes, old letters, and faded photos. When they came across a small blue box with a key on a soft leather necklace? Would they wonder? Would they pause to try to read the aerograms, probably faded to invisibility, before tossing it all into the trash?

Jane chortled. *It is what it is*, she thought. She was who she was. And who she'd been. What she'd done, mostly for love, had made her who she was. It was too late for regrets.

But maybe she could go down to the basement herself one day soon, get her son to line up a dozen boxes by the couch, and start sorting. Would she find a small blue box? And what other secrets might still be buried, what memories remained to be triggered?

If she could count on her dreams, there were decades still to come.

COMING HOME
SHIRLEY PEREZ WEST

Sacramento Valley, California
1966

Maria Morales was an hour into her afternoon and three Tom Collins to the good. She'd been on her way to confession at St. Joseph's in Marysville—a thirty-minute bus ride from her hometown—when they passed the Matsushita's farmstand and she got knocked off course, back to Okinawa and her gang of fellow travelers; girls like her who took teaching jobs abroad as a way to see the world.

Maria had been gone almost three years—two years in Germany and close to a year in Japan—when her brother, Art (Arturo), had called her back home.

She missed her gang, the way they kept the jukebox spinning with Sam Cooke and Martha and the Vandelas and danced till the barkeep made last call. Inevitably, one of them hooked an escort home, but since they all bunked at the same cracker box, a girl rarely went all in.

Maria was no prude. She'd read *Sex and the Single Girl* ("Good girls go to heaven; bad girls go everywhere") and celebrated senior year at college with a couple of tumbles in the hay. But it was not easy getting birth control in Okinawa, or anywhere, if you were unmarried and she didn't like leaving it up to her date, so she rarely rolled the dice.

Her last drink was down to melted ice, but instead of feeling the soft purr of the gin, the sweating glass made Maria want to pee. She stowed her horn-rimmed glasses—oddly effective for warding off male attention—stood—whoa, she should have eaten something—and shuffled toward the dark hall at the end of the bar. The scent of ammonia reminded her of walking into her parents' house the day she'd gotten home. Exactly two months ago.

THE CALL HAD COME TO MARIA'S ROOMING HOUSE AFTER MIDNIGHT when she wasn't there. One of the girls had taken it, covering for her with the not-unlikely story that she was babysitting on the base. Her brother had left a curt message that told her next to nothing.

Mom ill. Come home. Art.

The Morales kids had been raised to be discreet about family matters, but jeez, five words. When Maria got through to Art it was three a.m. in California. Yes, Mom's alive. No, she can't walk. Yes, she can speak.

It had taken three days to get home, or two depending on which time zone your watch was set. Her half-brother, Eddie (Eduardo) who lived on the peninsula, had met her at the San Francisco Airport and driven her the two hours northeast in his pickup that smelled like the inside of a lunch pail.

"You cut your hair," Eddie observed. "No more Zelda."

She'd worn bangs and a ponytail since she was fifteen and Eddie had teased her that she looked like the girl from *Dobie Gillis*. She hadn't minded because she knew it was Zelda's braininess Eddie was commenting on. But yes, she had hacked off her ponytail after going abroad—never the bangs—and kept her dark hair in a short bob.

Maria was the only girl and the youngest of eleven surviving siblings. Her mom had married four times. Eddie was Maria's favorite of the Cantu brothers; sons of Maximillian Cantu, their mother's third husband. They hadn't been raised together, but when she got her first job as a student teacher near San Jose, she'd spent weekends with him and his family in Sunnyvale. He liked jazz and his kids were well-behaved, and his wife was just a few years older than Maria (with four kids!) and Maria liked putting ideas in her sister-in-law's head. On the drive home, Eddie talked about his wife getting ideas in her head and now they were getting divorced. Maria wanted to object. Four kids.

"Do you want my advice?"

"About my marriage?" Eddie gave her a side-eye. "Why is it you Moraleses think you've got all the answers?"

She promised not to mention the divorce to their mother given her condition, or to any of the Morales brothers who did think they had all the answers.

When they pulled up to the house, Art's car was parked in the driveway, so Eddie turned his pickup onto a strip of gravel alongside the garage. By the time they unloaded Maria's two suitcases, overnight bag, and bag of gifts of Geisha dolls, and rubber coin purses that squeezed open bought at the Okinawa airport, Art had come onto the porch to greet them. He gave Maria an awkward hug then shot out a hand toward Eddie. Eddie's hands were full of luggage, so he threw his chin out by way of greeting.

"I see you're still driving that old Ford," Art said, as if that pickup and its loaded toolbox hadn't bailed the Moraleses out a time or two.

"That a Corvair?" Eddie asked with another thrust of his chin.

"How's Carmen and the kids?" Art countered.

Maria shot Eddie a look and asked Art, "Is Pops in with mom?" It was hot on the porch, even with the overhang, but she was in no hurry to go inside.

"He came home for lunch, but he's back at work."

"Didn't he retire last fall?" Their father had worked for the railroad for thirty-five years, and it had taken a lot to convince him his pension would provide enough for him and his wife to live on. Maria had chimed in from Okinawa, telling her dad to trust Art's numbers.

"He's still taking on jobs here and there. Yolanda's been coming every day after she gets Davide, Jr. to school." Yolanda and Davide—the son of their mother's first husband—had been childless until they'd taken in a baby boy orphaned when his mother was caught in an immigration raid at a local farm. "But now that you're here..."

Maria left Art and Eddie on the porch to dance around old grudges.

It was cool and dark inside the house. The caustic smell of ammonia or some other cleaner assaulted her nose. A woman she didn't know was mopping the kitchen floor. Maria stepped tentatively into her parents' bedroom where her mother lay like someone pinned as though by a stronger gravity. One side of her face had given up the fight and Maria had to clasp a hand over her own cheek to keep it from twitching in sympathy. Her gut swelled with guilt for being away for so long, but it was her mom who'd always cheered her adventures.

Contrary to what Art had told Maria, her mom couldn't speak, not in English. And since Maria's father—her mother's fourth husband, Anselmo Morales—had insisted his kids speak English to each other, the Morales siblings learned choppy Spanglish from their parents.

Maria asked after her mom's comfort but couldn't make sense of her replies. She felt helpless. Thank God Eddie burst in like he was arriving to a party and grabbed their mom up into a hug. He stroked her arm and her one perfect cheek with the back of his hand, spoke to her in smooth Spanish. His teasing tone coaxed a quiver of a smile, a trace of their mother.

———

ON HER WAY OUT OF THE LADIES', MARIA PASSED THE GRUMBLING barkeep, bucket and plunger in hand, heading toward the men's hole. She hadn't chosen The Seven Seas Club with any forethought except that it was between the bus stop and St. Joseph's. She was on her way to confession—first time since she'd come home—when memories of

Japan, the whole wide world for that matter, caught her by the throat. Two months. It was time to have a talk with her father.

She'd had no idea when she left Okinawa how long she'd be gone. She'd paid the other girls her share of the rent for the month and left behind a couple of cute skirts—above the knee!—and snug sweaters. Today she was dressed for church, a cotton dirndl skirt, short sleeve blouse with a sweater around her shoulders and scarf around her neck to slip on when needed, which was probably a good thing since a girl sitting in a bar alone could attract the wrong kind of attention. So far, she'd been left to herself. Plenty of time to think about family and the obligations that implied.

Their mom had married four times—to Martin Herrera, Davide's father, who died in the Mexican Revolution; to Teódoro Garcés, Teo Jr's father, who died in the influenza epidemic; to Maximilian Cantu, father to Frank, Eddie, Tom, Alex and Mike, whose fate Maria was fuzzy about, though the family secret was that he was a bad man; and to Anselmo, father to Art, Phil, Ruben, and Maria. Her older sister Teresa had died when Maria was four.

When she was in high school all the brothers had come together to build their mom a new house next to the three-room shack they'd lived in since the thirties. The Morales boys were in college and the Cantu brothers, who had carpentry and plumbing skills, had jobs and families, so the project lasted through Maria's sophomore year, on again, off again. And every time the brothers worked together, they clashed. They finished the house, though. They did what good sons do.

Now, according to Art, she was supposed to do what good daughters do: take care of her aging parents. He'd made that clear the moment Maria had returned. It seemed to be the one tradition of their Mexican heritage Art was willing to embrace.

"Now that you're home, you can take over and Yolanda can get back to her family," Art had declared, like that settled everything.

"Give her a couple days to get over jet lag," Eddie said with a wink at Maria.

"There's no such thing." Art had been a peace-time fighter pilot to make up for being too young to fight in WWII, like Davide and the Cantu brothers had.

Art found a couple beers for Eddie—the Morales brothers didn't drink—and the two of them walked around, inside and outside the house, apparently looking at things that needed work, until it was time for Art to go home to his family.

Eddie stayed. Maria, having never learned to cook, reheated the dinner Yolanda had brought, and he and Anselmo talked late into the night. The next morning, Eddie scrambled eggs with a jar of nopales their mother had put up, something Maria would never have thought of, and tried to show her how to make coffee on the stove-top percolator.

Her father insisted he didn't need help tending to her mom when Maria offered. Thinking about it, they had always been a team, divvying up the work at home and sharing supervision of the kids, though Art thought he was the boss. Maybe it was losing a child that bound them. They'd always kind of been in their own world.

As he left for work, her father said he'd make it an early day and would be back by *lonche*. He shook Eddie's hand and thanked him for coming.

"Do your best," Anselmo said, shaking Eddie's shoulder. It was something he always said to Maria and her brothers as they went out into the world. She wasn't sure if she liked him saying it to a Cantu brother.

"What were you and Anselmo up so late about?" Maria asked when they were alone.

"Oh, you know." Eddie leaned back in his chair, sipped his coffee. "He wanted to hear about all my brothers, who was doing what, the kids. I talked to him a little about me and Carmen."

"Good for you Eddie. What'd he say?"

"*Un hombre necesita mantener sus promesas.*"

"A man needs to keep his promises," she repeated. "He makes it sound easy, doesn't he?" Her pops had always tossed out simple declarations to her and her brothers. No whining allowed.

"You know, works for him," Eddie said, then shifted the conversation to her. "So, what are your plans? You back for good?"

Maria's shoulders straightened. "I'll help get Mom situated then I'm going back to teach in Okinawa. If I can swing it." She relaxed. This was Eddie.

"Yeah, well, I'm just asking because Art might have other ideas."

"Such as?"

"He wants me to add a room off the back. A big one, like an efficiency apartment."

Maria smirked. "Why? Is he hiring live-in help?" She knew better.

"It's for you, Mare." Maria had been called Mary since kindergarten, but when *West Side Story* hit the screen, she reclaimed her name. Most of her brothers still called her Mary. "He thinks you need to come home. He doesn't like it that you're so far away in case something happens. Like, you know, what just happened."

LEFT ALONE WITH HER MOTHER, MARIA REALIZED SHE DIDN'T HAVE a clue what could help with her recovery. She spent the morning chasing down an old schoolmate who'd become a nurse. The next day, Carol drove down from Yuba City thrilled to reconnect with Merry Mary, a nickname Maria thought made no sense.

"How's our world traveler?" Carol called from the open window of her Volkswagen. She was dressed in yellow capris and a sleeveless button shirt with a blue headband holding back her blonde flip. Same old Carol.

"Grounded," Maria called back, watching as Carol pulled a clipboard and what looked like a white lab coat from her backseat.

They hugged. Carol smelled like Juicy Fruit.

"I'm so glad you called," Carol sang out, then caught herself. "I'm so so sorry to hear about your mom's stroke. How's she doing?"

"Fine, considering," Maria said, taking Carol's clipboard so she could don her lab coat. "Honestly, I have no way of knowing. I can't understand her speech, though she nods a lot whenever one of us talks to her or does anything for her. Kind of an encouragement or thank you. Who knows?"

"Does she write notes?" Carol took back her clipboard and readied her ballpoint pen.

"Well, I don't think anyone's offered," Maria said, a little surprised and disappointed with herself that she hadn't thought of it. Of course, her father understood his wife's mumbled Spanish just fine and she supposed Yolanda did as well.

"Is she bedridden?" Carol asked softly with a puppy-dog look.

"Mostly," Maria said. "My father carries her to the toilet and to her bath."

"Awww," Carol said, her pen scratching across the clipboard.

Maria had shared her mom's diagnosis with Carol on the phone. According to Art, the doctor said that at age sixty-seven, her mom would not recover her strength, so there were no plans for physical therapy, which Carol thought was a real shame.

Carol wanted a tour of the house, which took about five minutes, before meeting Maria's mom. She asked a lot of questions. Who else lives here? Was her father home during the day? Did her mom ever seem to be in pain? Then gave Maria a lot of specific instructions.

"Your mother needs a wheelchair so she can get out of bed and outside for goodness' sake."

There were contraptions that sat over the toilet that would make it easier for Maria's dad to help his wife on and off, Carol told her. And stools and shower attachments to help him bathe her.

Within the week, Maria had Art take her to Sacramento to shop for everything Carol recommended and arranged for a county health nurse to come for regular visits.

Her pops loved taking her mom outside, the two of them sitting quietly or Pops talking softly. Pretty soon he stopped taking on extra work and made their outdoor excursions his new job.

Maria fell into a routine during the next month, though she didn't feel she was being all that helpful. In the mornings she made bad coffee—she preferred tea—while her father tended to her mother. He showed Maria how to cook an egg in a spoon of lard on a high flame until the edges were a crisp, brown lace. At noon she made sandwiches, though he preferred the *burros* her mom used to pack into his lunch pail. And Yolanda usually brought dinner on her daily visits.

Every now and again Maria would put her transistor radio on low volume and half-heartedly wipe counters and sweep floors, even though a woman came twice a week. On Wednesdays her brother Ruben came up from Sacramento and took the family's laundry to the new laundromat downtown. He'd spend the afternoon, biding his time between wet and dry loads, at Clive's Pool Pocket. Maria knew because he'd tell her who he saw there from high school or summer farm work. "Guesss who'ss back in town?" he'd ask, his esses sizzling. He'd tell her how so-and-so landed back in town and shake his head with genuine wonder. To all Maria's brothers, except Davide, leaving this podunk place was the goal.

I'm back in town, she wanted to say. Me.

As it was, she had a lot of time on her hands which she filled by reading—the closest library was in Marysville—writing letters—no news from here—and talking on the phone to her sisters-in-law—why hasn't so-and-so been to see our mother yet?—and a couple college friends. Her dear friend, Marie, who she'd student-taught with was starting graduate school at UCSF the coming fall. "My aunt has this houseboat in Tiburon she's letting me use. There's room for two of us. It'll be a gas."

———————————

DOWN AT THE FAR END OF THE BAR, TWO MEN WHO LOOKED LIKE regulars sat talking sports. The Giants, they agreed, wrenched from New York six years before, weren't going to amount to anything. Maria would wait for the barkeep, settle up, then find a lunch counter to get a sandwich or something to calm her stomach and clear her head before going home. She was in no shape for confession. It was time to have a talk with her father.

The padded leatherette door of the Seven Seas squawked open, throwing unwelcome light on the tired interior and a gush of hot sidewalk breath. Maria glanced up in case it was someone she knew, or her brothers knew, who hadn't gotten farther in life than a half-hour bus ride from home.

OVER THE WEEKS, MOST OF THE CANTU BROTHERS CAME UP FROM the peninsula to see their mom. On those days, Maria felt the pull of family, the sense of belonging to something bigger. She'd lay out the treats sent by her sisters-in-law, sip beers on the porch, and listen to her half-brothers' stories of their childhood. On one of those visits, Frank, the loudest of the Cantu brothers, told her how he and Eddie had first met Anselmo.

"We were shuffling around outside the Durst mercantile waiting for the old man to give us sacks for frog hunting—we used to get five cents a frog from the Southern Pacific brakeman—when this man walks up looking like he'd fallen off a train car. One side of his face was bruised and scraped, some of the rest of him torn and worn, but he didn't look dangerous. Besides, we were used to seeing hobos camping near the tracks.

"This man was as brown as we were. He asked us in Spanish if the storekeeper was a good man. I don't remember what we said, but we followed him inside. The old man was jawing with some farmer and they both kinda came to attention when they saw this Mexican hobo and me and Eddie.

"The old man yells to us, 'I'll get those sacks when I'm done, like I said.' Both men are looking the stranger up and down. Ever since the trouble, you know, with our crazy father, people around here paid attention when a Mexican man showed up.

"So, Anselmo turns to Eddie and tells him to ask the storekeeper if he wants to buy a gun.

The storekeeper said no thanks and pointed the stranger out the door.

"'I work. You gotta work?' Anselmo says to the storekeeper and the farmer. The storekeeper tells him to ask us boys because our family hired now and again. So, we all leave the store and we make a deal. If Anselmo shows us his gun, we'll take him to our uncle Antonio.

You know the end of the story."

Maria nodded.

HER MOM DIED ON ONE OF THE HOTTEST DAYS OF THE SUMMER.

Maria's tears mixed with sweat as she wandered around the house, picking up small items and moving them as if they were out of place.

Frank had brought a window air conditioner when he came to see their mom, bellowing that it was hot as hell in the house. But Art said it was extravagant and would block the window's light. A day before the funeral, after which the whole family would cram into their parents' little house, Art gave in and installed the unit in the dining room. The four Morales siblings—Art, Phil, Ruben, and Maria—sat around the table drinking 7-Ups and telling stories about their mom. Their father was outside in his vegetable garden napping under a shade cloth.

Inevitably, they repeated stories they'd heard about their mom's first three husbands. Davide's father was a farrier who'd been conscripted by one of Pancho Villa's generals, Art told them. No one knew much about Teo's father except that the influenza epidemic took him before Teo was born. It was her third husband, Maximillian Cantu, who brought their mom and her two boys up from northern Mexico. None of them knew exactly where she had been born. As for when their mom crossed the border, they guessed it was before nineteen twenty-one, because Frank was born that year in Texas. It hadn't occurred to Maria that her mother's history had died with her or that leaving a place meant leaving your history.

After a while, Art brought out a blue cardboard shoebox.

"I found this in Mom's old trunk," he said.

"You've already cleaned out Mom's chest?" Maria hated Art's efficiency sometimes.

"I didn't want Pops to have to do it."

Maria had been in and out of that old wooden trunk so many times through her childhood and adolescence she couldn't believe she'd missed this shoebox. The trunk had been full of musty old clothes, not worth keeping, including stuff she and her brothers once wore. And there was an old pair of her mother's dress shoes, maybe from the thirties, but she never saw a shoe box.

The box held unframed sepia photos of Davide and the five Cantu brothers in their military uniforms, their white borders freckled with age. Maria remembered the photos used to sit in frames on a side table. Now the only family photos on display were of her and Art and Phil posing in mortarboards and gowns.

Under the photos lay a small burlap sack cinched closed.

"I'll be damned," Maria said when Ruben pulled a small pistol from the sack. Frank's story must have been true. But why would it be in her mother's things?

"I think it was Pops's," Ruben said.

"It was," Maria said. "Frank had a whole story about the day he and Eddie met him."

"And there's this." Ruben pulled out a palm-sized burgundy velvet box with B-U-L-O-V-A lettered in gold along the bottom edge.

"I gave that watch to Pops when he retired," Art said. "He didn't understand why there weren't numbers on it. You know, just lines." Arts's own watch had a face full of dials and numbers.

When Ruben cracked open the box, instead of a watch, there was a pendant necklace.

Ruben held it up by its delicate silver chain. "You ever ssee Mom wear thiss?"

"Never." Maria reached for it. "I think it's white gold, or it would be tarnished," she said, smoothing her thumb over the etched face. She unclasped the locket's catch, spilling crumbled bits onto the table. "There are old hairs in here." She snapped the face closed and brushed away the fallen bits, then wondered if she'd dishonored something precious to her mom.

"Put it on," Ruben said.

"Why would I do that?"

"You're the only girl," Phil pointed out helpfully.

"Give it to your wife," Maria snapped.

"Don't be cheeky." Phil scowled. He'd been engaged twice since college and now lived a bachelor's life in Monterey teaching high school lit and coaching football.

"It's Mom's. Let's have them put it on her." Maria set the necklace back into the Bulova box.

"Are you sure it's herss?" Ruben asked.

"I don't wanna bother Pops with this." Art's final say on the matter. "I'll take it to Sullivan's."

Maria had picked out her mom's best dress, flowery and wispy-sleeved with a lace collar, probably from before the war when she and Pops used to go into Sacramento for the Mexican dances. The people at Sullivans had told her they'd make adjustments if the garment no longer fit, assuring Maria her mom would look lovely and peaceful at the showing.

"What about the gun?" Maria asked.

THE FUNERAL WAS BLEAK, WITH THE MORALES BROTHERS AND Davide and their families in the first pews with Anselmo, and the Cantu brothers and their families scattered among the town mourners. Teo, the hermit, didn't come. Maria made a few attempts to rearrange people but was met with a lot of pinched mouths. There'd been a brief controversy about pall bearers—too many brothers—but

Anselmo shut it down quickly and picked the six oldest to carry their mother.

Later, at the house filled with family, and women who'd brought covered dishes, and sisters-in-law supervising kids and food, or just smoking and gossiping, someone asked Maria about the necklace fastened around her mom's neck. "Where'd that come from? I never saw her wear jewelry." "What necklace?" another sister-in-law asked.

THE NEWCOMER WHO'D DRIFTED INTO THE SEVEN SEAS HAD obviously come from Beale Air Force Base, double chevron on his shoulder, a khaki crusher hat. He scanned the room as if he might be meeting someone—did his glance hesitate a moment on Maria?—then stepped up to the unmanned bar.

Maria decided she'd have a cigarette while she waited and took a stab at climbing onto a bar stool. Why did they make bar stools so tall? Men was why. A whole world built to fit men. She was not so tipsy she didn't notice the newcomer watching her in the mirror. She hefted her bag onto the bar; an unfashionable but practical bucket bag made of *Basho-fu* cloth, and swiveled to loosen the awkward twist of her skirt. As she fussed, the limp fabric of her bag melted onto the polished wood, spilling its guts onto the floor.

The newcomer slid off his stool and squatted to help gather her stuff: pens and gum and horned rim glasses, coin purse and pack of Lucky non-filters, Japanese candies and matchbooks. He reached up and dropped each item on the bar, pivoting to see that he hadn't missed anything. He stood with a small grunt and regarded her with a dry smile, mostly in his eyes.

"May I?" He held her glasses open. No rings or suntan lines on his fingers. Before she could answer, he slid the arms of her glasses over her ears until they settled in place.

"Brian," he said. "Walsh."

With her glasses on, she saw he was close-shaven, though a shadow was beginning to darken his otherwise pale cheeks. His mouth narrowed toward a pensive pucker.

"Maria Morales." She offered her hand and he took it, a forthright grip, but soft palm. A desk job. He grabbed her Japanese matchbook to light her cigarette, then read it, or pretended to.

"Don't tell me, you just came in from Okinawa."

"Chicago, actually." He winked. "I have a thing for languages."

"Spy?"

"Translator." The cheap match flared and spit as Brian lit it. "Yeow." He shook it loose and they both watched it dive to the patched linoleum like a shooting star. Brian went for the dropped match.

"What languages do they speak in Chicago? Cubs?" Okay, the drinks had dulled her wit.

"Hell-lo," Brian said to the floor. "I'm shipping out to Italy in a couple weeks for a Bulgarian intensive," he said as he stood. He took the empty stool between them. "Almost missed this." He held up a white gold locket with an etched face.

Maria froze. *Mom gone. Mom buried. Locket buried.* She looked around expecting to see one or two of her brothers yukking it up at her expense. The older ones, the ones raised by other fathers, were always seeing ghosts, witnessing miracles, watching for signs. But the older ones didn't live anywhere near their hometown anymore, except Davide.

"I have to go." Maria slid off the stool and stuffed everything into her bag, leaving a fiver to cover her drinks. She pushed through the door and trotted toward the bus stop, glad she was the kind of girl who wore flats.

The bus ride home took forever. She'd stuffed the necklace into her squeezable coin purse but felt its presence like heat coursing through her bag's thin fabric. Fortunately, Davide lived within blocks of the bus stop. She found her older brother in his backyard chopping wood.

Her hand trembled as she squeezed the coin purse open and pulled out the necklace. Davide chuckled.

"I thought you might never find it."

"So, it was you." Maria took a breath, surprised that she'd been so spooked by the whole thing.

Davide's eyes twinkled.

"Is it supposed to be a joke?"

His face fell. "No, no." Davide dropped his axe and sat on a stump. "I hadn't seen that necklace for years and years, then someone puts it on my dead mother."

"We found it in a box with photos of you boys from the war."

Davide lowered his head. "I didn't think she kept it. I saw her looking at it one day, crying. She said my father gave it to her. That was all she had left of him after he died in *La Revolución*. Well, and me." He looked at Maria sad-eyed like he carried all their mothers' pain. "She said she wore it until she married Maximillian Cantu. He didn't like her remembering my father, so she hid it. I only saw her looking at it that one time." He bowed his head. "But then that night Cantu went crazy, he said people saw her wearing the necklace and they were talking about it. He tore through the house looking for it and hurting her. When I tried to stop him, he hurt me too. Finally, someone heard her screams."

Maria felt like she might throw up. She wanted to ask how Cantu had hurt her mother, but she already knew. Though her mother dressed modestly, Maria sometimes caught a glimpse of scars, bits of raised or colorless skin.

"I thought the necklace was maybe cursed, but when Anselmo came, I thought it had brought her good luck, a good man like my father. Anselmo was a good husband, a good father, *que no?*"

"*Claro,*" Maria said, her Spanish returning.

"I thought, a girl like you, a single girl, that the necklace might bring you a good husband, a good life."

Maria took her time walking the half-mile home, sweating away the last traces of the three Tom Collins she'd swilled shamelessly in the middle of the day. Yolanda, bless her heart, had fed her a fat burro filled with molten beans and rice and two cool glasses of watermelon water. And Davide. She'd always thought of her eldest half-brother as big-hearted, if not emotional, and maybe a little simple: a magical necklace? But his words, his wishes, stuck with her. He thought the necklace would bring her a good life. What made up a good life these days? Most of her friends seemed set. A few married, a few still working on their futures, a few doing both. What was she working on? She'd succeeded in leaving home, getting out from under the watchful eyes of her brothers and having some freedom and fun minus the hangovers but it wasn't always a picnic. More than a few guys didn't take her seriously, and while she kept up a good front, it stung.

At home, Maria washed up and changed into a pair of Madras print shorts and a sleeveless blouse, relieved to shed her nylons; the darkest shade, suntan, was two shades lighter than her skin. She found her pops in his garden filling a basket with tomatoes and chiles. He pulled a slightly wrinkled chayote from a vine and brought it to his nose.

"*Para la cena*," he said, balancing it on top of his bounty.

The thought of dinner made Maria burp behind her hand.

"Can we talk?"

Inside the kitchen, Maria switched on the air conditioner and helped her father wash the vegetables and set them out on towels to dry. Finally, she got him to sit at the table by opening a bottle of root beer, his favorite. She took the necklace from her pocket. If he was surprised, her father didn't show it.

"This didn't get buried with Mom." She held it in her palm. "I don't know how but Davide took it off her at the funeral." Her father seemed to be listening intently. "He told me a story about it. Did you know she had this?"

"*Si.*" He nodded but didn't offer more.

"Art found it in an old shoe box she kept in her trunk. There was a gun in there, too. He said you had him bury it."

He nodded.

"Why did she have a gun, Pops? The boys think it was yours."

"*Si, si*. I found near *fortencock, mas alla del bridge*."

"Fortencock? Where is that?"

"*Tejas. Forte* Hancock," he repeated. "I thought I could trade it or sell. When I come to California on *el tren*, I come here and *esos jovenes*, *los* Cantu, bring me to *una ranchito* and I work for their *tio*, Antonio. He had *una* saw for cutting the big oaks. The farmers were clearing for orchards, so we had work. Me and some other men and the older boys. That's where I met your mother." He smiled at the memory. "She and her sister raised chickens and kept *una huerta*. They fed *todos* —seven boys and five men, including me. It took time, your mom had been hurt by *ese* Cantu. It took a long time to convince her to marry me." He chuckled then his face changed with a new memory. "I bought two bullets for the gun, and I gave it to her. I told her, 'If I ever do anything to hurt you or your boys, you should shoot me dead.'"

Maria gasped. Normally such a sentiment would prompt her to roll her eyes. Too much made up drama. But there was real love and trust in her pop's gesture. And geez, her mom must have been thirty and already put through the wringer with two dead husbands and a third one who nearly killed her, when she married for a fourth time. That had to take some faith.

"You two were lucky." Maria took her pop's hand and looked away while he blotted his eyes with his handkerchief.

———

DAYS LATER, MARIA MET CAROL AT THE SEVEN SEAS. SHE WANTED to buy Carol a round or two for all her help with her mom. A part of her hoped Brian Walsh, the linguist, would show up, give her a chance to explain her odd behavior.

Carol, friendly as ever, snapped her gum and winked as they passed a couple guys seated at the bar. Within a few minutes they'd insinuated themselves into the booth Carol and Maria had settled into. Carol asked, "What could it hurt?" She accepted their offer to buy a round.

When the drinks arrived, the guy sitting next to Maria stretched his arm across the back of her seat and said, "So, do you come here often?"

Maria rolled her eyes at Carol and sipped her drink just as the door squawked open. She nearly spit out her cocktail. Something strange was afoot and she wasn't going to buck it. Up went her arm in a big, and maybe a little desperate, welcome wave to Brian and his companion. She half stood, awkwardly trapped in the small booth.

"Sorry fellas, our dates are here."

Brian and his buddy Carl—Carl meet Carol, Carol meet Carl— were quick on their feet, playing along, apologizing for their delay. The foursome drank and danced, found a late supper, and settled in on blankets along the Feather River. Though Maria was half-due for a romp, it turned out Brian was a talker. When his tour ended, he said, he planned to finish college and maybe get into law school. Raised in the Windy City, Brian said he liked what he'd seen of central California —the easy pace of life and the ever-present sun. Maria didn't disagree, but still felt an urge to move on.

"I'm a different person when I'm out in the world," she said.

"I kinda like the one that's here," Brian teased.

He came to see her the day before he shipped out, greeting Anselmo with impressive Spanish. After Brian left, her pops asked Maria, for the first time, what her plans were. She told him what Art and her brothers had been pushing for and that she wanted to get back in the classroom, but maybe down near San Francisco. Anselmo laughed.

"Let him add to the house. Fine. When you come home, you'll have a place."

———

WHEN EDDIE ARRIVED TO START THE ADDITION, HE CAME WITH good news: he and Carmen had patched things up.

Maria told him how she was ready to get back to work.

"Yeah, Art said you were applying at the high school."

"Hah!" Maria threw back her head. "Could you imagine, teaching at the same school I attended?"

"At least they'd know you. Sure bet for getting the job."

"God there's jobs everywhere. Haven't you heard? There's been a baby boom since the war and now all those kids are in school."

She told him her plan. She'd applied for a job in Marin County where things were really exploding, and she was moving into a houseboat with her friend Marie.

"I'll come down and see Pops on some weekends and school breaks —she didn't mention summer break because the last place she wanted to spend her summers was the Sacramento Valley. Something in the back of her mind told her Italy was next on her travel itinerary.

"It sounds like you've got this all sewed up. Does Anselmo know?"

"He does. He said he'd have a *talkee* to Art."

Eddie chuckled.

"So did you hear we found a gun in Mom's things?"

"That's how we met your dad," Eddie said.

"I know. Frank told me the story. He said all you boys were living with your aunt and uncle on a ranch outside of town."

"Yeah, those were some good years. We were kids."

"What happened to your father, Eddie?"

"That's another story."

———

MARIA CUT THE NOTICE FROM THE PAPER AND POSTED IT WITH A magnet on her refrigerator. They had reprinted a Polaroid of her and Brian on their wedding day in nineteen sixty-seven. She remembered the knee-length white dress. Brian is wearing a white shirt and slim black tie. Or it might have been a dark blue tie to match the velvet band around her empire waist. The reprint is black and white. She could barely make out the locket.

50TH ANNIVERSARY: WALSH

Wheatland residents Brian F. and Maria Walsh celebrated their 50th wedding anniversary July 8 in Milan, Italy with their children and grandchildren. Brian and Maria nee Morales met in 1966 and were married July 8, 1967 at St. Joseph's Catholic Church in Marysville.

Originally from Chicago, he retired as a Yuba County Superior Court judge and works in the Assigned Judges Program. He served as a Bulgarian linguist in the U.S. Air Force, and is a graduate of the University of San Francisco and McGeorge School of Law—teaching at Anna McKenney School in Marysville while attending law school.

A native of Wheatland, Maria retired from teaching at the Wheatland School District after 30 years in a 36-year career in education.

CONTRIBUTORS

Kim Taylor Blakemore is an author, developmental editor and founder of the Novelitics Writers Collective. Her passion for storytelling and nurturing authors led her to establish Novelitics (come write with us!). She loves coaching and supporting novelists on their creative journeys Her passion for the written word extends to teaching editing and craft workshops to organizations like History Quill, Women's Fiction Writers Association, Sisters in Crime and more. Her novels include *The Deception*, *After Alice Fell* (Killer Nashville Silver Falchion Award, Best Historical), *The Companion* (Tucson Festival of Book Literary Award winner), *Bowery Girl* (NYPL Best Reads for Teens) and *Cissy Funk* (WILLA Award for Best Young Adult Fiction). Her latest works, *The Good Time Girls* and *The Good Time Girls Get Famous*, (written as K.T. Blakemore), introduce readers to the Wild-Willed Women of the West Series, featuring bold women who take no prisoners and succeed through sheer grit, determination, and a parcel of luck. Learn more at www.kimtaylorblakemore.com.

Kerry Cathers provides research resources for authors of historical detective fiction. She founded and runs the website, *A Curiosity of Crime*, (www.acuriosityofcrime.com) and produces a monthly publication, Bandit's Roost, (https://acuriosityofcrime.substack.com). Her first reference book, *A Writer's Guide to Nineteenth-Century Murder by Arsenic*, was published in 2022. It will be followed up next year with *A Writer's Guide to Nineteenth-Century Murder by Poison*. She has given talks at the Historical Novel Society's North American conference as well as for Sisters in Crime, Crime Writers of America, and Kiss of Death's COFFIN series.

Elyse Garrett, a California and Honolulu native, overcame childhood trauma and pursued a Master of Social Work at USC, specializing in healing traumatized individuals. Her novel *Cleft* awaits a publisher to fall in love with it, and explores the intertwining lives of two women both claiming the same daughter in Russia and Honolulu. Simultaneously, she finalizes *Matt,* set in post-Soviet Russia and Belarus, where an American mother searches for her daughter in hundreds of overcrowded orphanages. Residing in the Pacific Northwest, Elyse is a devoted mother of three, enjoying e-bike rides by the Columbia River and cultivating giant dahlias. Learn more at www.elysegarrett.com.

Carrie Hayes writes about characters from the past who wrestle with issues that modern readers are still dealing with today. Her debut novel, *Naked Truth or Equality, the Forbidden Fruit,* tells the little-known story of spiritualist sisters Victoria Woodhull and Tennessee Claflin, who ran for political office long before American women could vote. Its sequel, *Well Dressed Lies,* was published in September. She lives with her family in New Jersey. Follow her on Medium (carriehayz.medium.com) and Substack (hayesc.substack.com).

Sue Ann Higgens writes fiction and reads obituaries in Portland, Oregon. She finds leaving the routines of home–to the Bitterroot mountains or a troglodyte village in Tunisia–unfurls her creative canvas. She's been a birth doula, a pastry chef, a high school teacher and principal. Her writing looks at 20th century women, cultural friction, and entangled families. She aspires to make peace and very thin lefse.

Susan Kraus lives in Lawrence, Kansas, and worked for decades as a therapist, custody mediator, and award-winning travel writer. Then she segued into novels: *Fall From Grace, All God's Children, Insufficient Evidence,* and *When We Lost Touch.* Her novels have been called 'socially conscious' fiction, with characters that compel connection, page-turning plot lines, and themes that make readers think about their own beliefs. You can check out her work at www.susankraus.com.

Gail Lehrman is an expatriate New Yorker relocated to the Pacific Northwest. Though Gail traded the canyons of Manhattan for the mountains of Oregon, New York's voices continued to sing in her ear. Those voices are the force behind her debut novel, *Across Seward Park*. Gail holds a B.A. and M.A in English Literature and an MFA in Creative Writing. A frequent hiker in Oregon's lovely Columbia River Gorge, Gail is also an enthusiastic participant in the rich literary community of Portland, Oregon. Learn more at www. gaillehrmanauthor.com.

Tonya Mitchell's short fiction has appeared in various journals and anthologies, including *The Copperfield Review* and *Glimmer and Other Stories and Poems*, for which she won the Cinnamon Press award in fiction. Her debut historical novel, *A Feigned Madness,* won the Reader Views Reviewers Choice Award and the Kops-Fetherling International Book Award for Best New Voice in Historical Fiction. Her sophomore historical novel, *The Arsenic Eater's Wife*, is forthcoming February 2024. She lives in Cincinnati, Ohio with her husband, three boys, and an overweight golden doodle. You can learn more at www. tonyamitchellauthor.com

Katie Nelson lives and writes in Portland, Oregon. An event coordinator by day and a historical fiction author by night (or early mornings, or lunch breaks, etc.), Katie's love for historical stories runs deep. She received her Master's in History from Portland State University and is a historical research consultant with her company River City Historical. Her clientele includes journalists, historical fiction authors, and documentary filmmakers. When she's not working or writing, Katie enjoys camping with her husband and dogs, bike rides, themed parties, good food, captivating books, and bad reality TV. You can learn more at www.rivercityhistorical.com.

Gail Priest's degrees and work in theater and counseling psychology with a focus on family therapy, inspire her stories of healing from trauma and secrets within both traditional and nontraditional families. Her *Annie Crow Knoll* trilogy explores four generations of a family living on the Chesapeake Bay. The final novel was a Kindle Book Awards semi-finalist. *Eastern Shore Shorts*, Gail's collection of short stories set in various Eastern Shore towns, was an International Book Awards finalist. Gail is a member of The Women's Fiction Writers Association, Eastern Shore Writers' Association, and the South Jersey Writers' Group, where she was named Writer of the Year. Learn more at www.gailpriest.com.

Micah Thorp is a physician and writer in Portland, Oregon. His novels include *Uncle Joe's Muse*, winner of Forward Reviews Book Award and Next Gen Indie's Award for Humor, and *Uncle Joe's Senpai*. Other literary works have appeared in *Cleaver Magazine*, *Blind Corner* and the *Fictional Café*. Learn more at www.open-bks.com/library/moderns/uncle-joes-muse/about-author.html

Annie Tupek, originally from the Midwest, took a vacation to Alaska and never went home. After spending over a decade in the frozen tundra she moved south and now resides in Oregon. Her work has appeared in *The Normal School*, *The First Line Magazine*, and *The Pacific Northwest Reader*. Her story "Entanglement" was shortlisted for the 2019/2020 Quantum Shorts Flash Fiction Contest. When not making up stories, she can be found working in the tech industry, exploring the Pacific Northwest by land and air, and neglecting her website at www.annietupek.com.

Journalism took K. Fufkin Vollmayer from Alaska to Washington, D.C. When one of her kids parroted the same frontier myth learned in school—of brave, white pioneers in covered wagons—she remembered the captivity and slave narratives she read with her professor, Michael P. Rogin. Combing through the Lewis and Clark journals, she focused on writing about York, the Métis, and the other enslaved member of the expedition, Sacagawea in her novel, *I've Known Rivers: York's Account of the Lewis and Clark Expedition*. In every Latin American country she's visited, she's learned about maroon communities and the Black African diaspora. Learn more at fufkin.co.

Shirley Perez West was born and raised in the San Francisco Bay area among the remnants of cherry orchards, redwood forests, and Spanish ranchos. She holds bachelor's and master's degrees in journalism and is still trying to work out how not to let the facts get in the way of a good story. She currently lives on the north Oregon Coast where she enjoys paddling for a women's dragon boat team, and connecting with both local writers and far-flung members of the Novelitics community. She is author of *El Sueño*, a family saga of early California.

Sharon Woodard grew up on the east coast but spent most of early adulthood on Southern California beaches so she speaks both coasts fluently. She is settled happily in the verdant playgrounds of the Pacific Northwest biking, hiking, and paddle boarding. She spawned two now fully-functional adults who grow nervous when she dons her "be careful or you will end up in my novel" T-shirt. No family or friends were harmed in the generation of this story but all bets are off for what comes next.

ABOUT NOVELITICS WRITERS COLLECTIVE

Our community is a gathering place for dedicated novelists who are passionate about storytelling, mastering their craft, and navigating the world of publishing. We believe that connecting with like-minded writers is essential in creating a supportive and inspiring environment where everyone can thrive.

Here, you will find a diverse group of novelists at various stages in their writing journeys, from aspiring authors to published professionals. Whether you are just starting out or have several novels under your belt, joining our community will provide you with the opportunity to connect with fellow writers who share your enthusiasm.

We prioritize the exchange of ideas and feedback. We encourage members to share their work and seek constructive criticism, enabling everyone to grow as writers. Additionally, we create an annual anthology of short fiction, host regular discussions on various writing-related topics including techniques, plot development, character building, and offer workshops on the craft of fiction and the ever-changing landscape of the publishing industry.

Novelitics has both a virtual and local footprint, with virtual meetings, write-ins, and workshops and local Portland, Oregon area retreats and meet ups.

By being a part of our community, you will not only have access to invaluable resources, but you will also find motivation and encouragement to keep pushing forward. Our supportive network fosters an environment where writers can celebrate their successes, seek guidance during setbacks, and find inspiration in the accomplishments of their peers.

If you are serious about your writing journey and are looking for a community of dedicated novelists who share your aspirations, our community is the perfect place for you. Join us today and embark on a transformative experience that will propel your writing to new heights.

Learn more at www.novelitics.com